FOUL IS FAIR

ELISSE HAY

CITY OWL
PRESS

FOUL IS FAIR
Something Wicked, Book 1

CITY OWL PRESS
www.cityowlpress.com

Cover Design by MiblArt. All stock photos licensed appropriately.

Edited by Lisa Green.

For information on subsidiary rights, please contact the publisher at info@cityowlpress.com.

Print Edition ISBN: 978-1-64898-196-8

Digital Edition ISBN: 978-1-64898-195-1

Printed in the United States of America

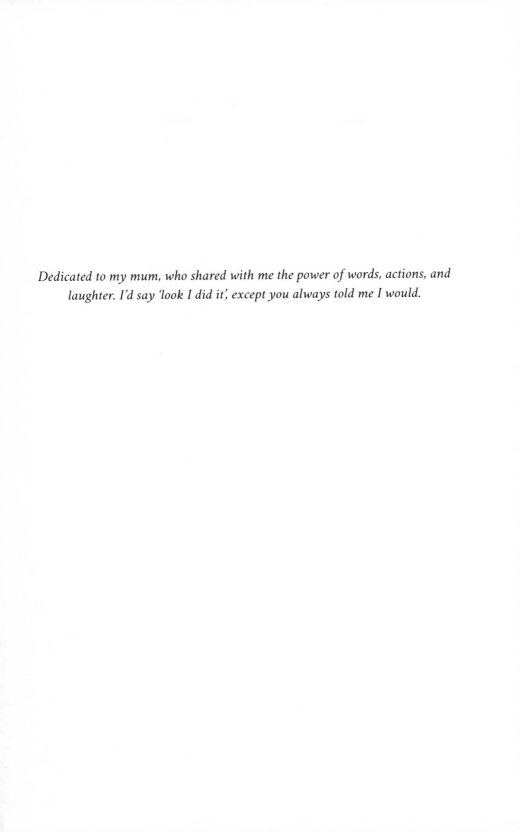

Dedicated to my mum, who shared with me the power of words, actions, and laughter. I'd say 'look I did it', except you always told me I would.

AUTHOR'S NOTE

This story was written on the Wadawurrung lands of the Kulin Nation and is set in the lands of the Bunurong Boon Wurrung and Wurundjeri Woi Wurrung peoples of the Eastern Kulin Nation.

I pay respect to First Nation Elders past and present. Sovereignty was never ceded.

PROLOGUE

EIGHTEEN MONTHS AGO

I SCANNED THE BUSHLAND AROUND US, UNEASY.

"Hunting mythical pumas," Brandon said lazily, the words directed along the barrel of his high-powered rifle. He looked down over the national park stretching out beneath us from our rocky eyrie. "Feels almost wrong to be paid for going hiking."

He didn't think there was any danger and I understood why. We'd stomped all over Mount Difficult for days. We should've known by now if there was any threat. In theory.

"Spot any?" I asked, just to annoy him. After all, the lump may as well be my big brother. His baby sister and I had been fast friends since we'd figured out the joy of stealing Brandon's juice when we were three.

A witch had to live up to expectations.

He snorted and straightened. "Yeah, right. Shit, Rory, I'm overqualified for shooting feral cats."

I knew in my bones it wasn't a feral cat, even if the rift had only been open for a split second, and the one witness who claimed to have seen a puma was pissed as a nit. The higher-ups needed to take it seriously, sure, but chances were slim we'd find evidence of anything, and Buckley's to none that we'd actually stumble across something.

I could imagine the report. *I believe there is a supernatural creature currently residing in the Gariwerd National Park. It is my professional opinion that all civilians should be evacuated immediately to minimise mind control, disembowelment, and/or general shitfuckery.* And, like usual, they'd ignore my very sensible advice while their screw-ups kept my payslips coming. Sucked to be anyone who wanted to visit this slice of paradise, though.

Meanwhile, I had an honorary big brother to torment.

"Feral cats can get to be like, two meters, I hear." I pretended to take his measure. "That's bigger than you, Mister I-Failed-Year-Nine-Maths. And they have *claws*, Brandon. *You* don't even eat pizza without a knife and fork."

Silently, he held up his gun. His very big, very serious gun.

I was colossally unimpressed. "You're setting yourself up for some body shaming there, mate, and I am *this* close to not rising above it."

He wrinkled his nose childishly and shouldered the weapon with a practiced shrug. The contrast should've been jarring, but it suited Brandon. "No rising over my body, thanks. That's basically incest. Also, I just helped set you up with Nic."

I flicked my fingers dismissively. "You're a passable wingman," I gave him graciously. I'd done most of the work myself, but he'd tried.

He could be very trying.

A flock of black cockatoos screamed their way across the sky. The early afternoon sun was warm as it filtered through the eucalypts. Quiet descended in the wake of the birds' cacophony.

I took a deep breath, lifted a heavy boot up onto a rock, and hauled the rest of me after it. It was an hour back to the car park on foot. Another thirty minutes to modern conveniences, give or take the five minutes required to put down anything unlucky enough to try to get between me and coffee.

I steadied myself on the rock and clambered down after Brandon. Two days of fruitless recon, and we were almost back to the path. Luxury. We'd even spotted hikers down there about half an hour ago. Real, human hikers. Well, probably human.

The birds were silent.

Foreboding trickled down my spine like ice water, but I kept my voice steady when I said, "Hey. Listen."

He hopped onto the next rock gracefully, then paused, his head cocked. And brought his rifle to the ready.

I breathed. Lifted my eyes over the outcrop above us. Scanned, slowly, watching for movement. Determination and purpose drummed through me.

The air felt warm and humid as I drew it deep into my lungs. Spells swam in my head, but I put no power behind them. Not yet. I could only have one spell active at a time. I needed to make sure it was the *right* one.

He lifted his head, then shouldered his rifle. "You're jumpy, Rory."

The hair on the back of my neck raised as those words echoed in the silence, and his boot heels scraped, sending a few rocks tumbling away into the deep ravine beneath us. Without meeting his eyes, I forced myself to move, lifting my arm. And, just to prove him wrong, I casually flipped him the bird as I picked my way past him towards the base of the waterfall that marked the home stretch to the car.

Jumpy. As if.

The hikers approached. Laughing, joking, playing their music. Their ruckus grew steadily, bouncing off the rocks and ravines around us. Who in the seven hells went into the bush to play music?

Brandon shot me a look and moved his chin a few times to the beat, pursing his lips dramatically. As he started to click his fingers and mouth the words to the eighties rock ballad, I rolled my eyes and got on with it, moving across an exposed area that dropped away sharply if you strayed from the footholds cut into the rock.

The sensation of being watched made my belly tighten.

You couldn't actually *feel* eyes on you, though. That was superstitious bullshit. And anyway, there was nothing to worry about.

The music stopped.

I stilled.

Brandon sighed and, for a split second, we were just kids again, headed home. "Come on," he said, kindness, not mockery, in those two words.

Fury pulsed through me. In a moment, I could see myself throwing out my arm, forcing him to take me seriously, demanding we do this right. I wasn't just *jumpy*.

Then the music started up again. New song, same vibe. I had no idea what it was called, but I knew the chorus. Brandon's hand on my arm, and the quick, supportive squeeze as he looked ahead made me want to light the whole place on fire. Instead, I unlocked my jaw and lifted my boots, frustrated with myself.

The bridge appeared before me, a steel and wood construction just a few meters long but wide enough for us to walk abreast. Though the path ahead looked empty, I braced for the tourists' reaction to the sight of Brandon and I in our tactical gear as I jumped down the last few rocks and onto the path this side of the bridge.

A big, retro-looking boom box sat positioned in the centre. Timber beams vibrated as music belted out of the speakers. But there was no tourist to be seen.

Spells snapped into my mind, humming with power as adrenaline rushed through my limbs. My fingers bit into the wood of my wand but damned if my hand would shake.

Brandon snorted. "Jesus. Music to piss to? Really?" He lifted his weapon and set his feet. "Don't kill it until after the guitar solo, yeah?"

I didn't bother rolling my eyes at him. Beneath my boots, the wood felt strange after nothing but rocks and dirt for days, but the breeze felt cool and the afternoon sun was beautifully warm. All we needed was a few beers and some snags.

A safe perimeter.

Wand in one hand, eyes on the empty trail ahead of us, I dropped down on one knee and murdered the music halfway through the guitar solo Brandon was so keen on.

Silence descended. My own breathing sounded loud in the sudden quiet. I stood slowly, listening to the murmurs of the bush around us. "Hello!" The word got tossed back at me from the rocks. "This is Officer Aurora Gold," I called, cutting over my own echoes. "Come into the open slowly."

The response was the soft sigh of wind through the eucalypts and wattles.

Well, if they wanted to be temporary Australians, that was their business. Still, I gave one last, impatient, "Hello?"

The word echoed off the rocks. *Hello. Hello. Hello.*

With a hard roll of one shoulder, I unlocked some of the tight muscles in my neck and turned back to Brandon.

He stood exactly as I'd left him, of course. Gun cocked, feet set.

And behind him was a giant.

Fucking.

Lycanthrope.

The words of my ward spell flashed hot and bright through my mind. *Through this dome none shall leave or come unless it is with me.* The spell landed, an impenetrable sphere formed around us with enough power to send up a shower of rocks and sheer a branch. While I breathed, not a thrice-cursed thing was getting in or out without my say-so.

Brandon dropped to one knee and spun, following my gaze, his movements elegant and economical. I heard him reloading with silver bullets but didn't watch to see the standard ammunition fall away.

Movement beside the bridge made fury rush through my veins. My silver knife was in my hand before I'd registered what I saw.

A man, stretching lazily as he stood from where he'd apparently been lying on a rock on the slope beside the bridge. Within my shield.

Maybe a man.

And I already had one spell on the go.

Before I could consider re-casting, a growl came from the ravine below. The rise and fall of it struck primal terror into my heart that sent familiar waves of adrenaline through me. The lycanthrope on the other side of Brandon leapt, hit my ward face-first with the sound of a striking bell, and fell away. Its momentum carried it off the ledge and into an old gum. I didn't watch as the century-old tree collapsed over the fallen creature. It didn't matter. We were surrounded, because why not? They could throw a fucking party out there. They couldn't touch us. Nothing outside my ward could.

So I focused on our vulnerabilities. As if he felt my full attention, the guy said, in an infuriatingly accurate impersonation of me, "Hello."

"On the ground." Brandon's demand was underscored by the snap and click of him readying the rifle.

I would've just shot him. But, shit, I would've just shot a lot of people.

"Hello," the man said again, smiling at me, then Brandon, as he stepped through the bracken. His shirt had the national cricketing team's logo and was sagging massively in the front, like he'd been grabbed and yanked, hard. He had thongs on his feet, the ones with the Australian flag on them, but no shorts. One of his hands reached above his head, planted on the metal railing, and he lifted himself effortlessly over it.

As if he hadn't just performed a feat of inhuman strength, he nonchalantly lifted a bottle of beer to his lips and took a pull. The movement showed a spray of dried blood across his forearm.

Hells, I didn't think you could get much worse than a standard bogan, but here he was, the Lycan Bogan. Lycy to his mates. Probably.

"Officer Brandon Reeve requesting backup at the bridge west of Beehive Falls, main path. Lycanthrope pack."

Brandon's words seeped from the now-hot comms charm in my ear.

"I hate to say you're right," he added softly, just for me. I didn't glance over but I could see how steady he was from the corner of my eye even as he let out a long, drawn out sigh. "Feral cats do get pretty damn big."

The guy's gaze swung in my direction as if he understood Brandon's fart-arsing around. The lycan was close enough I could see the brilliant green of his eyes, the gleam of his teeth as he smiled. He drew in a deep breath then skimmed his eyes over me like I was the last piece of leftover pizza in the morning. My skin crawled. I settled myself more firmly, lowering my weight just a little.

The silver knife in my hand wasn't made for combat. It was to channel spells. Well, I had a spell in use already.

Looked like today, my pretty silver foci was going to do double duty.

"On the ground or I shoot," Brandon said, the words matter-of-fact now.

"Hello," he mimicked again, then laughed.

Around us, snarls sounded, violent, gleeful sounds that melded with the roar of blood in my ears as the sun warmed my skin.

They were playing with us.

There was ice in my veins and time slowed. I knew how fast lycanthropes could move, even in human form. I knew how strong they were. I couldn't drop the ward without letting them all in. They were everywhere. They'd be on us in an instant.

We'd done this dance, and I knew every fucking step.

But we'd mis-stepped.

Over the lycan's head, I met Brandon's eyes, and my heart sank. An eerie sense of calm settled over me. We both knew.

Maybe one of us would get out of this.

Determination shot through me, hot and hard, shattering that peace. But I could already see a grin spreading over Brandon's face as his attention swung to the lycan. Rage rolled through me. He'd always been *faster—*

And, into the moment of quiet, I heard him murmur, "Here, kitty kitty."

ONE
PRESENT DAY

HALF-A-DOZEN HEAVILY LINED FACES BEAMED AT ME. WHY? WHY WERE they *beaming*?

"You must be Aurora," the shortest, roundest one said, her words so fizzy with excitement it made my eyes water.

Oh. Shit. Me. They were excited about *me*. One of them took my arm and towed me further into the room. "Your grandmother told us all about you, dear." Hellfire. I hoped that was an exaggeration. "It's so good to see a young witch coming on board! Look, everyone, Aurora is here!"

"It's Rory." But my protest was lost beneath their effervescent welcome.

I just wanted to get to work, but apparently stage one of my induction involved a spread that could've come off a bake stand at a school fair—and, before witches were legalized, that probably would have been a common side hustle.

Scones, breakfast muffins, slices, cakes—all homemade. The tea was weaker than the water I used to wash my dishes. To top it off was a handwritten banner that read *Welcome to the East Melbourne Coven, Aurora!* It had been decorated with pressed flowers.

"Hi, Rory," said a woman wearing paint-splattered pants and a wary smile. "I'm Janet. I'll be working with you for all your Koori clients. I'm the district Elder."

Trust the First Nations elder to have heard my preferred name. "Hi, Janet. Looking forward to working with you." I caught a jar of jam as it slipped from the nicotine-stained fingers of a grinning witch. Grimly amused, I watched the way she turned the situation to her advantage, using my momentary pause as I held the jar to press a plate into my hand.

I felt like a kid while I tried to smile, remember names, respond appropriately, and not drop the scone all at the same time. *Note to self: next time I want a change, I'll get a new hair color, not a new job.*

Behind the veterans, a younger woman with awesome jet-black hair and sapphire-blue highlights sent me a look of sympathy before she quietly removed herself from the fray. Smart woman. I should've gone sapphire blue, too. And also hightailed it out of there.

Some of the cream wilted down the side of my scone to puddle on my saucer as the jam-fumbling witch planted herself beside me, blocking the nearest exit, filling the air with chatter. "Oh, and you really ought to try Suzie's blueberry bar before we get caught up on the humdrum. Suzie's grandson owns a blueberry farm out in Silvan. Brings her fresh berries, doesn't he, Suzie?" Her eyes glittered. "He's a handsome young lad, isn't he, Suzie?" she went on, patting my arm knowingly. "Great butt," she said under her breath in an aside to me. "Looks like he knows how to use his hands, too, if you know what I mean!"

I estimated the likelihood of said grandson knowing the difference between a clitoris and a haemorrhoid as slim to none.

"I should find Arthur," I said firmly, before the grandson idea could gather any momentum. "I'll be back for that slice." Gazes of a half-dozen women, who were all obviously accustomed to people submitting to their affection, swung to me. Well, curse it, if I'd wanted to be fussed over, I'd have gone to work with my own grandmother. "This is such a great welcome. But I won't feel right until I know what I'm doing."

The jar-dropping witch, who might've been Bernie or Becky or even Esmerelda, for all I knew, made a harrumph of disapproval. "Well, you won't get that from Arthur. Half the time, that boy doesn't even know what he's doing, and the other half of the time, he's pulling on his own—"

"Hush, Bernie," another said with a disapproving frown. "I'm sure Aurora knows all about wizards." She cleared her throat, and I tried very hard to smother a grin. "Well, you go on up, dear," she said, her frown melting as she gazed up at me like I was the one grandchild who hadn't spilled food on their party dress at Solstice. "And when you come on back, we'll get you all settled in. Let her go, Bernie. She's quite right. Whether we like it or not, we all have those to-do lists now."

"The old days were much simpler," said a woman whose handmade name badge read *Cici—she/her*. Cool. Pronouns. I could get in on that. "No data or performance reviews. Just you, your wand, some herbs and foci, your coven and your flock. Now there's *paperwork*."

Plus a wage, superannuation, sick leave, holiday pay, and tax deductions.

I kept that to myself, sending them all my warmest, I'm-a-good-kid-with-good-manners smile as I went past the fussily decorated table in the direction I'd been pointed.

There wasn't space to get lost. Budgets being what they were, I hadn't expected a massive, multi-story complex. "Cozy" was a nice description for the little townhouse with its high, old ceiling and narrow rooms overflowing with furniture, plants, and piles of Really Important Stuff. Still, it had character that even the governmental grey paint and grey-flecked grey flooring couldn't overwhelm, vases that overflowed, doilies, donated mismatched furniture, and candles. Of course. Put a coven in a place long enough, it'd become a home, albeit a fussy one, if it was an old-school coven. And this was a very old-school coven.

I kept my face neutral as I went up the stairs. Well, I wanted different. I wasn't going to get anything as different from my last job as this, was I?

Should've gone for the blue streaks. Or maybe purple. I'd look great with purple hair.

A thirty-something, weekend-warrior type looked up from a coffee machine that perched precariously on a hallway table. His expression was equal parts curiosity and commiseration. "Aurora?"

I put out my hand. "Rory," I said, as he took it and shook.

"Arthur. I heard the welcome party banging their drums. Forgive me for not being present, but it sounded like they had you covered." He took an extra coffee cup. Not a flower in sight. "Anyway, word on the grapevine is you're a hard arse, so I figured you'd be okay. Coffee?"

He didn't look at me to deliver any of that. I didn't care, just sighed in pleasure at his offer. "Please."

He smiled down at the coffee machine. He had dimples, and he knew how to work them.

The coffee-making ritual gave me time to look around. He mentioned a few key points of interest: a bathroom, storage, his office—which he didn't share with anyone, I noticed—a meeting room, and the tech hub of the coven, currently unstaffed.

"It's not much," he said with false humility. "But we're two blocks from the local police station, and the tram line right around the corner makes travel a breeze."

"Uh huh." I wasn't here to give a real estate appraisal.

Inside Arthur's office, I was waved towards one of the chairs across from his desk.

I glanced around. Big windows overlooking the neighbour's brickwork. A few framed landscapes. His staff mounted on brackets on the wall.

Old school.

And he definitely had the most space in the building. The rooms I'd passed showed desks and office chairs crowded in so close I'd have my knees in my ears trying to work there.

With some grim thoughts about middle managers, I settled into the chair.

"So, I thought I'd give you a quick rundown of the coven's core values before we get into the nitty gritty of your work."

I folded my hands, reached for patience, found some, and marvelled. "Sure."

"Mutual respect and equality is, of course, the foundation of this coven," he began. This from behind his big desk, sitting in his new leather chair, in the one office that didn't have seven other people crammed into it.

"Mmm." I shifted a little, wishing, not for the first time, wizards came with a *skip* button.

"I know you've heard that before," he said in a way that he probably thought was charmingly self-deprecating. "So, I won't bang on about it. You'll see it in action. Accountability is, of course, critical. Risk assessments and case notes need to be kept updated so I can manage any situation that arises. We aren't police; we're here to tend to our flock, to keep them on the straight and narrow." He nodded at his own wisdom. It was kind of like being near someone sniffing their own farts. "To engage supernaturals in our society, help smooth over any bumps, and to ensure magi use their powers wisely. We're first responders."

So he didn't know what a first responder was. He did know what paperwork was though, obviously. That was the bottom line.

He flashed his dimples again. "And, of course, we need to discuss integrity," he went on, leaning forward.

At that point, I totally zoned him out.

When he finally fell silent, I said, "Thanks, Arthur. So, about the work. I'm assuming I'll get a rundown of my caseload from one of the coven?"

He nodded his agreement. "Unfortunately, you won't be able to do a thorough hand-over due to the nature of your predecessor's departure."

Sure, sour grapes didn't give much juice. I ignored the opportunity to garner gossip. I didn't value this guy's opinion. There would be someone in the know I could talk to. Confidentiality between a coven and the world was sacrament, but I was on the inside now.

"Aurora—"

"Rory."

His smile turned apologetic. "Rory. Most of what you need to know is in the handbook." He pushed the bound manual that had been sitting exactly at right angles to his laptop toward me. *Metro Procedures for Caretaker Witches.* "This is an established coven," he went on. Just what I needed, some light bedtime reading. "Most of the witches here are very... set in their ways."

That was so obvious I had planned on letting it go without saying.

The thing was, as much as their scones and welcome poster amused me, there was a reason the traditions were what they were. We didn't always even know what those reasons were, until we messed with them.

Anyway, they were cute. In a terrifying, grandmother-level-omnipotence sort of way.

Out of nowhere, without any sort of lead-in, Arthur declared, "I'm a feminist." And then he paused.

I met his eye and bit my tongue. He just sat there as if it was my turn to say something. Perhaps dig out a gold star.

When I just waited silently, content to let the awkward pause grow even more awkward, he shuffled a little in his seat and then went on.

"I know you're from the country, and you would be used to wizards getting in your way, telling you to go back to the kitchen and cook love potions."

I had been told exactly that. Still, I wasn't giving him the satisfaction of sharing my righteous indignation.

"Love potions are a Class B substance." My words were brisk.

He grinned at me again, as if trying to get me to share a joke. "Regardless, I want you to know you have my full support." I nodded and went to stand, because surely, this was the end. "I figure a strong, independent woman like yourself wouldn't necessarily want that."

Oh, wow, there was no irony. None. Was that…even possible?

"I just hope you never need it," he said with such concern that I was taken aback.

"I think this should cover me for now, though." I added, holding up the manual. If I ever needed Arthur to bail me out, I was in very dire straits.

As shields went, it might be useful.

He stood and walked me to the door. "Part of your caseload is a local lycanthrope pack," he said with a nod. "They're considered high-risk. I'm the district expert, so you don't need to worry. We'll work that together."

My feet were lead, and ice rushed through my veins. *Sun warming my face as blood began to dry on my hands. Black cockatoos screaming their way across the sky.* I looked down at the floor beneath my feet, drew in air. I was standing on carpet. Not bridge. Not rock. Carpet.

Lycans already? Shit. Suddenly, I didn't care that I'd just been patronized.

"Who's their Alpha?"

"Beo Velvela. Police are investigating them, but we're to keep up our surveillance until charges are laid."

I ignored the clutch of anxiety in my breast. I could deal with lycans.

"Can you email me the name of the officer in charge of the investigation, information on relevant parties, and crimes they could be linked to?"

He nodded. His arm went behind me, his hand resting on the door. I stepped out of that intimate circle without thinking, but he didn't react.

"Betty—your predecessor—and I were going along to where the Alpha works as part of our surveillance. *The Playground,*" he added as I opened my mouth to question him. "Mixed Martial Arts dojo and gym. Beo runs Brazilian Jiu-Jitsu classes, and his whole pack—that we've identified—attend. I've been sparring with them once a week for about two months. Betty sat and knit. She posed as my mother."

Rolling with a lycan pack as undercover surveillance? If this was normal, where the fuck was my hazard pay?

Arthur was either totally ignorant, absolutely amazing, or very brave. I highly doubted he was all three.

"I don't knit. And I don't roll with lycans." *Bones crunched, a splintering, wet sound.* My stomach rolled. Nope-ity, nope, no.

I had goals. One day, I wanted to spend a whole week eating ice cream, chips, and having amazing sex, preferably with someone else.

He shrugged. "So, you can be my girlfriend. Scroll through social media, send some snaps. You and I know you're not that sort of woman, but they'll see what they expect."

There he went again. I was tempted to hit back, but I bit my tongue.

"Is it a mixed class?"

The words popped out of my mouth while my brain held back my ample vitriol. I wondered if he heard my teeth groaning as I clenched my jaw shut.

He nodded, a faint frown appearing on his face. "The pack isn't all male, and there are some human players. It's useful for me to have someone on the sidelines. I'll need you armed and prepared if there's trouble."

On the *sidelines?* "Arthur," I said through my teeth, trying to keep hold of my last shred of patience, "if you're on a mat in the middle of a lycan pack who actually want to hurt you, there's not a damn thing anyone can do, even armed, prepared, and perfectly positioned." Okay. My vote leaned towards totally ignorant. "I'll get up to date with the information, and we'll figure out how to play it." I emphasised the *we* part, because obviously, Arthur's decision-making skills lent more towards finding opportunities to inflate his own ego rather than keeping his insides on the inside.

His frown deepened, but he nodded his agreement. "I've been going on a Tuesday. Five-thirty until seven."

"We'll keep your pattern." Although why he had a pattern for undercover surveillance, I had no idea. Tuesday night gave me a whole two days, if I counted today, which I absolutely did. Urgency drummed through my veins. *Of* course, *it's lycans. That's just great.* "Any other high-risk cases I should know about?"

"Just Beo. You've got a few moderate threats, but mostly, it's nonviolent."

Well, that was something. I went to leave, then paused; I didn't want to go off half-cocked, even if it was sort of my specialty.

"What belt are you?"

He blinked at me. "With the BJJ? White. It's just a cover."

Because anything he wasn't good at didn't matter, I suspected. Yeah, he was toast if they decided they wanted a snack. Shit. "Any combat training or hand-to-hand combat experience?"

His brows rose. "I'm a wizard, Rory."

My heart sank. Yep, that told me everything I needed to know...and confirmed my worst suspicions.

Lucky for both of us, I was a witch.

Two

My desk still held Betty's embroidered *magick happens* in a frame leaning against the wall and an indoor plant that crowded the edge of the desk.

I eyed the plant unhappily but didn't go with my first instinct of tossing it. Who knew? Maybe it was actually more than it seemed. Or maybe it would die of natural causes and I could sidestep the chiding I would no doubt receive for trashing it.

There was clutter, but no witch, at the desk to the left of mine. That wasn't so unusual—out of necessity, our hours were flexible. As long as we put in the right amount of time over the two-week cycle, ticked our boxes, and kept our noses clean, the union generally kept the government off our backs about it.

Cici, the witch who'd been sighing over the old days, strode in and saw me setting up my laptop. Her eyes grew overbright, and she turned away, but not before her face went as pale as her smile became determined.

With an inward sigh, I figured it was never too early to start putting together the pieces. And she looked like the first piece.

"Doesn't sound like there was a lot of love lost between Betty and Arthur."

Cici slid into a chair with a squeaky coaster on my right and tapped a few keys on her keyboard. So, she was my neighbour. I was kind of sad it wasn't the bawdy Bernie.

"Arthur loves himself quite enough." Her tone held no innuendo but plenty of disapproval. "Saves us the hassle. Has he asked you out yet?"

"No." I thought of that oh-so-casual arm, the judicious employment of those cute dimples. *Not yet.* "Wizards." I wrinkled my nose a little in case she didn't hear the distaste in my tone.

Her smile was fleeting, strained. She cleared her throat. "I can help you with getting to know your caseload. Betty liked to chat about her clients."

Well, that made my day a lot easier. "Thanks, Cici. I missed working in a coven." Maybe that was an exaggeration, but her smile grew a bit stronger. "I know, when a long-time member leaves, it has an impact. Covens aren't just staff lists; we're families."

She let out a long, shaky breath. "Yes. Yes, we are. What happened to Betty... Well, it's shaken us all. But I'm sure the police will take care of it."

Alarm bells rang in my head. I kept my expression carefully neutral, though. "Can I ask?" Which was a bullshit way to ask a question, really, but it was the gentlest thing I could think of to say on the spot.

As if on cue, Cici's eyes filled. She dashed the tears away angrily. "She was killed by those horrible lycans on her way home from some last-minute meeting. It was—" The words ended as she drew in a sharp breath.

She didn't need to tell me what it was. I'd seen it myself. Still saw it sometimes. Grief and dread tugged at me. I put it aside to look at later and tried to focus on Cici.

"But it's being investigated." Her words were stronger, almost forceful. "Don't you worry. We aren't down and out, oh no." She drew a tissue and dabbed at her eyes, still scowling.

With a sinking feeling in my belly, I flipped open the lid of my new-to-me laptop. "Beo Velvela?" I asked her grimly.

"One of his," she said with a hard nod. "Good-for-nothing, testosterone-fuelled bags of teeth and ego, they are." And she nodded again, as if to reinforce her judgement.

Shit. I thought of Arthur's flimsy excuse for me attending the surveillance. Betty had been made, and we were still doing this as if we were undercover?

"They're on my caseload. I think I want to meet the cops handling the case." Because while a lycan's ego might be massive, I had a sneaking suspicion Arthur's would rival it.

She looked at me in horror. "You...but... They killed Betty! We aren't here to take over from the police. We're just the Caretakers. He shouldn't be on *anyone's* caseload."

I distinctly remembered my conversation with Arthur and once again bit my tongue.

"Why, I have a mind to go up and let that young buck have a piece of my mind. His no-good, money-grubbing uncle will have put him up to it, you mark my words!"

I certainly did. The magickal world was full of nepotism. There wasn't much getting around it. We'd been able to legally practice for only a bit over a decade, and to even train before then had been risky. How else would information have been passed on, but through families and long-standing friendships?

And those ties meant both alliances and feuds that were a lot older than me.

It was worth keeping Cici onside, so I sighed and said, "I was looking forward to working with folks who weren't criminals."

Her lips still tight, she shot me an unreadable look.

"We're all guilty of something." Her eyes dry, she stood and shook out her skirt before striding off towards the stairs, her shoulders square and her orthopaedic shoes striking the linoleum floor like battle drums.

Somehow, I kept my eyebrows from disappearing into my hairline. I turned back to my work. There was no shouting, but that didn't mean much. By the time I got myself set up, Cici had come back down, looking grimly determined as she conferred quietly with paint-speckled Janet on the other side of the room, shooting worried glances my way.

Feeling my newness very acutely, I took out the new work phone from my induction package and followed the instructions to set myself up so I could get to the real work.

Something about Betty's case notes felt wrong. I started my own notebook and searched for key info. Contact details, important dates, key facts—anything I considered a red flag. Nothing stood out amongst the monotony of this witch's last days.

Janet marched over and, all business, passed me a name and number. "The detective working Betty's case," she said firmly. "He's not the worst of them."

Well, as recommendations went…

"Thank you." My eyes skimmed the information. Taig O'Malley. I added it under Beo's important contact details. Cici vanished out the side door with a box of tissues and some secateurs. It seemed safest to let her take her grief out on the comfrey, so I flew solo until my belly told me it was time to eat.

The cream had collapsed, but the leftover scones were still good. In the tiny excuse for a kitchen, I found some instant coffee in a giant tin that had probably been moved from whichever government office had been raided for our furniture.

I tried to scrape some powder out, bent the spoon, considered pouring boiling water into the tin, and discarded the idea. A knife, perhaps? I eyed off the selection of mismatched butter knives in the drawer, considered the apparently diamond-hard coffee, and, with a sigh, shoved it back in the cupboard and took out a teabag.

After quickly checking the manual for policy regarding social media, I logged into the account I had made for my last job—nothing personal, but nothing deceptive, either—and began to go through local community pages and interest groups that could be relevant. I posted a picture of my sad mug of stewed tea on the desk, making very sure nothing except the generic backdrop of the plant perched behind it, no reflections of anything that could cause me problems later. I captioned it *can't get a decent coffee even in Melbourne*, put some emojis behind it, and popped it up. I'd start adding groups or people I wanted to keep an eye on later. It amazed me how willing people were to add anyone, and the things they'd post—or would be tagged into or comment on—could be useful.

I put in a call to Taig O'Malley and left a message when he didn't answer. The rest of my afternoon was spent touching base with relevant stakeholders, or at least trying to. It was refreshing to introduce myself, even just via phone, to people who I wasn't watching because they'd either committed a crime or were considered at risk to the general public. Other witches, a few wizards, a family with a magickal heirloom of middling importance; all more or less happy to talk to me.

I was accustomed to having my own car but had no wish to fight for parking spots, so I made do with the groceries I could carry and dealt with the tram. It was, apparently, a juggle I'd have to learn to manage.

Dad called while I was debating just eating a bag of chips for dinner. I chatted to him about the boring parts of my day while I cooked myself a real meal, complete with meat and green stuff. I felt better for it, especially when the chips became dessert.

It wasn't until I got into work the next day that I realized I'd forgotten to bring half drinkable coffee.

It was almost eleven before I broke and, really, I considered that to be nothing short of proof of my heroic dedication to my new duties.

I pulled open the front door to the coven and felt the slightest push. I stepped back, but whoever was on the other side didn't come barrelling through.

The guy was probably only slightly taller than average, with hair that might've been auburn ten years ago and now was salt and pepper. He sported one of those professionally friendly expressions slapped on like he'd known I was coming.

Which he had. Because he, like me, had felt the tug of the door.

My eyes narrowed ever so slightly when he didn't step aside. "Caretaker Aurora?" he asked, and, curse it, he had a sexy voice. Following up on that was not on my to-do list.

"Yes." If he knew me, he was probably a client. Elders take my coven for not having coffee. "I was just stepping out. If you call, I can make an appointment to see you at a later time."

"Sure," he said, easily. And now he did, finally, step aside. "I was just here to see Arthur and figured I'd come a bit early, try to catch up with you, too."

I stepped past him. The narrow footpath meant there wasn't a huge amount of personal space. He smelled like sandalwood and coffee. Fuck him. "Fine. Well. I'll be back in ten."

"Ten?" His hands were tucked in his pockets as he looked at me with mild interest. "Going on a smoke break?"

"Coffee."

"Ah." He glanced in the direction of the nearest cafe. "Mind if I join you?"

I really did, but said, "Yeah. Sure," and strode off in the direction of coffee.

The jerk fell into step beside me on the footpath. I bet he didn't even need a cuppa. I bet he'd had one five minutes ago. My head pounded.

"Sorry. In the confusion, I didn't introduce myself. I'm Taig O'Malley. East Melbourne Supernatural Detective. Welcome aboard."

Now I had to be polite. "Rory." I offered him my hand without breaking my stride. "Been in Melbourne long, Detective?"

"At this precinct for a good seven years now, working one job or another." He smiled a bit as he opened the door to the cafe. "Let's save the small talk until after you're caffeinated, hey?"

So maybe he had a soul. I shot him a look of gratitude. "What's your poison?"

"Regular latte. Thanks, Rory." And he slid into a booth.

Somewhat off-balance that he hadn't argued about buying his own, I went and placed the order. Takeaway. It made sense, really; I'd invited him to join me. Sort of. Hadn't I? Anyway, who cared. I grabbed the coffees, considered setting his in front of him and walking off. I was pretty sure he'd just fall in beside me if I tried it.

So, I sat and sipped. "Well," *Come on, brain. You can do it.* "I'm keen to get what information you can give me on the investigation into"—Betty wasn't her real name. Shit. What was it?—"Elizabeth Brown." Hells, I had an awesome brain. As a reward, I had another sip of coffee.

"Of course. I can't tell you much, unfortunately." Even with his words brisk, he still sounded a bit rough, a bit sexy. He'd missed his calling. He would've been an amazing voice actor.

"Because you don't have much?" I pressed, shifting the scarf around my neck absently, a little warm now I was inside the cafe. "Or because you can't talk about an active case?"

He sighed. Sent me an apologetic look. "Both, unfortunately."

I sat back, drank a bit deeper, and considered him. He'd followed me to get coffee. Maybe he liked coffee. Or maybe he knew a bit more than he was letting on.

"The lycan pack led by Mr. Velvela are my clients," I pointed out, quite reasonably. "I understand that gives us some leeway to exchange information." In fact, it should mean we worked hand in hand. I'd read *that* part of the damned procedures book.

"Of course," he agreed blandly. "And to be honest, I don't have much on Mr. Velvela. Actually, I don't have anything…bad."

I shifted and glanced out the window, watching a pigeon bop along on the concrete, hunting for something to snack on. "So, he's a model citizen."

Bones shattered. I could feel the warmth of the sunlight on my skin, the ice-cold terror in my veins. I kept my face perfectly straight.

"As far as I know," he said with a sigh.

And wasn't that the clincher? We just couldn't keep up with supernaturals. We didn't have the technology, the experience, to afford them innocent until proven guilty. It just was what it was.

"He had a speeding ticket a year ago. That's it. Squeaky clean."

Well, fuck. I'd done worse than that—and been caught. I turned back to Taig. He sat back with his ankle folded up over his knee. Comfortable? Or taking up extra space? I wasn't sure yet.

"Any other lycans active in the area, aside from Velvela and his pack?"

He considered me over his latte, his head cocked ever-so-slightly to the side. The professionally friendly persona was gone and, I had to admit, I liked his hard-eyed cop expression. It felt honest.

"I don't know if I can tell you that, Caretaker."

Of course, he could. "It's my area," I reminded him calmly.

"You're one of the witches in the East Melbourne Coven, that's true."

He lifted his cup to his lips. I let the silence stretch out.

And so did he.

So, O'Malley could be a hard arse. That was good to know. Sometimes hard arses made good allies.

Sometimes I climbed over their corpses.

"All right, then." I stood. That was a whole lot of nothing. I didn't thank him. I figured his coffee was thanks enough. I walked back out into the winter wind and started back to the coven.

Jerk. He definitely knew something. Now I'd have to ask Arthur, who I didn't trust as far as I could throw.

Back at my desk, I flopped down into my once-ergonomic chair and it creaked alarmingly under my weight. I caught myself, opened up my case notes and, with keystrokes that were firmer than they needed to be, summarised the absolutely nothing conversation with sexy jerk detective.

I heard him return, of course. He didn't go straight up to Arthur but greeted a few of the witches before stealing Cici's unoccupied chair beside me. I shot him a quick, annoyed look, and he leaned forward. "Quietly. Between you and me. I've got unsubstantiated reports that we've had riftrunners in the area. Lycans working with some faeries to sell pixie dust." His eyes bored into me, and his voice lowered further as he said, "But you don't know that, and you don't talk about it, yeah?"

I took that warning seriously and stood. "I want some sun," I explained when Bernie, on her way to Cici's desk, wiggled her brows at me and shot the detective a loaded look. "Be right back." I jerked my head for him to follow me out into the tiny spit of a car park, skimming the area quickly for anyone coming or going before I turned my gaze on him again. "First. Why am I not talking to my coven about this?" I demanded of him, but I kept my voice down.

He stepped close and said quietly, "Unsubstantiated reports that I need to take seriously. Trust me on this."

Magi.

He thought there was a magi involved.

I paced away. I wasn't surprised that drugs were being moved. But faeries? Shit. Faeries were next to impossible to track down. They were like the sneaky rogues of the supernatural world, where lycans were just the big, scary barbarians that, while tough, you could still take out through sheer physical force.

I suddenly felt grateful I was dealing with a lycan pack, and that surprised the shit out of me.

The devils I know.

I paced back to him, hands on my hips. "Why are the lycans

riftrunners? Why not faeries? Since they're involved already… They're damned impossible to get a hold of. The lycans would make better knee breakers."

"I've got some theories," he said, looking at me with speculation. Then his eyes narrowed slightly. "Where were you posted last, Caretaker?"

"Ballarat." I didn't want to go down that line of questioning. I'd kept some of my qualifications out of my job application. Well, one key qualification and a shit ton of experience in that key field. "Hit me with your theories."

He held up a hand as if to pause me. A ring glittered on his pinkie. "You're new on the job."

I rolled my eyes. "Yes. I've never been a witch before yesterday. You caught me."

A bit of a smile tugged at his mouth. "Classically trained. That's what your file says. Start and end of it."

"Classically trained" was the nice way of saying "part of the illegal magi movement that we're now going to pretend we never persecuted" and I was grumpy enough that I was just about willing to have a crack at him about that. But I didn't. "And? Theories, Detective?"

He considered me. And then, as if testing me, he said, "The rift has a stable entry and exit point. I suspect the Overworld exit point is in lycan territory; they take a cut of the profits, let the faeries do their business."

"Checks out." Didn't seem like super-secret information, though. I cocked a brow at him. "What's this got to do with a dead witch?"

He paused and said mildly, "You asked about other lycans."

"You told me my pack are pure as driven snow," I reminded him, just as mild. "The logical conclusion, then, is to look for other lycans. I assume we know Betty was killed by a lycan; that isn't speculation."

"There isn't anything like a lycan kill." His face was painfully neutral as he said it.

Bones shattered, splintered, broken. I managed not to shudder. "No," I agreed, then had to pause to swallow down the lump in my throat. "No, there isn't." I glanced away. Light traffic. Parked cars. A cyclist juggling their headphones. A bin chicken looking for lunch. "So, are these riftrunners traceable?"

He shifted a little, his gaze following mine as he positioned himself beside me rather than facing me. "Not yet. We aren't even sure how many there are or where the rift on our end is…exactly."

They had a good idea then. Fine. Good. "And Mr. Velvela is just letting these lycans use his territory for their drops?" I asked, underwhelmed by his leaps of logic.

"My thoughts exactly," he agreed. "But I can't find a single link. Unless there have been some very quiet shifts of territory control, this must be happening under Velvela's nose."

So, untraceable lycans, drugs, and faeries. Day two of my new job felt a lot like my old job except with more indoor plants and less hazard pay. And less coffee. *So much for a change of pace.* "If you find out anything—even if it's a maybe—I'd really love to be kept up to date. And I'll return the favor."

"Of course," he agreed. I didn't believe him for a moment. "Before you go, though, Caretaker…are you familiar with laws around banishment spells?"

Ah. The standard "don't bring a nuke to a knife fight" talk. "I am very familiar, Detective, with laws around many uses of magick, force, and a number of other things too." It never ceased to amaze me that, somehow, we'd managed to hold on to the banishment spell as a bluff.

Just like a nuke, banishing anyone had serious consequences.

The look he shot me was one of amused speculation. "Well, that should keep us both on the same side, then, shouldn't it, Caretaker?"

The threat, however mild, wasn't lost on me. I wanted to tell him I'd stay on my side, and I'd see where he wandered. I didn't. "Following the rules keeps our lives simple. I like simple. Thanks for your time, Detective. I'll be in contact if I learn anything."

"A pleasure, Caretaker."

Curse him, he sounded amused.

THREE

By the time I got back to my desk, my irritation at the detective was forgotten. Primarily because a cat I hadn't seen the day before decided it belonged on my keyboard.

"Look, I can't afford real estate either." I worked on the theory that it was a coven cat and probably more capable of understanding me than most masculine members of my own species. "Let's bunk together for now and eat the rich later."

Whether it agreed or not, I couldn't tell, but it let me shift it onto my lap so I could keep working.

The day waned, and I forced myself to stop when the office grew quiet. Without any interest, I ate my leftover chicken and the salad that sat limply in the bottom of the container. I needed to figure out where I could buy hot chips around here.

Arthur breezed downstairs in shorts, trainers, and with a brand-name sweater that cost almost as much as a week's rent. I was reasonably sure that brand had seriously horrible Bangladeshi sweatshops. I doubted Arthur cared.

I eyed the bag he held. It was too small for a gi, if he even owned one. He wouldn't need it tonight, regardless. So why have a bag? Didn't he have pockets? All guy clothes had pockets. Proper ones.

"Got my wand," he said, following my gaze and patting his sports bag. "Figured we could head off early so you can get a feel for the place before we go in."

A wand. He had a bag for a wand. Seriously. What was this, the nineteen-hundreds? We had holsters for that shit now.

"I'd like to have a bit of time to look around," I agreed, keeping my thoughts to myself. Specifically, I wanted to identify all possible exits.

I'd decided, at some point, I'd go along with his plan. There were a number of reasons in both the 'for' and 'against' columns, but the bottom line was he was on the mat, not me. Right now, I wasn't very invested in Arthur's survival. And with him at the forefront, my chances of walking—or running—out, increased.

Whatever worked.

As we left, I questioned him on the tram lines we'd take. I'd only been in Melbourne a few days, and it sure wasn't second nature yet. Before the tram even arrived, I plugged our route and destination into the tracking app.

He watched me, his brows raised. "That's for client tracking."

"It'll help if we get audited on our timesheets," I told him, appealing to his inner bureaucrat rather than telling him the driving reason: safety.

His face lit up. "Can you add me, too?"

"Already done, King." The jibe slipped out before I put my brain into gear, but he didn't hear the sarcasm and instead grinned at me as if we shared a secret joke. I felt a bit bad and dug into my bag for some gum. It didn't fit in dainty pockets, curse it. When I offered, he accepted, then leaned back on the seat beside me.

We climbed off the tram, and I made a careful note of landmarks while skimming the tram timetable. I wouldn't remember which lines ran at what times, but they stopped about every seven minutes, and that was good to know. If we had to go fast, a tram probably wouldn't be fast enough. It certainly wouldn't be if we just missed one, and that information could save a life.

We wandered. The winter air had bite, so I pulled my blazer closed and fluffed my scarf.

A huge blonde approached on a giant fuck-off motorcycle. He shot me a glance as he went past, studying me. Apparently, he hadn't heard of protective gear; even his helmet wasn't secured.

If Detective O'Malley played nice, I'd let him know there were some traffic violations they could pick that lycan up on. Because there was no way that particular blonde wasn't a lycan.

"We've got time to grab a coffee if you want," Arthur offered as we neared a cafe with cheerful umbrellas rattling in the wind.

"No, thanks." Much as I desperately wanted coffee, I didn't need to pee in the middle of his class. Being separated seemed like a bad idea. Unless I was throwing him to the wolves. When I thought about it like that, coffee wasn't such a terrible option.

I chewed my gum absently and didn't stare as the huge blonde parked his bike, lifted a small bag off the back of it, and strode across the street. Arthur cocked a brow at me, and I nodded.

I'd made him. Hellfire, half the block had made him.

Arthur looked at his watch. I glanced over too. "I don't want to be in there too long." I lied without a qualm. "We've got time to stroll around the block, right?"

"It's cold," he complained but kept pace beside me. I didn't peer into The Playground as we passed it, being more interested in the building over the road and those beside it.

I gave him a friendly nudge. Hey, he'd been half decent for a whole twenty minutes. Maybe I'd been wrong about him. "King, I'm from Ballarat. This isn't cold. You know what's cold? Snow is cold."

His sulk instantly ended. He had blue eyes, I realized, as he flashed me those dimples. "Sure, but you're not wearing shorts." And his gaze rolled down my legs as if imagining me with fewer clothes on.

Nope, my initial assessment was on point. "You're right," I agreed blandly. "Good thing you're hairy, isn't it?" And, before he could figure out if he was insulted or not, I feigned interest in a group of businesses working out of the one building. Access would be easier here. Did it connect to The Playground?

I didn't try to scout it out now. We didn't have that much time. But maybe later.

By the time we made it back, Arthur was rubbing his hands together to combat the cold. He went straight to the desk while I sized up the facilities. I had an excuse.

Ground floor was a gym. It was quiet and small, mostly free weights. I went over to them while Arthur paid for his class. The fire exit was behind some empty benches, but not marked as well as I thought it was supposed to be. I noted the weights, the number of bars, and the variety of plates available. It was all fine, but was that actually a fire door? Something else for Detective O'Malley.

Arthur waited for me at the base of the stairs. I could hear people talking up there already, and the occasional burst of laughter.

Upstairs. Only downstairs would've been worse.

Dread coiled in my belly. I wish I'd sent my best friend Aspen a message and told her how awesome she was.

Ignoring the normal reaction to walking into a pack of lycans, I forced my feet to move and went up alongside Arthur.

The universal smell of BJJ—sweat, bleach, and body odour—was familiar and welcoming. I didn't let the sense of homecoming lull me as I scanned the area, lightly skimming my eyes over the gathered people.

"Hey, Arthur," someone called, and he lifted a hand in response, steering us to the side. "Brought some fresh meat?"

The question was good-natured, the speaker a bit shorter than me, wiry, and with a smile that was as friendly and authentic as a bunch of plastic flowers.

"This is Aurora," Arthur said, putting a possessive hand on my lower back. It sat there like a chunk of ice. "She's here to check things out."

The hair on my neck stood up. I stepped away from Arthur's hand, and locked the correction I wanted to give behind my teeth. If there were less than five lycans there, I'd eat my charmed earrings.

In the face of those odds, what was the point of getting in Arthur's face about appropriate boundaries?

"Hey, Aurora, you going to get on the mat?" the friendly guy asked me directly.

I saw the quick look Arthur sent him, the shake of his head, the roll of his eyes. And I ignored Arthur completely.

"Rory," I told Friendly Guy, offering my hand. "I'm new to the area, just seeing what's around."

He stepped closer, and the smile became fixed. His eyes flickered down to the ring on my hand. "Yeah," he agreed, as he gingerly shook my hand the way you'd touch a coiled snake. "Jeff."

I filed his description away in my head. Young, easy going. Wary of me. Cool and normal.

"Many of your club fight professionally, Jeff?" I positioned myself at his shoulder, going for the non-threatening vibe. I looked over the space, not the people in it.

The space was long, well-lit by big industrial lights with big fans that would be important in summer. A big man strode towards us. Everything was big.

I hated it. And, curse it, I kind of liked it at the same time.

I didn't let myself stare at the incoming mountain of lycan, but, Hellfire, every single cell in my body felt him approaching.

Beo.

Jeff didn't respond, his eyes flickering nervously over me. Oh, yeah, we were made all right. My shoulder blades itched.

"Let's run," the big man said in a voice that carried. Jeff was already off before I could so much as consider farewelling him, leaving me in the metaphorical dust.

Arthur, in the skin-tight rashie they all wore, passed me by as Beo took Jeff's spot at my shoulder. Anxiety hummed in the back of my brain. Silently, I let my favorite ward spell float through my mind, finding the words, feeling them and the power behind them, ready to be called upon.

"Hey," I said, offering Beo Velvela a hand. "You're the coach, right?"

The man looked down at the rings on my fingers. The settings for my charms were all stainless steel or gold, not silver. Was he trying to figure out the metal or just naturally suspicious?

I waited, leaving my hand outstretched, ignoring the reflexive social discomfort the long pause brought. His skin was brown, his face rough-carved, his hair only a hop, skip, and jump away from being shaggy.

And when he lifted his eyes to meet mine, his were green. Not light hazel, not blueish, but a real green that I'd only seen once before.

Oh, shit. He's related to Duke.

Even as the thought exploded through my mind, he took my hand, his fingers big and hot and strangely careful. *My fists, wet with blood. Bones shattered. The sun warm on my skin.* But there was no sun, no bones breaking. I drew in a breath, pushing the memory away.

"Pleased to meet you, Rory." He'd been across the other side of a room that hadn't been silent when I'd told Jeff my name. If I'd had any doubts, I'd have known then, for sure, that this person wasn't human.

Preternatural hearing? Tick. Heightened sense of smell? Tick. Amazing shoulder span? Tick.

"I'm Beo. You don't have any knitting with you."

His eyes bore into my soul. A wave of heat swept through me. Men jogged past, a dizzying array of bodies that made me feel like the world spun around us. I dragged my eyes forcibly away from his face.

Was hypnotism a lycan thing? Maybe an Alpha thing? I'd only heard it attributed to faeries. My heart beat too fast. I could feel it, trapped behind my ribs like a bird. I breathed, focused.

We'd been made, but they weren't throwing us out or tearing us apart. Either they were waiting for the opportune time, or they weren't planning on killing us. I'd hope for the best. I'd already done everything I could to prepare for the worst anyway, short of coming in here in my full Retrieval Officer kit, which was currently illegal for me to do anyway.

Hating the display of weakness, I tried to remember what he'd said, fumbling my words. Arthur loped past and shot me a carefree grin, completely oblivious, thank the Elders.

Knitting. Betty had knitted. I shook my head. Even knowing what he meant, I had no idea how to respond.

"Sorry, Coach, not following." Simplest, easiest. No games this way. "Are these your regulars?"

His face was impassive, or at least impassive enough that I couldn't make out much from the corner of my eye.

"More or less," he answered. "Sidestep!" he called, and the class all turned inwards and began to take running sidesteps. Arthur was holding up okay. I tried to focus on him, but not noticing the sheer presence of the man beside me took some work. "We've got a couple that you could partner with."

A couple? I could only see a few people who'd be my general height, and none of them were in my weight range. Drilling was always easier with someone who was close to your build.

"Anyone likely to come next week who'll suit me?"

I felt the look he sent me from the corner of my eye. It made my belly clench, and it wasn't in fear.

"Nothing better than what's in front of you."

Self-preservation was completely forgotten. I arched a brow, skimming my eyes over him in a very obvious assessment. Okay, so he was huge and stacked. He was also a lycan. I wasn't going there. He didn't need to know why, though.

"Pretty sure you're not supposed to flirt with students, Coach."

"Fine. Don't come train with us then. Reverse!" And though he didn't smile, there was a brief softening of his expression, despite the disinterest in my tone.

The chicken I'd eaten must've been a phoenix, because I'd swear that it had resurrected and was flapping around in my belly. He strode into the fray, joining in the warm-up, and I let my valiant legs carry me to a seat not occupied by someone's bag or drink bottle, sitting down before I fell.

I felt very much like Little Red Riding Hood, except my huntsman was a clueless, self-important bureaucrat, and there was way more than one big bad wolf.

Right then, the idea of being eaten conjured up some pretty amazing fantasies.

My fingers itched to text Aspen. Instead, I kept my eyes on the class as they did warm-ups. They were all incredibly fit. I'd expected no less. Still, they were sweating and breathing hard before the drink break.

Aside from the odd speculative look sent my way, it was all painfully normal.

This was the worst attempt at undercover surveillance I'd ever been part of, and I'd been in some doozies.

I pushed thoughts of Duke—*bright green eyes and face covered in blood*—aside. Slumping down in the chair, I watched without seeing as they began to drill transitions. My hands found their way into my pockets. One of them curled around my phone, the other around my keys. Two very comforting tools. I breathed.

Eventually, I gathered myself enough to do a headcount, to put names and faces to the lycans in front of me, going off Betty's notes, my case load, and Cici's information. When they broke for water again, I got up and stretched my legs, but kept my hands on my keys.

They rolled after a break, short bouts of low-pressure sparring. I kept my back to the wall and my eyes on the fray in front of me.

Arthur was, very obviously outclassed by everyone he fought with. They were gentle with him anyway. The lycans particularly were gentle with everyone—and each other.

I felt Beo's eyes on me from where he watched at the edge of the mat. A traitorous trickle of heat pooled low in my belly, regardless of my brain knowing it shouldn't. I ignored my body and assessed the enemy.

I wondered if Arthur could see that they let him flop like a fish on the line before reeling him in.

I doubted it.

He defended an armbar from a young lycan—Frankie? Probably Frankie. Part-time business student, part-time retail—and let his opponent set him up for an Americana. My face stayed in its neutral lines with little effort as I waited for Frankie to complete the transition, to lock Arthur down and submit him. I had to admit, I didn't mind seeing Arthur tap out.

And then Arthur rolled the wrong way as Frankie's grip tightened on his hand, and his weight shifted.

I surged to my feet, knowing what would happen next. "Let it go!" I shouted to Arthur, fear driving down my spine. "Left foot down, bridge! Roll in!"

It was too late, though. The crack of breaking bones was audible even over grunts and good-natured banter. A chill washed over me.

Frankie let Arthur go with horror, but Beo was already there, crouching over the infuriating wizard, white as skim milk and very, very still.

The mat cleared as I toed off my flats and waded into the space, giving up any defensible position as my heart hammered in my chest.

That hadn't been orchestrated.

That was pure bad luck mixed with a predictable amount of inflated self-belief on Arthur's part.

"Let's get you an ambulance," Beo was saying, his hands draped over his knees. Non-threatening. Supportive. Calm.

"No ambulance," Arthur said, between his teeth.

I rolled my eyes, grudgingly let go of my keys, and reached down to help him sit. "Look," I said, as he opened his mouth to protest. "Your arm is broken. We don't have a car. You want to sit on a tram right now, mate?"

He shot me a look that was shocky and, beneath it, scared. "I...I could call someone. A cab."

Briefly I considered breaking his other arm. "You don't have to pay for an ambulance," I reminded him.

Beo looked between us, his face impassive. "You could take him into the change rooms," he said softly to me. "See if he feels better after some time in the quiet. Maybe it isn't broken."

The offer was kind, insightful, and made my blood boil with its inferences.

Beo expected me to heal Arthur so we could continue our shitty excuse for surveillance, but he was too polite to come out and say, "Hey since you're a witch, you can fix that up, and we'll pretend not to notice."

Because Arthur didn't want it to end early, didn't want to be vulnerable, and certainly didn't want to be beaten...and Beo knew it.

Well, I wasn't playing either of their games.

"This is ridiculous," I told them both, standing so I could pull my phone out of my pocket. "I'm not a healer, and you're going to the cursed hospital, or you're going to tell the paramedics why." I punched in triple zero.

"Police, fire, or ambulance?" the impersonal voice asked on the other end.

"Ambulance."

"Putting you through."

Arthur spluttered his objections, his eyes all but bugging from his head. Maybe he hadn't realized quite how far gone the cover was.

I passed the phone to Beo, saying, "I don't know the address." Arthur now sat on the mat while Beo took the phone as he unfurled from his crouched position. "We need to get you downstairs. Think you can manage it, King?"

He started to struggle up, then paled. I grabbed him, and felt my back twinge as I hauled the heavy jerk to his feet.

"What are you doing?" he said under his breath, the words thick with disbelief.

"You had literally nobody fooled," I told him impatiently. "I'm cutting the bullshit. Walk slow. You're shaky. I'll get your gear. We can put your shoes on downstairs."

He was in no condition to argue with me. Beo had handed my phone to the big, shaggy blonde—Zane—and disappeared. Frankie and Jeff grabbed Arthur's stuff, Jeff taking it downstairs. I was left with the job of steadying the wizard.

Like usual.

Arthur shot me an alarmed look. "My bag—"

"We'll get it downstairs." As if he could think straight to cast spells right now.

He took a step and blanched as the hand cradled to his chest moved with his body. I waited, reaching for patience as my head spun. The ambulance wouldn't be quick; it wasn't like this was a life-or-death situation.

These lycans were confident we wouldn't find anything, otherwise they wouldn't have let us in and wouldn't have offered to let me heal Arthur to keep up this pretense.

Was Beo's confidence driven by innocence or arrogance?

Arthur took another step, and all I could do was stand there with him, a silent support, an outgunned guard. He began to mutter obscenities and what sounded like encouragement to himself. I let him have at it. I'd broken a few bones. The pain was real, even through adrenaline.

Betty had been killed. The assumption was that it was either by these lycans or someone they worked with.

There was no evidence, though, aside from the turf issue. I'd seen nothing that deserved their high-risk status so far, aside from the possibility for harm. And, really, if we were punishing people for their potential to do damage, then who had their eyes on our politicians?

Beo reappeared, his steps long and economical. "Three-minute rotations," he told the group. "Go easy."

Someone grabbed a phone, set a timer. They filtered back onto the mat. Beo's hands held some cardboard and a first aid kit, half of which made sense.

Following my gaze, Beo offered up the cardboard. "We'll splint this."

The furious look Arthur shot me made me raise my brows. "It's just a bit sore," he said between his teeth. "I'm fine."

The guy was sweating with pain. I didn't roll my eyes, and my restraint made me proud. "You can be more fine," Beo responded, the words mild, as he folded the cardboard and put a few bandages in as padding.

When he passed it to me, I held it carefully and observed Beo's ease with the supplies and the situation at large. He dug back into the box for a bandage. "I don't need this," Arthur said, taking another step.

"You're probably right," Beo agreed, still mild. "Put his arm into the depression there, Rory. It'll keep it stable while he's transported, save him some pain."

I fitted the makeshift splint over Arthur's grudgingly offered forearm, trying to be quick about it. He hissed in pain and made a choked noise. I took the bandage Beo passed me, working in silence to wrap it securely.

The potential for violence was huge while both my hands were occupied, but for some reason, there wasn't even a flutter of anxiety in my belly now. My early warning system wasn't wailing at me, and I had no idea why. But, shit, body knows best. Sometimes.

As soon as he was secured, Arthur shifted so he faced Beo, putting more space between them. The move was, very obviously, hostile.

Without a word, Beo picked up the first aid kit and left.

That was the second time he'd looked after Arthur—curse it—and been gracious about it.

Had he wanted me to do the first aid for practicality or so he didn't have to put his hands on Arthur? And, if it was the latter, why? Litigation?

Consideration? Not wanting to touch the wizard? I certainly understood the last one.

Arthur was able to walk more comfortably with the splinted arm cradled to his chest. "It's my wand hand," he told me, voice thick with impotent rage and pain.

Barefoot still, I escorted him downstairs and waited with him while the two lycans who'd helped stayed a few metres away.

I didn't talk. Arthur had nothing to say worth hearing, and I didn't want to be overheard anyway.

The paramedics arrived after Arthur had settled himself on a bench. One of them checked information with me, the other assessed Arthur. They admired the splint, approved of the fact it'd be fine to X-ray him in it, mentioned all the pain that Arthur wouldn't have due to Beo's thoughtfulness, and piled him into the back of the ambulance.

Barefoot, without a phone, and with a head full of confusion, I turned and went back in.

They'd done a lot more for Arthur than I suspected Arthur would do for them. Or for me, unless he thought it would get him accolades or leverage, which was beside the point.

Why? Why help him? Possible backlash? Murdering two of us in a semi-public place would make a splash. Was Beo so calculating that he'd done it to reduce suspicion? Was the suspicion that intense?

Cici talked about them like they were the killers who were just about to get caught, O'Malley like they were model citizens. They couldn't be both now, could they?

The class was rolling when I got back to the top.

Leaving without any acknowledgement of what they'd done felt wrong, but Beo was on the far side of the mat, his eyes on his students, his arms folded.

If it wasn't a lycan from this pack who'd killed Betty, they could be invaluable allies against the real killer.

"Thanks, Beo," I said, as if he was beside me. Maybe I could undo some of the damage that had been done by our—and the system's—assumption of guilt. "You and yours did more than you needed to. I won't forget that." His eyes lifted, met mine across the mat, and gave me a slight nod.

Approval? Acknowledgement? It hadn't been a big deal. I didn't owe him a life debt or anything. But I'd come to Melbourne to help people who wanted or needed to be helped, not to solve murders—certainly not to gather data to prove guilt.

I'd wanted a change, and innocent until proven guilty was definitely a change.

FOUR

"How're you doing, Oma?" I said, popping in the second earbud to free up my hands to cook while I spoke.

On the other end of the line, my grandmother let out a happy sigh. "I was worried about you today," she said by way of answer.

I scooped a bunch of vegetables out of the fridge. "Things aren't simple here. Hey, do you know Arthur Van Der Holst?"

"Arthur? No. But I know an Edward Van Der Holst. Some hoity-toity wizard in government. He was up in Darwin when we were legalized." She said *legalized* as if she was laughing down her nose at the officials, even now. "Worked up there for a bit, I heard. Did a stint in Canberra but didn't have much support, so he ended up in Melbourne. He had a brother, apparently a mediocre wizard—"

"Damned by faint praise," I interrupted, grinning.

She cackled with glee. "Oh, yes. He died, oh, two decades ago? Three? No, not three. Probably just the other side of twenty years, I think. He was only in his mid-thirties. Cancer. Terrible. Anyway, his brother...William, I think? Henry? Hm." I smiled as I broke stalks off celery. "Some sort of King name. Well, his brother married into some old money, because nothing's as sexy to a wizard as a young, pretty, virginal bank account, right?"

I grinned, playing along. "Wizards are scum."

"Ha! Well, anyway, William or Henry, whatever his name was, he had a child, who might have been Arthur. Or William? But, definitely, the boy was a Van Der Holst. And a ladder climber. Didn't I hear he'd gone to a private boys' school in Sydney? Or, no, it was Melbourne." Oma was off now. I rinsed the stalks, chopped them. Everything felt right in my world as I listened with half an ear and took out an onion. "Yes, Melbourne. I saw him in one of those viral videos, you know, standard misogynistic stuff." She cleared her throat and chanted, "'I wish that all the ladies were holes in the road, and if I was a dump-truck, I'd fill them with my load.'"

"Ugh, Oma." I looked down at the parsnip with disgust. "I'm making dinner. What in the actual fuck?"

"Sorry." She didn't sound it. "Can't remember their names, but by golly, that got my goat and stuck in my brain. Also, it rhymes, and you know how I am with rhymes." I sighed because it was true. "I'm sure it was him in one of those videos. Maybe not that exact one, but something like it. Haven't heard much about him, but I doubt there'd be anything good. Edward, though... Why, he's trying to get his finger in every pie around."

She moved from discussion about hoity-toity Edward to the thirdhand tales she'd heard about Arthur, and by the time she'd finished talking about friends of the family's most noteworthy accomplishments, I had a stew on.

Cici's name got a dramatic reaction. Not because Oma felt strongly about her, or even because the woman had done anything particularly scandalous, but just because of the depth and breadth of information Oma had to share.

"Three husbands, fine, good for her, but seven cats? Who needs that many cats?"

I had my laundry put away and, for lack of anything better to do, started mixing up a cake batter while she talked.

By the time she signed off, I had run out of housework to do.

Green eyes, the blood, on his face, the smug grin as he turned his face up into the sun while they silvered him. Brandon's body going cold just a few metres away.

I scrubbed my hands over my face. The banana cake was a good forty minutes away. I tied back the mass of black curls that was liable to become an actual OH&S hazard if left to its own devices, pulled on runners, stirred the stew, lowered the heat, cranked up fuck-you music, and set out for a run.

If Beo was some relation of Duke's, it didn't make Beo instantly guilty of anything. Every family had its secrets, and being within the family didn't necessarily mean you knew them all. I was a prime example of that. No information on my mother, at all. Life could be pretty weird.

But if Beo was Duke's relative, and they were cut from the same cloth, then we had a giant shitshow about to erupt, and Arthur had planted he and I both squarely in the center of it.

Add to that riftrunning lycans and I didn't even know what to think.

However, there hadn't been anything in Betty's notes that made the group seem high-risk. The siren working as a hairdresser who was classed as a medium risk and suspected of inappropriate dealings with a few clients appeared, on the surface, to be a much greater threat than a bunch of beer-swilling, protective-clothing-disdaining meatheads. But they must've been classified as such before she was murdered. Otherwise, Arthur wouldn't have had her knitting on the sidelines.

Regular, predictable attendance did not make good surveillance. Not when your job was known by the people you were supposed to be keeping an eye on. So, who had decided the lycans were high-risk, and why had they decided to post such a ridiculously predictable schedule?

The whole thing was off.

Regardless of how wrong it all felt, Betty was dead. The murderer was either one of these lycans or protected by them.

I thought of Frankie's face when Arthur's bones snapped like twigs in his hands and didn't like the wave of empathy that swept through me. I was pretty sure Frankie's file claimed he was twenty-one, but he looked like a kid.

Sucking in the cold night air, feeling the jolt of my running feet finding cement, I was suddenly struck by how old and jaded I'd become.

By the time I made it up to my second-floor apartment, I was steadier than I had been since hearing about the lycan pack on my caseload. I had questions, and they felt like the right ones.

I couldn't get answers yet, so, without bothering to change, I grabbed myself a bowl of stew, leaving the rest to keep simmering, rescued my cake, which I didn't even want—but, hey, banana cake was basically banana bread, which was an acceptable breakfast food—and settled down at the table with my phone.

While I ate, I searched for news articles on Betty's murder.

It was all neutral, polite. No super graphic descriptions or pictures that put me in jeopardy of losing my dinner. A few photos of police tape over an alleyway, a few photos of Betty as she had been, with a round face and rosy cheeks.

The woman could've been a garden gnome model.

The reports all said the same thing: the police were investigating, but due to the wounds inflicted, they suspected the murderer was supernatural. No reason to be alarmed, however, as this was the first case like it in Melbourne in more than six months.

There weren't many beings who inflicted damage quite like a lycan did, as the detective had said.

There were more dangerous supernatural folks, more crafty ones, but when you were talking brute strength and raw power, you were looking at vampires and lycans. And even then, the kills were so different there would be no mistaking it. I hadn't really needed O'Malley's confirmation.

If people said it was a lycan, then it was a lycan.

Sidestepping the memories of Duke's green eyes and everything that came after, I clamped down on what I'd learned.

A lycan.

They never hunted alone; there would've been more than one.

How many packs did we have in Melbourne? Our district had just the one, of course, but other districts would have one, or maybe two, maybe even three, depending how they divided their territories compared to our own districts.

Had any local witches managed to develop a rapport with a pack? Could we get inside information?

I shovelled in the rest of the food, my mind spinning. Lycans were loyal to their pack to a fault. Vamps, though, vamps would—and regularly did—turn on their own mother. But not lycans. I'd seen lycans fight and die for their pack.

Lycans didn't turn on each other. Period.

Would they betray other packs to protect their own, though? But none of the other Melbourne packs were being threatened. Betty's murder had been committed squarely on Beo's turf, and that meant the buck stopped with him.

It was worth investigating other avenues, but I had to focus on that one.

While I cleaned, I let my mind spin. I arrived at only one conclusion: I was going to have to stick my neck out to get more information.

FIVE

I SENT ARTHUR A TEXT CHECKING IN BEFORE IT GOT TOO LATE. DIDN'T HURT to try to keep on his good side for now. Anyway, my conscience liked me for it.

The next morning, I had a response.

Got a cast for you to sign when you come in today. We're meeting with the High District Wizard. 11:00 am.

He even capitalized the bloke's title in text. What in the hells?

Avoiding looking at myself in the mirror because I didn't need to know what the bed had done to my hair, I turned the hot water on as hard as it would go and impatiently waited for it to heat.

Spotting a notification of a new work email, I opened the app.

It was a calendar invite for a meeting at eleven with Master Edward Van Der Holst, High District Wizard, the power grabbing, ladder-climbing uncle.

Grimly, I hit accept, put the phone on the side of the basin, and threw myself into the shower.

I was debating whether I was really ready to get out, even though I was clean, when my phone rang. With one hand, I swiped some of the mist off the shower screen so I could peer through. Did I actually have to answer my phone at not-much-past-seven in the morning?

Detective O'Malley.

I scrambled out of the shower. These phones were waterproof, right? "Rory," I said, sounding satisfactorily awake.

"Good morning, Caretaker." His words were rough, his voice pleasant and slow, as if he had all the time in the world and wanted to chat just with me. I'd forgotten how sexy the man's voice was. Conveniently, I hadn't forgotten how annoying he was. "I'm sorry to call you so early. Is now a good time?"

With the phone held between my shoulder and my ear, I reached for a towel to stave off the winter chill. "No problems." Aside from me freezing. "Did something come up regarding the murder or lycans?"

I looked at myself in the small, steam-free part of the mirror. White as cheap bread, brows raised in exasperation, my familiar face looked back at me—one blue eye, one hazel, and the wet black hair hanging limply around my face. I looked like I'd just crawled out of someone's television after they watched a cursed tape.

"I was calling regarding another matter. I believe you were with Caretaker Wizard Arthur Van Der Holst last night?"

The bottom fell out of my belly at that gentle probe. "I was, yes, until he left for the hospital."

"He mentioned you witnessed what happened at The Playground."

There was only one thing he could be talking about. I didn't bother feigning ignorance. "Yes."

"Caretaker Wizard Van Der Holst is pressing charges," the detective said, his tone still unfailingly neutral. "I was hoping you might be able to give a statement."

I closed my eyes because I didn't want to see what expression I wore.

I hadn't even had coffee yet. This wasn't fair.

"Certainly," my mouth said, independent of my brain. "I have a late morning appointment, so earlier is better. Can you see me at nine?"

As soon as the call ended, I drew a deep breath and called Arthur. He'd sent me a text. He was up.

He answered on the second ring. "Morning, Aurora." He didn't say good. He didn't sound it, either.

"You're pressing charges?" I asked, glancing down at myself. The hand that held the towel around my chest was white-knuckled.

There was some sort of appliance noise in the background. "Sorry. Making coffee. Yes, I'm pressing charges. We need leverage against these arseholes. Maybe Velvela will talk if he thinks one of the young guys will take the fall."

Duke's brilliant green eyes and huge grin. Right there in the mist behind my shoulder. *The wash of warm sunlight.* Gritting my teeth, I swiped the condensation off the glass and dispelled the memory.

"Lycans don't talk, Arthur," I said, trying to sound calm and professional as my towel slipped down my body and anger started to simmer. "Besides, what's he going to take the fall for? Assault? It's a far cry from proving murder."

"Assault will get him ten years in SuperSec," he said dismissively. "If he doesn't cut a deal. And I expect he'll cut a deal." The sheer arrogance in his tone kept me silent for one beat, then two. "Look, he broke my arm. You blew our cover. We may as well play the cards we've got as hard as we can, right?"

I blew our cover? Beo had all but said, "Hey you wanna go do Witchy Stuff over there?"

And fuck Arthur for being so utterly oblivious to social interactions that didn't suit him.

I didn't even try to argue about it. What was the point?

"What if it wasn't Beo's pack?" I asked him, trying for logic and sidestepping the bullshit.

"Beo's pack is the only one in the district," he said, impatient now. "If it wasn't his pack, he'd talk to protect his own."

Unless someone bigger, badder, and scarier was around. The thought bounced in my head, and I had to consider it seriously because it just didn't sit right with me that Beo was a cold-blooded killer. He could've been an apex predator if he wanted to. He clearly didn't.

"Just think of it as giving the police some leverage. Good news, the lycans are off your case load if they're arrested. And we both know if one Lycan is in on it, they're all in on it. And so do the cops. So"—a spoon chimed against the side of a mug—"tell me when you're going in to see

O'Malley, and I'll bring you a coffee. There's a decent cafe just half a block away. We can chat about the meeting with the HW."

Shit on a stick. I looked at the phone in my hand for a moment, considered just hanging up on him. He wanted me to lie.

I wasn't even sure if he knew it was a lie.

"Are you feeling okay, Arthur?" I asked, making one last-ditch attempt to search for some sort of excuse for all the shitfuckery that was this man.

"Not going to lie, I'm pretty sore," he admitted. "And pretty shaken. It could've gone very, very wrong. But it didn't. I have drugs and coffee, and I've booked in to see an old family friend with some strong healing talent this afternoon. I'll be okay." I heard feigned vulnerability and a whole lot of smugness, as if my question confirmed something he'd suspected.

He thought I was asking because I cared.

That did it. I hadn't had coffee, and he was obviously drinking his. I was being asked to lie for my boss, who happened to be the nephew of the District Big Wand, and piss off our one possibly useful ally in the process.

There was no reason. No logic. Not even his ego could explain this.

I sat the phone on the edge of the vanity, picked the towel up, and began to get dry as he kept talking to himself. Walking out of the room made a dark jolt of satisfaction coil through me.

He'd eventually realize I wasn't there. He'd probably assume the connection had dropped out. I knew I was wasting his time, just like he'd wasted mine. It was petty, and I didn't mind in the slightest.

Meanwhile, I surveyed my clothes. What did a modern witch wear when she wanted to burn some bridges?

Heels. Really high, killer heels. And a dress—something fitted, something black. All the better to hide the blood, spilled coffee, or wizard's tears.

A dim "hello?" floated to my ears as I walked past the bathroom on the way to caffeinate. A smile tugged at my lips. I didn't fight it.

My curls mostly behaved themselves today, so I had time for coffee and to apply some warpaint. When I admired myself in the mirror, what I saw pleased me.

By the time the tram stopped near the police station, my anger had settled at a good simmer. I got off, my feet already weeping, but the click of the needle heels on the pavement and the sidelong glances I drew from people as I strode forward helped to steel my heart.

Three big motorcycles were parked out front. They couldn't have brought Frankie in already.

The anger bubbled under my skin, and the ground fell away beneath me. A man coming out of the precinct saw me and stopped, did a sharp about-face, stepped back, and held the door open, his eyes round.

Maybe I wasn't beautiful, but, by Hellfire, I could make them pay attention.

Beo waited in the front room with the blonde Zane, who didn't understand road protection, beside him. I didn't look at either of them, struggling to keep the anger from reaching a boil.

They *had* brought him in already.

Which meant there was an innocent—at least, innocent of this crime— kid, probably in silver cuffs, in pain and in distress.

I had a lot of words for that, and none of them were polite.

The desk clerk looked at me, blinked, and said, "Good morning, can I help you?"

"Aurora Gold." I felt the lycan's eyes on me and was furious to be in this position. That they were in this position.

Why hadn't the cops waited on my statement?

"I'm here to see Detective O'Malley." My work phone chirped in my bag. It was background noise, unimportant.

She glanced at the computer, blinked again. "Caretaker Aurora? I have two Aurora Gold's on the system—"

"They're both me," I said, impatient and angry, but not with this particular clerk.

She blinked again. "You—" she checked the file. "Can I confirm your practice number, Caretaker? I have two different ones on file."

"I'm licensed for different areas." I reached into my bag, took out my wallet, showed both my general witchcraft license I used for my current job as Caretaker, and the specialty Retrievals license to work with supernaturals who'd been identified as dangerous.

I didn't need my audience overhearing specific details of my prior work just in case they didn't know who'd brought Duke down. I also didn't need word getting to the District Ego Epicentre.

If I wanted to be in that line of work, I would be.

"The specialty isn't applicable in my current role, so I didn't inform the district of it when I applied for the position." But it didn't hurt for the local law enforcement to know.

"I see." From her impeccably neutral expression, I suspected she did. "I'll merge your two files in our system." She placed the slightest emphasis on *our* that made me grimly pleased. "Detective O'Malley will—" she broke off, glanced over her shoulder, a flicker of relief crossing her face.

I followed her gaze. O'Malley had brackets of worry lining his tired eyes. It suited the noir vibe he had going. "Caretaker Aurora. Thank you for coming in at such short notice." He offered me a hand.

I took it, shook, and put aside any appreciation for him as a bloke. "Rory." Pretty sure I'd already done this dance. "You didn't tell me you'd brought my client in, detective." And that was poor form.

"We always try to call as soon as we can," he said, waving me through a door to the warren behind the front desk. "As I knew you were coming in, I thought I'd save us both some time and just tell you in person."

It wouldn't have changed anything, but that didn't mean I liked it any better. "In the future, I'm more than happy for you to use my time," I told him firmly as he guided me through a series of beige twists and turns. "That's what I'm paid for, Detective."

He sent me an unreadable glance. "Noted. I'm sure you appreciate we're under pressure in this particular instance."

Which meant someone, probably Arthur or Arthur's big-wig uncle, was leaning on them. Or someone even higher. *Shit.*

"I appreciate the importance of processes in place to protect us all," I responded coolly. *Don't cut corners just because of politics*, I thought furiously.

He didn't respond, waving me into an interview room with a uniformed officer who took my statement.

O'Malley hung around for the first round, then left me with the beat cop to fix errors in her written version and ensure the validity of the final thing.

When he returned, I was about ready to sign. "I've just Googled these moves," he told me while the beat cop hunted up a pen that worked. "It sounds like breaking Arthur's arm was exactly what Mr. Marshall was attempting to do, however, you stated there was no malice and it was an accident."

"An Americana puts strain on the elbow and shoulder joints," I told him briskly. "Arthur broke his forearm because he moved wrong."

O'Malley nodded, then said, "You're familiar enough with Brazilian Jiu-Jitsu to be confident of that?"

No, I just said it to jerk you around. "Yes."

"Then you wouldn't have any problems re-creating this so we can film it."

I didn't bat an eyelash. Because fuck Arthur and his ego and his complete and utter lack of understanding of the entire situation.

"No, I wouldn't, if you can find someone else who knows Brazilian Jiu-Jitsu well enough to follow my instructions."

My brain went to Beo, waiting outside. Considering how hands-off he'd been with Arthur, I doubted he'd be excited by the idea. Still, my traitorous body hummed at the thought of getting close to him. I kept my lips firmly sealed.

He gave a brisk nod. "I'll get an officer. Can you set up for a recording, Sergeant?"

It meant more paperwork, but I suspected O'Malley was protecting us against the very same people I was pissing off, so I didn't mind. I didn't even object to getting down on the ground in my dress. The floor had been recently cleaned.

The person O'Malley brought in so I could demonstrate the moves in question was an older chap with salt and pepper hair and an impassive expression. He was quite polite about positioning me so the camera wouldn't point up my skirt and didn't mention my shoes, which was just as well. I wasn't taking them off, because I wasn't sure they'd go back on today, and I still had to drop the match on this bridge.

My practice partner knew what he was doing. I demonstrated, from Arthur's perspective and then putting the uniformed cop in Arthur's spot and showing how the different submissions could have been used to harm, had that been Frankie's true intent, and how it didn't match up with Arthur's injury. It went as smoothly as it could've, and the cop shook my hand before he left.

"Will my client be released now?" I asked O'Malley once the formalities were done.

He nodded, some of the lines of strain gone now. "We'll tidy this up, but we've no reason to hold him. Your report corresponds with others we've received and added important information that confirms this was an accident, not an assault." What he didn't say was that I was an impartial witness, not a member of Frankie's pack.

I stood as he did. In heels, I was taller than him, though not by much. If it bothered him, he gave no sign of it.

"I'd like to wait for my client then."

"Of course." He opened the door for me and led me back through the maze. "It'll be a few minutes."

I'd expected no less; in fact, I expected a fair bit more. I didn't bother looking at the time. I could always send an email apology if it took longer than it ought; it wasn't like I didn't have a good reason to miss the meeting.

"I'm in no rush." I had plenty of fuel to burn still.

He paused before the door to the waiting area out front. "Usually, I'd warn a Caretaker that their client might be unsettled after this sort of thing," he said, sending me a look of pure calculation. "Particularly as he isn't here alone. But I happened to glance through your file since our," he paused for a moment, "admin error was corrected." I was sent a very long, thoughtful look. "You're not the sort of witch I need to worry about."

The smile that tugged on my lips held no warmth. He knew exactly who was on the other side of that door. And he was betting that they'd be listening to this "private" conversation.

This warning was not for me.

I appreciated the sentiments, even if they did complicate my life somewhat.

"I'm in a new line of work, Detective. I'm kind of liking the whole innocent-until-proven-guilty thing," I said calmly because it was true. I wasn't hunting anyone down or holding anyone accountable. I wasn't setting out knowing odds were good someone would die and hoping it wouldn't be me or mine. Nope. I was just keeping track. Just keeping folks safe. "I'll be in contact."

He didn't say anything else, but gave me a nod to let me know the message was received and opened the door so I could return to the waiting area. As he did, he stuck his head around the corner and said to Beo, "He'll be with you in just a moment."

Beo, green eyes hard and jaw tight, said, "Thank you."

I walked over and took one lime-green chair directly beside him. "If he was mistreated in any fashion by the police, I want to know," I told him, reaching into my handbag and finding my work phone. Just on ten. Still plenty of time.

He sent me a look of mild disbelief. "And what would you do?" he asked me, the words quiet and vibrating with fury.

I skimmed through my emails with disinterest. "My job." I opened one about a young witch who was being transferred after a domestic violence issue with a wizard in her hometown in Perth.

Betty had done the initial intake. She was under protective watch, moderate-risk.

Due to the delay between Betty passing and me being brought on board to support, people on the Perth end had secured her lodgings. I didn't know the address, but I knew if she had run from Perth, and the Perth branch held intimate information, then she was in danger.

She was due tomorrow. I'd have emergency accommodations booked for her, and I might just forget to mention that to my Perth associates. Never hurt to keep something up my sleeve. Then she'd be able to look for her own accommodations. At least her work was secure. I'd organised that myself. She was a healer and potion maker by trade, and they were in high demand. Finding her a quiet clinic on short notice hadn't been hard. From there, she'd be able to rebuild her own life as she wished.

When the door opened, I glanced up and saw a surly faced Frankie rubbing at his wrists. Holding lycans in silver was standard procedure, for good reason.

Usually, I was grateful for that extra layer of protection. Today it infuriated me.

He looked like any teenager who'd been caught between their own sense of justice and the real world: sullen and defensive. Hellfire, I couldn't say I'd look any different if I was in his shoes. All he'd done wrong was be near a wizard.

I stood, putting my phone away to finish my accommodation search later. Frankie shot me a look that was both wary and furious. I ignored it. My own anger wouldn't help him.

"Did they give you a balm?" I asked him briskly, referring to the mix made by healing witches to soothe the hurts silver inflicted on lycans. Again, it was supposed to be standard procedure. It was sometimes overlooked, though, unlike the cuffs.

He nodded jerkily, took the helmet Beo passed him, then stood for a moment, waiting as if unsure. I turned and began to stroll towards the exit, deliberately putting myself in their group, then stopping to open the door for them.

"I'm going to send you all a text. Save my number. Next time," I said once the door had swung closed, "call me as soon as things look like they're going wrong."

"We know how this world works," Beo said, the words flat. "Your type stick together."

Well, that was the pot calling the kettle black, wasn't it? Pointing that out wouldn't be useful, though, so I raised my brows at Frankie.

"How'd that work for me, you reckon?"

A smile flickered over his face. "Shit," he muttered, but there was a spark of humor in his eyes.

Very deliberately, I offered him my hand. "You did good. I'll deal with my end, but I can't help if I don't know there's a problem. So let me know, okay?"

"Yeah, okay," he muttered. His tone said 'no way', but he took my hand and shook.

I turned to Beo, offering him my palm, too. When I saw his anger, I understood it. "You, too. I want you all to be safe."

And I wasn't even exaggerating. These guys weren't like the lycans I'd dealt with. But Arthur was exactly like the ego-centric, oxygen-wasting wizards.

Silently, Beo folded his fingers around mine. First one hand, then another. "You're going to get a lot of shit." For all his gentleness, his face was hard.

I raised my brows. "Going to bring me into the fold and protect me, too?" A smile twitched at his mouth, and I quite liked that, even if it was grudging. My hand was warm and welcome between his palms, and through the protective, simmering anger, I felt a tug of humor at the situation. "If you don't let me go, how am I supposed to go do my job, Coach?"

"I think you'd manage." But I was released all the same. "You going to hold Arthur's towel next Tuesday?"

I couldn't think that far ahead. All I knew was that I had some burning questions and a whole lot of fury. "You're happy for me to come back?" I asked, just so we were on the level.

He lifted one shoulder, then dropped it. "You pay your fees, you train."

I didn't have room for egos, not his or anyone else's. "No bullshit, Beo, I've got a meeting. Do you want me to train, or should I work from the sidelines?"

Amusement faded from his face. He hadn't shaved this morning, and the shadow on his jaw just made him look more like the dangerous predator I'd assumed he was. "I like to know who we're dealing with."

That was an answer I'd accept. It wasn't open arms, but if it had been, I'd have been watching for teeth. "I might not be able to blow off Arthur. I'll look into policy."

His eyes narrowed. "You do that."

I shrugged. I didn't like it either. "I'll message you." I turned towards the tram stop.

I'd make the meeting. I might even have time to get a coffee in beforehand. Today was not a tea day.

"Hey, Rory," Beo called, before I'd taken more than a half a dozen steps.

I paused, turning warily, not trusting my needle-point heels. "Yeah?"

"Gi tonight."

I paused, considering. My very vague plan had been to keep it pretty much nine-to-five until I figured out a rhythm. "I'm off the clock."

He lifted one shoulder, then dropped it, strolling over to where his motorcycle was perched between the two others. "Invite stands."

The smile that wanted to tug at my mouth was stilled and held secret. Anticipation hummed.

I was in trouble.

But I was also making progress.

Six

Arthur's eyes were flat when I walked into the meeting room two minutes early. I got exactly zero dimples, and it made me want to laugh.

I chose a seat, pulled out my phone, and saw I had a response from the earlier text I'd sent Beo: *saved*.

Well, if he had my number, the pack would be able to contact me.

"Office policy states phone use is restricted to breaks," Arthur told me stiffly.

I didn't even glance up. "Work phone, King. Smaller than hauling a laptop and more functional." I completed the booking for a midterm place for my family violence victim, downloaded the invoice, and sent it through to the business manager.

By the time I was done, Arthur was doing a sound check for the videoconference on the screen on the side of the room, his movements a little awkward with his arm in a sling. He didn't ask for help. I didn't offer it. I opened up the notes app and wished for a stylus.

When the face appeared on the screen, I saw an instant family resemblance. Same heavy jaw, same blue eyes, same sour cream skin, same expensive taste in clothes.

Same lack of dimples in my direction.

There were some issues with the sound, so I waited while Arthur tinkered with it. It took him almost a solid ten minutes before we could hear and be heard.

"Welcome onboard, Aurora," Edward said. "As District High Wizard, I wish I could be there in person to greet you."

His tone said otherwise, and I gave no fucks. "I understood your role had you placed in Melbourne," I said because information would be nice. There had been no mention of remote—no link given—in the earlier invitation.

His smile was thin. The dimples that creased his cheeks made me think of a demon's cowl folded over on itself. I very much regretted that he'd employed their use.

"I am indeed."

I gave him a beat, then two, to expand on his answer. When he didn't, I asked, "Is remote our standard method of communication?" I knew the answer. I wanted to know why there'd been a change in plans.

"It's an option," he said, neatly sidestepping my question.

I nodded and, in my notes, typed *why not f2f with DHW?*

"Don't mind me, I like to take my own notes," I told them, feeling Arthur's eyes boring holes into me. "You didn't attach an agenda to the invite, Edward." If he was going to use my name, I was going to use his, too.

"Ah, you're accustomed to working in a highly formal setting," he said with some satisfaction in his voice. "That'll be useful for data collection, I'm sure." He said *data collection* the way I'd say *hot chips*. "When I set the meeting this morning, it was to discuss how to use our leverage against the district lycans." He paused for a moment. I typed in a note: *DHW data driven.* I let the silence stretch out into that uncomfortable stage, let it hang there, let it writhe, before I raised my eyes to the screen, lifting my brows. "Unfortunately, it appears that leverage is gone, as are any hopes of finding out what happens by attending The Playground."

I sat back. Did I throw Arthur under the bus, tell his uncle how badly he'd misread the situation? *No. Keep it simple.*

"I've read the notes on the lycans," I said, completely ignoring Arthur and the whole shitstorm that was this morning. "I found no mention as to why they were flagged as high-risk."

"A group of lycans is dangerous," Edward said, smoothly. "One on one, most of us can hold our own against them, but they never hunt alone."

A chill ran up my spine. He knew something. "So, they're categorized as high-risk clients due to their supernatural typing?" I asked directly. Suddenly, I wished I'd read some of the policy book around risk factors. I didn't know if this was a smokescreen or systemic prejudice.

"Beo and his pack's role in the murder of Betty—" Edward began.

"The pack was high-risk before Betty's murder," I cut in, impatient. "According to the staffing." I needed to know what I was dealing with, aside from Betty's murder.

"Accurately assessed as such, yes," Edward agreed. "In order to contain them now, we'll need to apply for external intervention."

"Which will be costly." Arthur shot me a look with this barb, as if I should be worried this cost might be met from my own salary.

They talked like politicians. "Who assigns clients to witches?" Then, with an easy smile, I added, "Just wondering."

"I do," Arthur said. "But we're off topic."

"Who decides on the risk level of clients?" I asked, making a quick note of Arthur's answer. Had Betty been set up to take a fall? Had her load been low? Was she skilled in dealing with lycans? Just because she looked like a garden gnome didn't mean she was one.

"It depends on the situation," Arthur said, clearly frustrated. "We're supposed to have each other's back, so it shouldn't be a problem."

Yes, that was a nice idea, wasn't it? Like maybe giving me all the pertinent information rather than going in thinking we were undercover when actually every single lycan knew exactly who we were and what we were doing? If they hadn't been peaceful, we'd both be so very dead.

"So, is this meeting about the ongoing management of the lycans, Betty's murder, or both?" I asked them, tired of dancing.

"The two are so closely linked it would be impossible to separate them," Edward said, frowning with worry. "Now that the coven has lost all surprise and leverage…there are options to deal with them, of course. But we cannot have rogue lycans."

Arthur added something in support that I didn't listen to, just waiting until he'd finished with his blather while I brought up my case notes. "I have no evidence of rogue behaviour," I said when I could get a word in edgewise. "Betty's notes indicate that—"

"Just because we don't have evidence doesn't mean it isn't happening," Arthur cut in, frustrated. "They're violent."

I shrugged. "Further investigation would be needed—"

"Unfortunately," Edward said, his huge face on the screen lagging out of time with the frustrated words, "we lost any chance at that."

My smile was cold and hard. "Yes. It's a shame someone had tipped their hand. I assume that's why Betty was targeted, because she was known as a witch. And exactly what we would have been identifying via attending a public place on a routine basis, I'm unsure. Still, it's possible—"

"Are you questioning the validity of our methods?" Arthur asked me furiously.

"I was questioning what outcome we were looking for, however—"

"The outcome we want is to keep people alive," Arthur cut in again.

I raised my brows, speared him with my gaze, and lent back in my chair. "You were after that outcome before Betty was murdered? Had there been lycan-related murders—"

"Aurora," Edward said my name, low, smooth and enough to set my teeth on edge. "I feel like we've got a basic miscommunication somewhere. Is there something about these clients that you'd like to raise?"

The way Arthur's lip curled drove the probably-not-accidental double entendre home. I didn't let it bother me, even if I had experienced a few thoughts in that general direction.

I had already been given the runaround this morning. Did I lay it all on the table? The thing was, I didn't trust Arthur or Edward, except to protect their own backsides.

"I will not support external measures given the data I have," I said instead, keeping my words brisk. "The lycans should remain as my clients until—"

"With all due respect, Caretaker, that won't be your decision," Edward said, just as brisk as I.

Shit, I would've loved to throw down the gauntlet. I knew I'd lose, though.

"Of course, in the end, it would be your decision," I said with a hard smile, "with the consequences of your action falling solely on your shoulders, District High Wizard." Fuck, I'd said that politely. *Pat on the back, Rory.*

He could be stood down for mismanagement if it was discovered that he'd acted inappropriately. And we all knew it.

When the silence had gestated long enough, I figured I'd have another go. "My proposal, as things stand—"

"If you hadn't—" Arthur began.

I overrode him, raising my voice. "—is to increase surveillance on the pack to gather the appropriate data that will support whatever action we take next."

"—undermined our position completely," Arthur continued.

"Caretaker," Edward said, firmly silencing his nephew, "explain further."

I nodded, gathering my thoughts quickly. "It's true that the pack is aware of my role. I can make that work for us. So far, we've focused on Beo at his place of work. I can continue that, making my attendance unpredictable. I can also widen the net and visit all the pack members, as well as people within their inner circles, to keep a closer eye on them. This can—"

"I cannot justify the hours for two staff members," Arthur cut in. "My schedule is already full, and I'm the only one in the district qualified to manage lycans."

If qualifications were what he wanted, I could show him a thing or two. But it was more hurtful to dismiss him with a shrug. "So, downgrade the risk level. At the moment, with the data we have, we cannot justify their high-risk status. In fact, I couldn't even justify medium risk, aside from the murder of Betty, which we cannot link to the pack aside from their geographical location." I met Arthur's eyes squarely. "I am capable of working alone."

Edward nodded firmly. "I support this decision, not to downgrade the whole pack, but perhaps the younger members. Keep Velvela himself as high-risk."

I opened my mouth to point out that Arthur had marked himself as enemy in their eyes and was therefore a liability, but before I could speak Arthur said, "You can't think they're actually innocent."

"I think the information I have is, at best, pure garbage," I told him, feeling my temper slipping. "This has been mismanaged, and we need to remedy that before it causes problems that cannot be explained away." While Arthur's face turned red, I glanced up at the screen. "I'll also need to speak to other Caretakers of the lycan packs in the area." I made a quick note of suggestions I was throwing out because I didn't want to forget an important detail. "No one dishes dirt like rivals." It was true—of humans. I doubted I'd get any information about Beo's pack from other lycans.

But I could get a lot of information about other things.

Luckily for me, Edward either didn't know or didn't consider that angle. "I can get contact information for you."

"Excellent." I smiled at both of them. "Then I believe I have a working plan to continue with for now. Unless there's anything else?"

There wasn't.

This time, Arthur didn't get the door for me. He probably thought that was hurtful. I was just glad I didn't have to reinforce personal space boundaries yet again.

All in all, I'd pissed off absolutely everyone. And it wasn't even lunch.

SEVEN

IT SEEMED LIKE AN EXCELLENT DAY TO LEAVE THE OFFICE EARLY.

By the time I got home, my feet were one big hot ball of pain, and my anger had drained away. I was left feeling flat and sad.

I'd said I was off the clock, and even though I could've logged the hours, I didn't use the tracking app when I left home with my old, battered gym bag over my shoulder and my keys in the pocket of my hoodie.

Drumming up any actual enthusiasm for jiu-jitsu was a struggle. Not because I didn't love it—of all the combat sports I'd dabbled in over the years, jiu-jitsu was the one that had called to me. My coach had referred to it as chess with body parts. But it had been weeks since I'd trained, and I didn't feel like I'd bounced back yet from riding the wave of conflict this morning.

At least Arthur hadn't taken any shots at me after the meeting. He'd just closed the door to his office and sulked.

At the desk, I paid for a six-month membership, tried not to think of my weeping savings account, and had them email me the receipt. One perk of mixing business and pleasure was that money would be reimbursed, hopefully before my insurance was due.

The flight of stairs was a lot shorter than I remembered, and the class's ranks swollen with people. I found a spot against the wall—all the chairs were taken, but it didn't matter—and claimed it by dropping my bag.

I ignored the looks being sent my way by the pack because I was here by invite, and therefore, they'd accept me.

Or wait until the opportunity arose to eviscerate me. Whatever worked.

Like others around me, I scooted out of my pants ringside, mostly hidden by my hoodie and the boyleg underwear I'd opted for after my nap. The gi in my bag was my old, much-loved blue one with the emblem of my old coach on the back.

My gym was only a few hours away. I'd go back in a week or two. See Dad and Oma. Maybe go a few rounds with the team. Catch up with Aspen for coffee and cake, or wine and cake, depending on the time of day. Tell her all about the city-slicker bullshit.

The plan, vague as it was, comforted me as I knelt and tied my washed-out belt around my waist.

A few people chatted with me; one had been there last night and asked after Arthur. Beo didn't approach me, but that was fine.

It was all too easy to switch off my head and let the familiar ebb and flow of the lesson carry me along. I'd been the new girl at enough clubs to know the routine. I drilled with a few different people practicing transitions and got coated in my sweat, theirs, and whoever's they'd drilled with before. It felt like putting on comfy old slippers.

Beo circulated, offering instructions, mixing up pairs, giving encouragement, but not participating, much as he had during the no-gi class.

So, when we returned from a drink break to roll, it gave me a jolt to see him beside me, offering his palm to a white-belt to begin a fight. I focused on my own opponent until the timer went off and the pairings rotated.

Beo smoothly moved into place before me. I felt my heart do a slow roll in my chest. I missed the armour of my lipstick and figure-hugging dress. The hand I offered him was naked of rings, and the way he looked at me, I was sure he could see my every thought.

If he could, I'd be pretty embarrassed, because there wasn't much going on in my poor, hormone-overwhelmed brain. He slapped my palm lightly with his own, bumped my fist, and started to circle.

Hyperaware of the others on the mat and the fact that I was outclassed, I didn't engage in the dance but grabbed for his gi and pulled guard, settling for the neutral position and going to the mat.

He didn't try to overwhelm me. He could've, but he didn't. I was pushed, tested, but it felt more like an interview than a fight. And damned if he didn't interview well.

I saw him setting me up for two submissions and avoided both, inverting and going for a triangle choke that he defended. I ended up back in guard somehow, blowing an escaped curl out of my face.

He watched me like he was weighing my every move. I couldn't help it; I grinned up at him. "Did I pass the test?"

Some sort of glib "you'll do" was the response I expected, maybe a "we'll see." Instead, I was rag-dolled; the strength in his arms, in his legs, in his grips, and in his back left me scrambling to keep up through the whirlwind.

My heart rate kicked up, and I struggled to stick to the rules, struggled to reign in the instincts that wanted me to fight, to defend, with everything I had.

He took my back. Words formed in my head, spells to protect myself. I deliberately didn't sink any power into them, didn't reach for them.

As soon as his forearm slid smoothly beneath my tucked chin and I felt the warmth of his arm on both sides of my neck, I tapped. The Rear Naked-Choke was right up there with the swiftest, most permanent ways to disable an opponent, but he'd done it with infinite gentleness.

His hold loosened, but only fractionally. Before I could repeat the motion and force him to let me up—or show his hand—he said quietly, "What would you do if I kept this choke on, Rory?"

The question didn't hold any real threat, just idle curiosity. In front of me, I could see the mat, full of other people shifting and moving, focused on their own fights.

I wondered how many of these people would come to The Playground if they knew it was run by lycans. The thought made me inexplicably sad.

"I've been in a few pissing matches today already," I told Beo, letting myself flop back onto him. If he wanted to sit there, he could bloody well hold me up. And, anyway, it almost felt like he was hugging me. I managed not to snuggle in, but it was a near thing. Tension ebbed out of me. "I'm dry. Can we do this next time?"

His breath was warm against my ear. Jiu-jitsu required up close and personal. I'd been caught this way more times than I could count, taken others in this position. But it was different. He'd made it different. Or maybe my traitorous hormones were making it different.

"You're…"

"If you say 'not like most girls' I will absolutely curse you," I told him flatly. "I've already dealt with King Wand Waver today. I have literally zero patience."

The hold he had on me loosened a moment after I felt his laughter, the movement of his whole body around me. "I had a lot of words. They weren't among them."

I scooted back, turned on my knees, and took a moment to yank my gi top back to more or less where it belonged. "Oh yeah?" The impatience had ebbed. He sat back on his hands, studying me still, but at least now he was smiling.

"Yeah. Probably should call it there for the night." That he looked regretful made butterflies hatch in my belly. "Unless you're free later."

The quiet invitation turned those butterflies in my belly into rhinoceroses, but I laughed around their stampede. "Mate," I drawled, standing, "I'm top shelf. You don't get that for free."

He stood, too, as the buzzer went off. "Pretty sure you're not supposed to flirt with your coach, Student," he returned, in a fair imitation of my own laconic comment from yesterday.

Before my brain could engage to shut down the by-play, or at least diffuse it, I arched one brow and scooped back my hair. "Maybe I found something that suits me."

"I think you might've," he agreed, and damned if he didn't look just a little irritated about it. "Grab a drink," he called to the class, walking away from me.

Following the coach's recommendations, I drained what remained in my bottle. Work was nowhere in my short-circuiting brain as I enjoyed the hum of anticipation in my body.

Despite how unfairly tempting it was to linger and do some verbal sparring with Beo, I changed and slipped out with the crowd after the class, warm and limber and feeling dramatically more hopeful than I had last night. A text from Dad waited, and I responded on the tram ride home. Later, when I climbed into bed, no lycan stalked me through my dreams, no bones broke. I woke feeling energized and ready to save the world.

My first stop was to Lilith, the blue-haired witch I hadn't been able to get hold of in the office. I'd heard she was good at tracing supernatural genealogies.

Trade between worlds was a mess I didn't even want to think about, much less interfere with. The information we got was limited and tightly controlled. As a number of the supernatural folk we worked with had strong familial or tribal ties, being able to trace those ties was both important and pretty much impossible.

I stuck my head into her office—well, the room that her desk was in— didn't see her and headed upstairs to the tech hub. Arthur was in the corridor when I got up there, making coffee.

He looked me over head to toe, then turned away as if his silence was a punishment. I bounced past and knocked on the door. A young guy with a pretty oval face was crouched behind a series of monitors.

"Hi," I said, cheerfully. "I'm Rory. New witch."

He blinked at me from behind his glasses, then offered me a hand tentatively. "Vince."

I sent Vince a big smile and pulled up a chair that tried to massage my kidneys with its overzealous lumbar support. "So," I said, and he blinked at me over his coffee as if I'd just sprouted horns. "I need a favor."

His eyes flickered to the door, beyond which the coffee machine hummed. So, I had been feathered and tarred. Oh well. "Always happy to help," he told me with a firm nod.

I raised my brows at his declaration of loyalty. I mean, if it was me or Arthur, I'd choose me, too, but that wasn't the point. Bloke had met me ten seconds ago.

"I need to get in contact with Lilith, and I don't have any of her details. In fact, I've got only a handful of email addresses. Do we have a contact list?"

"Oh." He looked mildly perplexed. "No. Most of the witches have known each other for years, so it never really came up. But you're right. We should."

Of course, they all knew each other. That hadn't even occurred to me, and it should've. Did they even use their work phones? The thought of them not having the tracking app when they left the coven made worry worm its way into my belly, but Vince was already tapping away on his keyboard.

"Lilith's details?" I asked, peering over his shoulder.

"Yeah," he said. "And I'm cc'ing you into a group email. I'm pretty sure you were added to the distribution list already, but I'll make a note to touch base next time one comes through and double check. That isn't us, that's Headquarters." The sound of Arthur's door closing was solid and very, very surly. I'd met six-year-olds with more dignity.

"Awesome. If I gather contact details for a list—just for our coven— could you upload it onto the main folder in the cloud?" I had read-only access to all folders except my own, which was both mildly annoying and also kind of made sense.

"Yeah, of course. But did you want me to"—he waved a hand—"get the information? I've probably got most of it."

I shrugged. "Gives me an excuse to ask people their names," I admitted with a grin. "Now that I'm not trying to figure out which way my toes are pointing." I leaned forward a little, my smile fading, and I jerked my thumb in the direction of Arthur. "You don't need to pick sides, okay?"

His gaze darkened. "Walls up here are thin," he murmured. "I followed what went on yesterday—more or less. You don't need to ask me to pick sides. And, anyway, I know what he's like."

"Yeah, well." I stood, just as pleased with my flowy pants and comfy flats as I was in my man-eater getup yesterday. "You also know who sends work your way. Look after you."

He stood too, and rubbed his hands against his legs. "Don't worry," he said, his voice quiet. "I've got a solid contract."

With a wry smile, I shook my head. "Shit world we live in, isn't it?"

"Oh, I don't know." Mirth touched his eyes, brightening his face. "It's got better this week, I reckon."

I laughed, impressed at the smooth delivery. "The future is bright," I agreed, leaving behind the horrible chair and the sweet techie with a wave.

As soon as I got back to my computer and had Lilith's number, I sent her a text asking if I could meet her somewhere, preferably with real coffee. While I waited for a response, I dived into my work, determined to stay afloat in the sea of admin tasks awaiting me.

I'd just cross-referenced my schedule against my case list to make sure I hadn't left anyone off when I received a response from Lilith with the address of a coffee shop.

I'd be able to get a hire-car and get to the airport as long as Lilith didn't talk for more than an hour. From what little I'd seen of her, I figured I was pretty safe on that front.

Inside the warmth of the cafe, I spotted her sitting at a corner table with a coffee beside her and her laptop open. In the bright winter light, her eyes skimmed over the screen, a faint frown on her face as she found her cup without looking.

Unease unfurled low in my belly, and I glanced around, seeking the cause. The other patrons were all absorbed in their own pursuits, scrolling on phones, talking to companions. A server moved from the kitchen carrying three plates, and my unease increased. Without making it obvious, I did a quick scan of their body, but there was nothing obviously wrong.

That didn't settle my anxiety. I walked through the room, choosing the path least occupied by chairs and bodies, and took a seat opposite Lilith.

"Hey," I said, and she looked at me with a wary expression. I lifted a brow, then jerked my head in the direction of the server's retreating back.

She nodded, hit enter a few times, typed something on her laptop, and spun it around to face me.

Changeling.

The unease condensed and froze in my belly. Changelings were a bit like mythical ninjas, killers for hire that you'd never see and couldn't track. I gave a nod; message received. The information on changelings was pretty light, so it was safer to assume we could be overheard. "So," I said, settling back as she spun the laptop back to its original spot. "Have you recently discovered this place, or is it a regular haunt of yours?"

"Regular," she said, deleting the words and then closing her laptop. "They have good coffee, amazing food, and decent wi-fi."

So, the changeling wasn't her target then; identifying her was just chance. I nodded again, and when the changeling arrived with a sunny smile and blonde hair bouncing, I took the menu and glanced at Lilith.

"Lunch. What should I get?"

She looked a bit puzzled. "It's ten."

I grinned at this. "Sure, but I know what my day looks like."

"Want the day's specials?" the changeling asked me, their voice as sunny as the face they wore.

"If you like pesto…" Lilith looked at me like she was trying to figure me out.

I didn't think it was just about the pesto, but I ran with it. "I could live on pesto."

Lilith thawed a bit, amusement tugging at her mouth. "The pesto chicken focaccia is one of my favorites."

I wiggled my brows at her. "Want to join my brunch club and get one, too? Don't worry, I don't have an email list."

Her smile widened a little more. "But if I do… Oh, why not. And another coffee please."

"Yes. Coffee. A giant bucket of coffee. Black for me."

"And you're having the latte with two sugars?" the changeling asked Lilith.

"Good memory," Lilith said with a nod. "Thanks."

As she left, tucking the pen into its pad, I sat back with a sigh. The music was something welcoming and folksy, the air warm, and the hum of conversation just loud enough I figured it'd cover some of what I said.

"Thank you for seeing me. Especially out of the office. I really like that last part, I have to say."

Her smile faded a bit and her brows rose. "Why wouldn't I see you?"

I waved a hand. "Because time. And also fucks to give."

Some of the wariness left her face. Not much. Just a bit. She wasn't beautiful, but she was striking, with a long face and a wide mouth. I suspected I was going to like her.

"I am a bit short on those, I have to say," she admitted. "Are you just catching up with people, or..."

The calendar I'd drawn up popped into my head. The pace wasn't exactly hectic, but I'd be on the hop. That was the point, wasn't it, to work? "Not exactly. But before I get into it"—the changeling came and left us with our order—"tell me about Arthur."

Her expression became cautiously neutral. "What about him?"

I shot her my best don't-bullshit-me look. "I've pissed him off royally, and I've been here, what, three days? Did I misread him totally? Should I be apologizing?" What I really wanted to know was if she was part of his fan club. I didn't think it had a huge membership, but it didn't hurt to ask some questions.

She smiled a bit. "How should I know?" I waited, silent, and she sighed. "I'm not his favorite person. It hasn't made life simple, if you know what I mean, but..." She shrugged, sipped the coffee before her, and left the word hanging.

"Okay, okay." I sighed and propped my elbow on the table. "Maybe one day you'll spill the tea. Is he why you're not in the office much?"

One shoulder lifted, then dropped. Her black jacket whispered with the movement, and a coil of bright blue hair spilled down her front. She left it there, framing her face alongside the rest of the black-as-night strands. Lilith hid in plain sight.

"It isn't super comfortable, I have to say." Her black-nailed fingers drummed a beat on the table. Fast. Slow. She shifted, obviously uncomfortable. "Arthur isn't the only reason."

I waited, listening, watching as she silently debated what to say and how to say it.

When she remained silent, I had to temper my curiosity. "Look. It's cool. I don't want to put you in a position where you feel uncomfortable." I blew out a breath. I couldn't ask her to trust me when I holding back, could I? "I need help with a thing, and I hear you're amazing at genealogies." I paused, assessing her expression. Wary.

Waiting. "Off the books. Like, Bermuda Triangle off the books. No trace."

Her brows rose, but she looked more comfortable now; the nails stopped drumming, and she settled back a little in her chair. Silently, I wondered about her unease. Did he have some sort of leverage over her? Had he assaulted her, coerced her? The temptation to promise to remove his intestines via his nose was strong, but I bit it back.

"So, is this why we trash-talked Arthur?"

"I mean, he's an easy target," I admitted because it was true. "But yeah. If this gets to him, he'll use it, absolutely." Beo's face swam in my mind, those angry eyes that were at odds with his gentle hands.

She considered that as she nibbled on her focaccia. I barely tasted mine while I waited for her to think it over. "This is about the lycan pack that murdered Betty, isn't it?"

I raised my brows. "Did they?"

"Well…" She let it trail off, shrugged, then took another bite.

"It doesn't fit," I said, quieter. "Look, you don't know me, but something is off, and I don't trust Arthur as far as I can throw him. I have zero interest in covering up for dangerous criminals, but if it wasn't the pack and they get nailed for it, not only have we punished innocent folks, but the community is still unsafe."

She shrugged, then nodded. "Yeah, I'm following. I'm not scared of Arthur. So, what am I looking for?"

I leaned forward a little, lowering my voice further. "A few years ago, I had a run in with a lycan. Illegal jumper."

Her eyes narrowed.

I pushed away the memories, focused on the information I needed to get across. "I was on the Retrievals team. It was bad."

She nodded slowly, her focaccia hanging limply in her hand, all her attention on me.

"The lycan that escaped was known only as Duke. Brilliant green eyes. Think classic bad-romance green eyes." I felt sick and pushed away the food, drew a breath. "Beo, my lycan pack Alpha, has those same eyes."

She sat back, puffed out her cheeks, and blew out a long breath. "Well, shit. Has this Alpha given any hint that he recognizes you?"

I shook my head and picked up my coffee for something to do. My stomach was in knots. I nursed the coffee, glad of its warmth.

"None. But our Retrieval mission was successful. Duke wouldn't have been able to get word back—easily, anyway—and even if he did, would he mention me specifically? 'Hey, some horrible woman with weird eyes was in a team of meat-bags that nailed me' seems like it wouldn't be a likely conversational gambit between two super macho lycanthropes."

A grin lit up her face. "Your eyes are cool."

I grinned back. "Look, I don't know if there is a relationship, or if they even like each other. Some of us have shit families. If that's the case, why punish the guy, you know?"

Something flickered across her face for just a moment, but I couldn't read it, couldn't follow her thinking. "So why even look?"

"Because maybe they are in it together," I said with a shrug. "And because if I don't, I'm going to turn myself inside out second-guessing everything."

She gave a hum of agreement. "I'll do it from home. Got a personal number I can catch you on?"

I nodded and took the phone she slid across to me. It had the most gorgeous deep-purple, sparkly cover. I admired it for too long and it locked again. Without seeming to mind, she unlocked it once more for me to add in my details. And while I did, my mind spun.

Something was wrong. No one should be chased out of their workplace.

"Look," I said slowly, way out of my depth and desperately wishing I could channel Aspen, who pretty much always knew what to say. "I'm not sure what the story is, why you don't come in very often. And I don't want you to feel like you have to...if it puts you in danger or makes you uncomfortable. I just want you to know that if you ever need someone to have your back to kick arse"—something flickered again across her face, and she withdrew slightly from the table—"or just to, you know, be present, talk about shoes or music or games and compare memes, or just to listen, or..." What the hell did people do to support people who might've been totally isolated and abused? I waved a hand, helpless. "I don't know what I'm saying," I admitted, because honesty was pretty much the safest policy. "I'm getting a vibe. I care. Okay?"

She nodded, but the movement was jerky. "Sure. Thanks."

Fuck. I'd screwed it up. "Okay. I'm sorry if that was super awkward. I'm way better at not giving fucks than, um, giving them."

Her smile was faint, but there was a little pleasure in it. She took a serviette, her food forgotten, and folded the soft paper. I watched, my own anxiety increasing as the paper shrank into smaller triangles, some of them wonky.

"Arthur is shit. And so are some of our coven. I don't...fit. That's all."

Hellfire. "Um. That sounds like kind of a big deal to me?" But if she didn't want me to make a big deal of it, I could not do that. Or do that? Or whatever worked. "But if this is better for you, then the food is great." Both of us had barely touched it. "Well. Okay. Maybe it's great. You're fun. I like you. I love your hair." I looked at her, feeling like I was drowning. "I'm screwing up again. But I really do love your hair." She nodded, silent. She'd gone pale, and now I was really worried.

I couldn't just leave her alone if she was, like, being assaulted by Arthur and it was being covered up, could I? But, Hellfire, I didn't have a choice. I just kind of had to trust her to know how to keep herself as safe as she could.

"I need all the sisters I can get," I told her, honestly. "I've got some witch-eating lycans, a whole shitstorm with Arthur, and I have literally zero support network in Melbourne. All my people are back home. So..." I shrugged and sighed. "I don't even feel hungry now."

"Me either." Her voice was thick. "I'm trans."

As the words spilled out of her mouth, her eyes darted up like she was shocked she'd said them. And I sat there, trying hard to reframe all the doom and gloom in my head.

"Okay." That was totally okay. I drew in a breath. Shit, it was like, super fucking dangerous for her to say that to the wrong person, wasn't it? "Thank you for telling me." I shifted, uncomfortable. Heart to hearts were not my strength, and I was way out of my depth. "Like, sincerely. I know that's a big deal to talk about. And, like, live. Oh, shit, I'm absolutely going to fuck this up, Lilith, but"—*shit. Words. Come on, words*—"is it unkind of me to say it doesn't matter to me? Is that, like, minimizing? Because it matters that I know you'd face a bunch of prejudice and things would be harder, so I don't want to say like, *that* doesn't matter. It does."

She had picked up her coffee and was slightly hunched over it. "It's fine. Let's just forget it. I shouldn't have…"

Arthur hadn't hurt her physically. They were jerks to her. Righteous fury burned in my heart. I trapped it there because she didn't need to deal with it.

"Hells no, I won't forget you trusted me, even half by accident." I scowled then sipped. "But I won't make it a big deal. And I'll shut up about it. But I still think you're an awesome sister, and I've still got your back. Nothing's changed. Fuck it. I'm going to eat this pesto artwork and just sit here and be super stoked that you trusted me." And, putting aside all my useless frustration at the world, I did exactly what I'd said I'd do. "So," I said, as she took an awkward sip of her coffee, determined to make this as okay as I could. "What've you got on for the afternoon?"

EIGHT

DIERDRE SUMMERS WAS THE NEW NAME MY CLIENT HAD CHOSEN. BETTY HAD done the paperwork as a precaution alongside the Supernatural Police but hadn't got around to sending it through to the Perth office. There were some potential loose threads there, but I let them dangle.

The less they knew, the less they could tell.

She was easy to spot in a crowd. She wasn't short, probably average height, but she was shrunk so far into herself that she looked like a child with her big, sad blue eyes and her hands clutching the bag to her chest.

I introduced myself, keeping it calm and confident. She didn't have any luggage to speak of. She'd been in protective custody for more than three weeks but somehow still only had what was crammed into her bag.

I didn't ask for information on her ex. I didn't need it. I could see from the way she jumped at loud noises or sudden movements that she'd been hurt—exactly how didn't matter. Hurt was hurt, and it all needed care, kindness, and safety to heal.

During the drive, I explained to her the extra steps I'd taken: the name only known to the Melbourne police and coven, the address I'd organized, and the job she had. She looked overwhelmed, and I wished I'd stopped and bought groceries beforehand, but I hadn't been thinking. Guilt and helplessness gnawed at me, an ache low in my belly that wouldn't quit.

We did it together at the local supermarket so she'd get familiar with her surroundings. She didn't offer up much in the way of preferences, so I grabbed what I thought would be useful.

When I got her to the place I'd found and began to unpack the groceries, she explored, her steps quiet and small.

I slid things into about the spots where I'd look for them myself. The silence filled with the rustle of bags and packets, the clatter of cupboard doors opening and closing.

It felt empty. It felt sad.

It had seemed like so much stuff, but when I put it in the cupboards, it looked small with nothing behind it. No multiple tins of tomatoes bought over the last twelve months, no alternate brands because something was on special. No variety, no "Hey, I only need a small tin of beetroot today." It looked so…transient.

And, really, it was. The place was paid for six weeks. I'd had pushback over the length of time, but, come on, she was starting a new job—she couldn't even start to look for rentals until that was established and she got a feel for the area and her budget.

The woman deserved some time, didn't she?

With that in mind, I said to the cemetery-quiet apartment, "Dierdre, this is your home for the next six weeks unless you find something you'd prefer sooner. But if you can't, we can extend the lease." I'd damned well make it happen.

The answer I got was the whisper of bags being put down and small, tired steps coming towards me. For a time, she just stood there in the middle of the kitchen, looking at the bags as if they were Everest and she was a mountaineer. "I've got it," I told her mildly. "You should put on the kettle. We can have a cuppa."

But she took a deep breath, and from the way her body moved, I could almost see the effort it cost her to bend to look at the groceries. To identify what she'd take and where she'd put it. My heart bled for her.

I tried to give her space, lingered over putting away the vegetables while she selected her items so I wouldn't crowd her, wouldn't make her feel rushed. Her hands were full of shampoo and conditioner when she crumpled in on herself, her face buried in the items, huge sobs wracking her body while she half-melted into the sea of groceries and empty bags.

I dropped the head of lettuce in my hands and went over to her, feeling pretty damn overwhelmed myself. I tried to remember what I'd been told when I'd been hurting, tried to channel Oma or my dad, but she just wept in big, heaving, broken sobs, and I squatted there, helpless.

"Do you need a hug?" I offered tentatively.

She shook her head and wept harder.

"Okay." I blew out a breath. That was pretty much my arsenal for sadness gone. My mind went to the ice cream, but I didn't think that would work.

I hadn't bought tissues. Who didn't buy tissues?

Inspiration struck and I went to the toilet where I'd dropped the pack of toilet paper I had bought and grabbed a roll. "It's what I've got," I said, sitting and passing the paper over, feeling like shit. "Won't make it better, but at least you can be sad with less snot. Snot on your face makes everything worse, I reckon."

She nodded and took the roll, but just clutched it to her thin chest and kept right on sobbing.

The temptation to get up and finish putting away the shopping was strong. I couldn't help her. Well, I didn't know how to help her. Any words that floated through my mind were either out-and-out inappropriate or felt superficial. What comfort could I possibly give?

Regardless of my very obvious inadequate ability to help, I made myself sit there and be present. My hands itched for my phone. I laced them together. It was the least I could do, give the woman some respect when she'd obviously had so little of it.

The file I'd sent had been scarce on details, but as the grief flooded out of her, I thought of the myriad ways power could be abused, ways people could be isolated and hurt and cowed.

She'd gotten out. That was a whole world of struggle I couldn't even imagine. It didn't make her superhuman, but damned if she didn't deserve some acknowledgement.

Logically, I knew if the police were willing to throw money at her to keep her secure, there must be something big going on. Experience led me to be confident that big meant different things to the police and to people. I didn't need the cops to tell me shit had been horrendous for this woman.

And here I was, with nothing to offer and no way to help except by sitting on the tiles, surrounded by groceries, feeling that horrible sadness with her.

My arse and legs were asleep. I'd settled into a good brood myself when one spider-like hand reached out, unstuck the end of the toilet paper from the layer below, and unravelled it enough to take a chunk. Behind the curtain of hair, still punctuated by sobs, her movements were jerky.

"C-can you h-help me?" she whispered. "W-ward this place?"

Relief flooded through me at this task I *could* do, a tangible thing. "Absolutely," I said firmly. Right then, if she'd asked me for the sun, I'd have done everything I could to give it to her. "We'll ward it so hard that any wizard that comes near it will"—I swallowed the vile, probably inappropriate, and definitely anatomically incorrect suggestion—"forget why he was here, and go look for his car keys in his fridge while I track him down."

And then I'd do those inappropriate, anatomically impossible things to him. Because I was nothing if not determined.

She nodded. The curtain of her red hair rippled. "I...I think I want a cuppa. I work better with a cup in my hand. I used to."

My heart broke at those small words, at that self-doubt. "Sounds reasonable to me," I agreed, keeping it calm on the surface while unfolding myself. Blood rushed through my legs and sent prickles of discomfort into the limbs, but I kept it to myself. "Wards are actually one of my specialties." Probably my only specialty, aside from being a bitch, but I didn't tell her that. She'd probably figure it out herself. Any wizard who got close to her certainly would. "So, let's talk about what you'd like. I'm going to insist on a two-hour traceable signal, though. I want to know not just if someone comes knocking, but where to find them afterwards."

By the time I got out of there, I felt sad and drained. I left her with the car I'd rented for a few days and my number in the crappy phone she'd been given. I tried to call my Oma on the way home. She didn't answer. I sent Aspen a touching-base text, but she was busy. She wasn't a witch, but she was a woman and she'd get it.

My place felt as empty as my heart. I looked in the fridge but found no inspiration. I scrolled through social media, liked a few posts, read half of a work email about a new potion going around, and closed the app.

Frustrated and helpless, I changed into compression leggings and a singlet, put in my headphones, pulled on a hoodie, and headed out.

The weather was as cold and dreary as my mood. It should've been late afternoon, but the clouds covered the sun and with the misty rain, brought the gloom of dusk early. I let my feet carry me onto a tram, cranked up my tunes, and turned off my head.

When I found myself at The Playground, I almost walked away, but something drew me on. It was too early for a class, and I was in no mood for people anyway. I was peopled out. But inside the doors, the weights called to me, the area almost empty.

Hells. Why not?

So I lifted some heavy things, focused on my form, the smooth glide of muscles, the strength in my body. A few people filtered in for the class, but I zoned them out.

Right then, if they'd attacked me, I wasn't sure if I'd have ripped the heart out of everyone in the building or just lain down and let them have me.

Brandon's quiet laugh floated through the music, and I gritted my teeth, felt the bar on my hips as I bridged and lowered.

Slow. Smooth. In control.

It didn't stop my heart aching. It didn't stop the sounds in my head. *Bones splintering, a scream that turned into a gurgle.* I hated the feel of the sun on my skin, the memory of that day, and I hated that I let myself go there. I squeezed my eyes shut, but I could see Duke in his lycan form, his coat glossy and brown beneath Brandon's blood.

I bridged again, lowered. I *hated* having Duke in my head. I grabbed another ten kilos for each end of the bar.

A lycan I recognized from my file, not from training, appeared in my field of view. Her blonde hair fell perfectly in the tail at the back of her head, and her expression was one of deep curiosity. I pulled out one ear bud, digging for patience.

She had green eyes. Not romance-trope green, not like Duke and Beo, more like a hazel, could-be-green-in-the-right-light.

"Men are arseholes," she said definitively, her hands on her hips. "I'm Callie."

"Hi, Callie," I said, briefly. "I'm out of patience. Can we do this another day?"

She grinned at me. There were a lot of teeth involved. "So I see. Got class in fifteen. I can spot you 'til then. And I can help insult him."

Any other day, I'd have wanted to adopt her. "No words."

Her answer was a nod. I hesitated, partially because I didn't want to interact at all, and partially because I had no idea how much I could bench anymore. I assessed my rage and figured it was probably a lot.

After putting my music back in, I left off the glute bridges, went to the bench, and got into position. She was as good as her word, watching me carefully. When my form went from perfect to shit in an instant, she was there, taking the bar and lifting it effortlessly into place.

My arms felt like noodles, and I was still furious and helpless.

After passing me my water and giving me a quick rub on the back, she tapped her ear. Grudgingly, I pulled out the bud again. "Want a beer tonight?" she asked. "You look like you could use some decent company."

I shook my head firmly. "Maybe I could, but I wouldn't be any good myself. Thanks."

She just nodded again and loped off as I put the bud in and went back to my bridges.

The next day, I was stiff and sore in ways I hadn't been for a long time. Bracing myself, I checked in on Dierdre before I got into the office, then began to work through my list. I stuck my head in to see Arthur and said, "I'm planning on going to The Playground on Monday evening. Does that work for you?"

He frowned a little and said, "I have a meeting." I didn't know if he did or didn't, but I suspected it was a power move.

Rather than lower myself to his level and tell him to shove it, I just nodded. "Wednesday, then?"

"I can probably make Wednesday work." The agreement was grudging.

"Thanks, Arthur," I said, because politeness probably wouldn't hurt me. "Want me to send you an invite?"

He nodded briskly. "You're the Data Queen."

I was the Arse-Covering Queen, the I-Know-Your-Game Queen. "It's useful. And reliable." Sensing weakness, I said, "I'm going out to do some jobs. Want me to grab anything on the way back?"

Instead of an answer, he looked at me like he was studying a bug and asked, "Why didn't you back me up?"

I lent my shoulder against the door, considered my options.

I didn't trust him, but maybe the bridge wasn't as burned as I'd thought it would be. I wasn't above using his fallibility and ego to further my own goals.

"You were in pain, and we were totally outnumbered that night," I said, trying to soften the blow. "I've worked undercover, Arthur. I know what it's like, and I know how to do it. We weren't undercover. They knew who we were. Beo basically called me a witch."

He eyed me off. "I suppose they wouldn't have killed Betty if they hadn't known about us."

I didn't agree or disagree. It seemed pretty obvious. "We're never going to get them to knowingly turn on each other. Pretty sure that's rule number one of lycan club." I didn't apologize, just shrugged. "I wasn't in the loop, Arthur. I didn't know how to play it." Half lie, half truth, zero guilt. "Anyway. I'm off. Send me a message if you want something."

Before I left, I checked the address I was headed to and added in the Wednesday night session. I had to rearrange my schedule, but it wasn't a big deal, and Arthur'd been suitably pandered to. I'd just go on Monday without him and, if anyone asked, I was tailing one of the other lycans, the low-risk ones. Because they'd downgraded the threat on the pack members, I could get away with it.

Probably.

NINE

THE WEEK MELTED AWAY. I GOT A CALL FROM NONE OTHER THAN EDWARD Van Der Holst, Eternal Emperor of the Melbourne District, at it-isn't-even-eight on Friday morning while I tried to find where one of my earrings had disappeared to. I answered warily.

"Good morning, Rory," he said, his voice as hearty as beef stew. "I wanted to get you bright and early. I hadn't forgotten you wanted information on other lycan packs in Melbourne. Can I just say I very much appreciate how willing you are to get in and get answers? I wish I had more magi like you. Honestly, there are so many supernaturals all over the city that would benefit from your thorough approach and data-driven methodology."

That was a lot of words. "Thanks, Edward."

"Sorry. I think I laid it on a bit thick. To be quite frank, Rory," he sighed, "I'm quite worried about how this is all panning out. Obviously, Betty's murder is horrendous, but the idea of criminals just walking free? I don't want any more dead witches. So, if I was a bit over the top... Well, put it in context. I've got a massive problem, and you're the only one helping. So, I am grateful."

Okay. I glanced over at my mug and found it empty. Felt a little bit the same. He was right. Arthur wasn't doing jack. "I'm just doing my job."

"Maybe to you," he agreed. "I wish your interpretation of your job wasn't so unique."

Shit. Shots fired. Arthur must be seriously in the bad books with his uncle.

"But anyway. I think I might've found someone who can help you out. A lycan who doesn't get on with Velvela." I grabbed my personal phone since I was talking on my work one, opened up the notes app, and got a fresh screen. "Jay and Jaye—the second Jay is with an 'e'—Automotive. Jay with an 'e' is a lycan; he's on today."

I tapped in the information. "'On' as in at the auto shop?"

"That's right."

"Are there other lycans likely to be present?" I asked, quickly. A lycan might separate from their pack to work. I knew a bunch of Beo's did.

"Not according to my information," Van Der Holst told me, a little hesitantly. "I wouldn't do that to you, Rory."

Well, he'd failed the shit out of that for Betty, hadn't he? "Did the information come from Jaye's Caretaker?" I asked because there had been a definite hesitation there.

"No," he sighed slowly. "You're aware, I'm sure, that Arthur is the area expert on lycans."

From the corner of my eye, I spied my bespelled earring lurking beneath the fruit bowl, of all places. "Yes, I'd heard mention."

"Well…Arthur's had information on Jaye for some time."

That was it. That was his statement. I reached out, grabbed my earring. Edward was pissed at Arthur. I supposed that made two of us.

"So, you want me to get in and get it done?"

"I wouldn't have put it in as many words," Edward demurred. "But it does concern me that this lead hasn't been followed up yet. We need to move on this coal before it starts a fire, Rory. And…" The pause was pregnant, grew, then birthed. "I know you're licensed Retrievals."

My heart sank. "I see."

"I know you can get the job done, Aurora. That's why I wanted you. And so far, you've proved me right. You're an excellent witch."

He was right about that. And about Arthur. "Okay." I figured the man had an agenda. He was a bureaucratic wizard. Of course, he had an agenda. "So, I'm assuming Arthur won't be there."

"Jaye isn't high-risk," Edward told me. "Not as far as any information shows, anyway. But if you'd prefer to wait for Arthur, I wouldn't blame you. I know lycans can be highly dangerous, after all, and you're trained to reduce risks."

He had no idea. "It's fine. One lycan at work, I can manage."

"I'll call this afternoon," he promised. "Check in on you. I'm very interested to see what you can learn."

I turned the earring around in my fingers, curiosity piqued. The tone of High Dick Wafter's call was definitely an about face. What had Arthur done?

I let my brain kick into autopilot as I wrapped up the small talk, said good-bye to Mighty Wand Waver Edward, then stood and looked at my notes for a few minutes, frowning.

This was very off.

I had no clear Caretaker I could call, not even a clear district. I'd still follow up with them, of course. But it was a lone lycan at his day job; this wasn't a pack. I did a quick search, found the number for the automotive shop, and considered it.

My car was in Dad's garage. In Ballarat. A four-hour round trip away.

In my personal phone, I found Lilith in my contacts then hit dial. "Hey," she said after a moment. "Is today a real-coffee-just-to-get-up-and-running kinda day?"

"Oh, I'm up and running," I promised, putting in the rogue earring. "Look, you've got a car, right?"

"Right."

"Can I service it for you?"

She didn't like the idea of me paying for it, but I figured we didn't know what quality of work this place did. I called the auto place, booked in for that morning, jumped on a tram and zipped over to Lilith's. She didn't ask to see my license to double-check I could drive, but I knew she wasn't entirely comfortable with it.

"Promise," I told her, drawing a line over my heart. "I break it, I buy it."

She didn't look any happier but passed me the keys. "Go forth, buttercup," she said with a sigh. "Fuckery awaits."

By the Elders, I had an awesome coven.

Since I was paying for the service, and since I'd be filling the tank before I gave it back, I made a slight detour to the share house where Callie and Frankie both had a place, figuring I had enough time to do a quick drop-in.

I knocked on the door, and a teenager wearing sweatpants and a huge hoodie with a food stain down the front peered at me. "Yes?" she asked blearily.

"I was hoping to see Frankie or Callie," I said, turning on my warmest, most trustworthy smile.

She shrugged, stepped back, and let me in. A small study area was crammed to the roof with bits of paper, notebooks, textbooks, unwashed mugs, charging cords, and the odd bottle. A clothes rack stood with a few shirts hanging limply on it. I didn't blame them for looking so despondent. The place didn't scream "Hey, you're home!" More like "Hey, let's crash here until we find a better cave!"

The kitchen was pretty much as bad. Someone had cleaned the dining table recently enough; a laptop there, books somewhat organized around it. The mug here sat on a coaster.

"He'll be here in a minute. She's at work." The girl disappeared back into her own room and closed the door.

I tucked my hands in my pockets and peered at Callie's notes. She was studying accounting. I was pretty sure anyway. Or maybe Frankie was studying accounting? One of them was. The other was doing a certificate in community something-or-another. I thumbed through the pages idly. Neat headings, subheadings, and precise handwriting.

A door opened and Frankie emerged, his hair poking up in every direction yet chartered. He smiled at me, looking like he'd rolled out of bed and also managing to be awake without caffeine.

"Hey, Rory," he said a bit awkwardly. "Is everything okay?"

"Hey, Frankie. Yeah, things are good. Can I sit?"

"Oh. Um." He looked at the table, and an expression of relief crossed his face as he realized he could offer me a seat without shit piled on it.

"Yeah, of course." And he sat, too, his hands dangling between his legs. "So, this isn't, like, a bad-news visit?"

"Nah." I settled, crossed my legs under the table. "You look like you had a late one."

"Yeah." He scratched his cheek, a bit sheepish. He didn't look hungover, though—just tired, a bit pale, and puffy around the eyes. "I, um, went out. Hung out with a friend."

The blush rising up his neck made me wonder exactly how his hair had gotten so exciting. I wiggled my brows, jerked my thumb towards his room. He went redder, nodded. "Mate," I said with a grin, "bacon and eggs. Super romantic. Go!" And I stood to let myself out. Because, really, I'd seen enough. I was just here to check in after all, make sure there were no corpses sitting around, no lines of pixie dust, see if they actually lived where they said they did. Those little things.

They were just being young folks. And I wasn't going to rain on Frankie's parade.

Not today anyway.

He walked with me to the door, his hands in his pockets. "Didn't you, uh, want anything?"

"Nah. Just like to check in. Looks like things are going swimmingly." He went an even deeper shade of red, and he was so wholesome I wanted to hug him. "Hey," I said as I opened the door myself, "do you know a Jaye? He runs with a different crowd, but..." Frankie's expression had become fixed. "You do know him."

"I, uh..." He stepped back, hands buried in his pockets. His eyes danced around as if he didn't know where to look. "Yeah, I mean, I don't *know* him, I know *of* him. But I don't know what I should..."

"What you should tell me," I finished, when he seemed to lose the ability to find words.

He nodded, looking miserable.

That was fair, I supposed. I was the outsider, after all. "All good. I appreciate your honesty, Frankie. You have an excellent morning, won't you?" I hesitated then said, "You can at least make them a coffee, right?"

"Yeah," he told me miserably. "Don't think there's any bacon and eggs."

"Cafe breakfast?" I looked at the holes in the shirt he wore. Budgets were a thing. "Quick grocery store run?"

"Yeah. Maybe." He shifted. "You're not going to go see..."

"Jaye."

"Yeah. Jaye."

That was worrying. He was definitely uncomfortable with the idea. Maybe Arthur hadn't dragged his feet just for the sake of it?

"It's fine. He'll be at work. Public space. Also"—I wiggled my fingers—"I'm magick. But thanks for your concern. I'm leaving now."

He watched me, looking embarrassed and worried as I climbed into Lilith's comfy sedan with plenty of leg room. He was still there, wearing that torn expression, as I eased out of the cramped car park.

Worry sat in my belly like a brick. First that strange call, now that very strong reaction. No question, Jaye was trouble.

But that was fine. So was I. They just didn't know it yet.

The place would have been easy to miss if I hadn't been watching so closely. Inside, the door hadn't even closed behind me when a guy wearing a grubby shirt with the mechanics' logo on the breast was there, checking the calendar and saying, "Help you?"

I leaned on the counter, didn't miss the way his eyes dipped down to my breasts. He was about as attractive as the furball I'd scooped off my chair yesterday afternoon after the coven cat had decided it was a prime spot to puke. Not physically—he was tall, strong, rugged. But there was something icky about him that wasn't just the way he eyeballed me.

"I've booked my car in. Actually, it's my friend's car," I admitted with an apologetic smile. "I've borrowed it because I don't have access to one." All perfectly true. "And I figured I better get it all sorted before I hand it back, you know? But I was hoping to speak to the mechanic, because..." I shrugged, didn't have to work too hard to look uncomfortable.

"Yeah, sure," he said, his words vaguely accented in a way I couldn't quite place. He cleared his throat. "Jaye's in. Come on back. We don't usually have people out here but..." His gaze swept over me as he opened the door to the workshop in the back. "I'm sure he'll make an exception."

I hadn't spent much time in workshops, but I recognized the smells of oil and dust, the sight of all those tools. It looked like an auto workshop, smelled like an auto workshop, probably was an auto workshop.

A few guys glanced our way as I was taken into the interior. It was dark after the bright winter light outside, with a radio somewhere playing from a local station. Even with the hum of the city in the background and the occasional conversation between mechanics, it felt isolated.

Alarms rang in my mind, as they should've. I was about to chat with an unknown lycan. Smart women didn't do that lightly, and—okay, maybe I wasn't smart, but, shit, I was good at staying alive.

Maybe "alive women didn't do that lightly" was more accurate?

"Hey, Jaye," my guide called. "Someone for you."

A lean, wiry guy about my height looked up from the bowels of a car engine, wiping his hands on a rag stuffed into his belt. He did a quick skim of my body. Unlike my guide, he must've been a hips man; his eyes lingered there before coming up to my face.

"Good morning," he said with that same accent that made his words almost guttural. *German?* "What can I do for you?"

I spun him the same totally-not-bullshit story, waiting for the guide to leave so I could get down to business. Asked him about his qualifications, for references. That part was absolute bullshit. I'd already booked the car in, after all.

My guide didn't fuck off.

I passed him Lilith's car keys and shot him a smile. "Sounds like you've got it covered. You should bring it in."

He took Lilith's keys, nodded, and still didn't move.

My internal warning system cranked up from "I don't like this" to "look for the nearest fucking exit." I put my hands in my pockets. One on my phone, one on my keys. "I was hoping to speak to you in private," I told Jaye directly and sent the guide a meaningful glance.

Jaye nodded to the guide and steered me towards a little room beside the bathroom. The office was crowded with filing cabinets and a desk half covered by an old, well-loved desktop. Into the tiny cubicle we went. I didn't love him closing the door after us, but I'd asked for private and I got it.

My survival instincts warned me that now the nearest escape was a lot farther away.

"So." He indicated I should sit. I did but kept my hands firmly on the tools of my trade. He slid onto the desk, positioning himself uncomfortably close, before stretching out his legs between me and the door. "What, you wanted to know what it's like to have a lycan between your legs?"

Well, that saved beating around the bush, didn't it?

"I want information on the riftrunners."

His eyes narrowed. "Do you?"

Having just said I did, I felt no need to repeat myself. I ignored the crawly, sick feeling I was getting from this place, leaned back, folded my legs, then waited.

"Seems to me a pretty, young witch should have a lot of ways to get information," he offered, tilting his head to the side. "I hear there are some really hot spells you bitches can use."

Blokes. Why?

"I have one that can burn someone so hot that their bones turn to ash," I offered him, my tone pleasant. "Is that what you mean?"

He grinned at me. Not with me—at me. "You're on my turf threatening me if I don't help you out? Seems like a bad play."

"I was going to ask politely," I admitted, keeping my tone as carefree as I could. "But, hey, turnabout is fair play. I can be nice if you can."

His grin twitched then widened. "Nice was never really my thing. Tell you what. You've wasted my time here today. You make it up to me, you walk out, we have happy afternoons."

He wasn't talking about the old time-is-money thing.

"Or, what? You rape me here in the office, with all those guys out there just pretending not to hear, and dump my body in the Yarra?" I lifted my brows, ignoring the way my heart was trying to drum its way out of my body and get back to the car.

I didn't even have the keys.

He scratched his jaw. "The guys, they like fun, too. And anyway, I was thinking something closer than the Yarra. But you've got the gist of it."

I realized in a rush that Jaye wasn't just a lycan; he was an Alpha. And, following that train of logic, at the very least, the guide who had the same accent and hadn't wanted to piss him off was also a lycan.

Possibly, they all were.

Fuck you, Arthur Van Der Holst, Head Shitfucker of the East Melbourne Coven.

Fuck.

You.

Adrenaline sharpened my sight and flooded my limbs with strength. "So, I walk in, ready to play nice, and I get ultimatums." I stood, fully prepared to bluff my way as close to the door as I could or, if I couldn't, to blast my way out. "You know what, Jaye? I'll get my filters changed somewhere else."

Bracing myself, I stuffed down the terror, hard, and headed for the door. I expected not to make it, but I couldn't just sit there.

I let go of the phone and took my hand out of my pocket but kept a death grip on my keys. Thank the Elders I hadn't needed to hand over mine, just Lilith's.

One step toward the door. Two.

His arm shot out with dizzying speed, a fistful of my shirt his prisoner. My legs went. I was jerked off-balance towards him.

I locked my free hand over his. My key-weighted fist swung straight up into his face. I dropped and spun. Stitches popped. He snarled.

I got one long step closer to the door, heart in my throat. *Almost there.* He caught my leg and I staggered, off-balance, and smashed into the cubicle wall. It shuddered behind me. Sheer luck let me rip free and half-fall out of the door into the shop.

The rattle and grind of the big roller doors coming down stretched and expanded until it was all I could hear. Three men still holding tools covered in grease were arrayed between me and the rapidly disappearing exit.

Lycans. Not men.

The odds were shit. I couldn't outrun them, and I couldn't fight them all off.

So, I did what any smart witch would—I drew up my magick. *Through this dome none shall leave or come unless it is with me.* I let the spell run from my mind through the wand attached to my keyring and coalesce around me. And, as soon as it did, the panic began to ebb.

Maybe I was stuck, but they couldn't touch me. I drew in a deep breath and waited for my mind to clear, for my heart to stop the urgent beat of *run-run-run.*

Jaye wandered out of the office, wiping blood from his face and looking both furious and grimly pleased. "I gotta say," he told me, strolling over as if he was king of the fucking world, "you've made my day a much more interesting one, witch."

Then he ran into my ward.

His face contorted into instant rage. "How dare you?'" he snarled. "Get the tools!"

I rolled my eyes as one of the nearby men lifted a crowbar. "Yeah. Sure." I reached for my phone as they struck it. A sound like a big church bell filled the garage as I glanced at the time. *Detective O'Malley first, or my coven?*

Fuck, I was going to cop flak over this, and I didn't even care.

As I unlocked the device, I swore to myself I'd never, ever trust another wizard as long as I lived.

I'd just opened the calls app when I realized the men around me had turned towards the door with their makeshift weapons ready, fierce expressions on their faces.

The air became soup. I couldn't breathe. If a regular Joe arrived... I couldn't hold two spells at once.

Why was I the one witch who couldn't hold two spells at once?

My heart roared in my ears. I went into recent calls and skimmed through for O'Malley, feeling the shaking set in.

This could get ugly fast.

I dialled as I heard the service area door open. They'd turned off the radio. When had they turned off the radio? Or could I not hear it over the roaring in my ears? But I could hear the way the phone just rang and rang.

O'Malley's voicemail kicked in, and I hung up as a large figure blocked the sun streaming through the door to the service area.

Just beside my ward, Jaye snarled something in a language I didn't recognize. I didn't need to. "Get off my motherfucking lawn" was universal.

My heart skipped and tumbled as I saw another figure come through behind the first. They were backlit, and my shitty human eyes couldn't see who they were, but obviously Jaye knew them. I swallowed. *Turf war?* I glanced down at the phone and quickly changed it over to keypad. Emergency service response was shit when it came to a supernatural clusterfuck, but I couldn't hang around all day.

"You've got our witch."

My head snapped up to find more figures.

Seven of them, fanning out. Someone hit the button for the door, and it began its slow, agonizing climb. Sunlight washed in, and I recognized Beo, with the shaggy, blonde Zane beside him.

I was being rescued.

Whatever Jaye snarled back pissed off Beo's pack. I didn't like the way Jeff was pacing, the way his eyes had settled on a specific target. A few threats went back and forth between Jaye's lycans and Beo's.

I was not doing this.

"Look," I said over top of them. "I can call the fucking cops, or you can give me my car keys and let me leave. Personally, I don't care if you get torn to ribbons, except that it's more paperwork. I'm safe and cozy right here."

"Shut your mouth unless my dick's in it, bitch," Jaye snarled.

I shuddered. "I can't ever unthink that. Well, cops it is."

"You going to explain this to them?" Beo asked Jaye. "What do you think they'll find when they go over this place? And they will."

Jaye spat something in his language, and I hesitated because if I did call in the regular cops, odds were excellent there would be fatalities. And a Retrievals team would take time. *I* had plenty, but locking down the area so there was no collateral damage? That was dicey.

"I told you. She's our witch. We just lost our last one. This one's been useful. We'll keep her, thanks." Beo started towards me.

Jaye turned his face, spat out a wad of blood and spit, and said something I couldn't understand.

A set of keys flew through the air. Beo caught them, tossed them back to Zane.

With much skulking and snarled parting shots, Jaye fell back, and I locked my phone, waiting until Beo was right beside my ward, his eyes still on the mechanics.

"Go," he told me, quietly.

I breathed deep, prepared for the worst, and let the words to end a spell solidify in my mind, felt them pulse as the power flowed back into them—*as I will, so shall it be.* And even though my brain screamed *run*, I tempered my pace, letting my long legs carry me out into the patchy sunshine, past the pack. Zane passed me the keys wordlessly.

They stood in the parking lot like a guard until I finished the five-point turn I needed to get out of there and nosed into the traffic.

The flood of relief made my head spin. I drove in the vague direction of the office, trying to keep it together.

When I saw Albert Park Lake, though, with its easily accessible car parks, I pulled in, put my head on the wheel, and just breathed.

"I am never trusting a wizard again," I told myself out loud, because things I could hear were way less scary than things I couldn't. I buried my hands in my hair, felt the soft glide of the curls as they wrapped around my fingers. *Normal.* One of my hands banged off the wheel rhythmically. "I am never. Trusting. A. Wizard. Again."

A tap on my window made me jump, my heart racing. I met Beo's eyes and took a moment to register that he stood beside the car, peering into the window, watching me. I gulped in some air, looking away, and struggled to compose myself.

I'd had it under control. More or less. I hadn't needed a rescue.

I hadn't, but other people would've.

I buzzed down the window, and a blast of cold air blew in. I looked back towards him, trying to gather the thoughts flickering through my head. "You want to get out, stretch your legs, take a breather?" he asked me, his hands in his pockets, the pose infinitely non-threatening.

The memory of him rag-dolling me, taking my back, going for that rear naked choke, flashed in high definition into the fore of my mind. "What would you have done if I'd gone for offense, not defense?" I asked him, remembering how prepared to do violence Jaye's pack had been.

"Want to go back, find out?" he offered blithely.

"No." Curse it. "I was told there would be one. Not four."

"Seems like you did okay for yourself."

On cue, my hand started to ache. I looked down at it, surprised, and realized my foot hurt, too, though not as bad. I lifted my hand, inspected the knuckle, made a fist, then with a long, shaky sigh, let the hand fall on the wheel. "I don't want to get out. If you're going to hover, you'll have to get in. But I'm fine, now, honestly. Thank you."

From the corner of my eye, I could see the way he peered at me. I just kept my eyes on my aching hand on the wheel.

Four lycans. I should've levelled the whole fucking place.

And...what did Beo mean about what the police would find there?

His shadow fell across the bonnet. A moment later, I heard the passenger door open then close. I buzzed the window up again, resisting the urge to lock the doors.

"Tell me about Jaye."

"He's your typical scum of the world," Beo said, adjusting himself in the seat a bit, settling back. "Word is he's dodged more than three rape convictions. Witnesses and evidence keep going missing. Pretty sure he does some chop-shop work. Again, investigations tend to lose traction."

Fuck. "I can't just ignore all that."

He shrugged. "What're you going to do, create some evidence?" He gazed at my hand. "You must have a mean swing. Haven't seen many humans do actual damage to a lycan. Is that a combat spell?"

I shot him an annoyed look. "Yes. It's called Punch-A-Fucker, and you do it with the magick of muscle and bone."

"My favorite kind." He settled back, and I watched a woman herd what looked like a million small children across a green area and towards some playground equipment.

If things had gone differently, I'd have a dead lycan, my practicing license would be suspended while I was investigated, and there would be an entire shitstorm.

But I'd gotten lucky. Because Frankie had called Beo. Because Beo had...

"Why did you come?" I asked without looking. If I knew he was walking into some sort of fiery ball of nasty, I'd go, but I was *paid* to.

He shrugged, shifting a little. "Frankie said you were expecting there to be one. I figure you're smart enough to know your limits. If it'd just been one, I would've stayed out of it."

"But you knew there'd be more."

"Yeah. His whole outfit are lycans. I wasn't sure how many would be there, but I didn't like the idea of you being ambushed." He considered it for a moment and nodded. "Felt cheap."

Fucking wand-waving, ego-defending wizards. "Thank you. And thanks to Frankie, too. You didn't have to, but it made it a lot simpler."

He turned a little, looked me over. "You're pretty calm for a witch who was almost dinner."

Bones crunched in my head, and I shuddered, braced my hand against the wheel. "I was very prepared to call the police, let them do their jobs. I could still go and report what he did." I flexed my knuckle, reconsidered. "Actually, there's probably more evidence against me than for me."

He was quiet for a few moments before turning to look in the back. "You got a spare shirt?" he asked, rummaging a bit. "Whose car is this?"

"Friend." I glanced down at my shirt, remembering the way Jaye grabbed me, the way I'd weaponized that grip. "Well, shit." The robin blue, drapey fabric bagged dramatically between my breasts. Some of it was torn.

If I'd killed him then and there...well, laws were laws. Maybe I could've proven self-defense, maybe not, but either way it would've been a whole circus.

"You should go back to whatever you were doing before you rescued me. I'm rattled, I'm not going to deny that, but I'll be totally fine. I just need to go home and change."

He considered me for a moment, as if weighing my words against my presentation. "I'm not sure if you're being polite, cautious, or honest. But I'll go since you asked."

Completely taken off guard by his words, I watched as he reached for the door. I didn't know which of those three options I was either. Probably not cautious. I doubted I could claim that anymore. "Thanks, Beo. I mean it."

"I know you do." He swung his legs out but half-turned and met my eyes. "You looked after Frankie, that day. Not in a small way, either. You were a witch headed to war. Do you need a hug, Caretaker?"

Trying to follow the conversation was giving me whiplash. I did need a hug. I hadn't even realized how much until he offered. Somewhere warm and dark and small and safe was exactly where I wanted to be to let my tired, over-excited brain whir and spin and rest.

But there were boundaries I needed to at least sort of adhere to. "I would. But I don't think I'm allowed."

"What, you worried those kids over there are going to report you?" he asked, raising his brows.

I said nothing, just sighed and ran a hand through my hair. "I hate wizards. Really, really despise them."

He swung his legs back in and opened his arms. I eyed him for a moment, his typical biker jacket open over a black T-shirt that looked as soft as the now-ruined robin blue one I wore, and all that warm strength beneath. With another sigh, I let my brain switch off and leaned over.

My head rested on his chest. The gear stick poked me in the hip, but I ignored it. I just breathed, resting against him, feeling the slow, steady drum of his heart. And with every beat, a little more tension eased out of me, until I was all but lying in his lap, his arms warm and solid and totally undemanding around me.

I could've quite easily gone to sleep there, gear stick or no. But my phone buzzed, and then, a few minutes later, a call jarred the peace. I dragged myself up to check the screen just as it rang out.

Lilith. Shit. I sent her a quick text. *Not dead. Car is fine. Not serviced after all. Talk soon.*

After I'd sent it, I realized I should've chosen a better description than "not dead." But that was pretty much where my standards were after going toe-to-toe with an unfriendly Alpha, much less with a few cronies along, too. I put my phone down, ran my hands over my hair and scooped it back.

"Thank you. I do feel better." I eyeballed the kids on the playground. "Maybe a curse so they lose all memory of today." A beat of silence passed, then another. I glanced over, saw his carefully neutral expression, and grinned. "That was a joke, Beo. Memory wipes aren't a thing."

A little relief flickered over his face. "I wasn't sure. They're a fae thing, after all, and you're..."

"I'm?"

"Hard to read."

I was pretty sure I was an open book, but I let it slide. "Okay. Sure. Well, now I owe you for a rescue and a hug."

"We should probably stop keeping score," he suggested, throwing one leg out the door. "I like you. You like me. Let's keep it easy."

My throat tightened. "Okay."

He climbed out, shut the door, and wandered around the car. His bike was parked illegally on the grass a few meters away. How I hadn't heard him arrive earlier, I had no idea. But he didn't go to it, instead coming back to my window and tapping on it again.

I realized when I buzzed it down that I'd left the damn car running that whole time. Poor Lilith's car. At least I was warm.

"I know what kind of folk Jaye is," he said, meeting my eyes. "I know what he would've said and done. I'm pretty sure now wouldn't be a good time to kiss you, but I'm not really confident, so I thought I'd throw the choice to you."

Kiss me. He wanted to kiss me? I was so far away from wanting anything sexual it wasn't even in the same postcode.

"Yeah, I'm not feeling super excitable right now." Holy shit. *Right now* meant at some point I could see myself kissing him. Yes, I definitely could. "I really like that you asked."

His brows rose. "Are you allergic to the word 'no'?"

I eyed him warily. "Are you?"

"No."

A bubble of humor filled my chest. "Well played. I need to go now. But thank you. Sincerely. I know I said it already, but you made what could've been really horrible into something that was a lot simpler. More than once." And I wished I could just take him home and use him as a pillow.

He shrugged. "Say it again if it makes you feel better. No score cards over here, Caretaker." He stepped back and held out his empty hands. My heart did a slow roll in my chest as I threw the car in reverse.

TEN

EDWARD CALLED ME THAT AFTERNOON, AND, OH BOY, DID I LET HIM HAVE IT.

He was surprisingly conciliatory about the whole thing, promised to go back over Arthur's notes with a fine-tooth comb, and sent me contact details for Jaye's last known Caretakers. "I don't know how this could have been so poorly managed," he said, more than once. "I cannot apologize enough, Aurora. This isn't how we do things in Melbourne."

Well, it was certainly how Arthur did things. Or didn't. "I understand Arthur is your nephew," I began cautiously. "However, perhaps this needs further investigation."

"You're right," Edward said heavily. "I know you are. To be honest, I knew it before that meeting the other day. Betty was a friend of mine. I have to wonder…"

Exactly what he wondered he didn't say as I stood in the narrow, little parking bays in the sparse winter sun and waited.

"Aurora," he said, eventually, "can you…keep an eye on Arthur for me? I think a fresh view on what's happening in that coven will be…useful."

Unease trickled down my spine. Hello, stratagem, my old friend. "I'm more than happy to do my job." And that was it. Full stop. End of offer.

"Of course. I wouldn't ask more of you. I just wonder if…" I waited. And waited. And waited. "I wonder if you might be willing to discuss things of this particular nature with me. I'm concerned about the flow of information."

That was a lot of inference, none of it subtle. He thought Arthur was dirty. He wanted me to prove it. "I'll case note everything as usual."

Edward was quiet for a moment, then asked, "Did you notice any discrepancies in Betty's case notes on the lycan pack, compared to her other clients?"

I paused to consider. Had there been a difference? Maybe. The lycan pack had next to no information listed. I'd have to double check.

"Who has access to case notes?" I asked him, watching the traffic chugging past.

"Arthur does," Edward admitted quietly.

Fuck.

Fucking fuck-it-y fuck-stickles.

"Okay," I said slowly. I was going to have to play this carefully. "I can let you know what I'm doing." And keep my own, separate notes, not on the coven cloud. "But I'll still case-note as usual." And then if anything happened to me, well, he'd at least be able to know if Arthur was rewriting history. The idea left me cold. He couldn't seriously think his own nephew, the dimple-wielding, weekend warrior Arthur was in cahoots with lycans. Could he?

"That's an excellent solution," Edward said, relief in his voice. "I wouldn't ask this of you lightly, Aurora. You're clearly a highly capable witch. I'm glad we have you."

Yeah, that and five bucks would buy me a decent coffee. "It's no big deal," I said, even though it was. "I'd best go write this up."

"Maybe this specific incident shouldn't be written up," Edward said warily. "In case someone notices."

The someone who would notice was quite obvious. "You want me to lie."

"No. Just wait on this. Please, just until we have a little more information."

He'd said please. Something about that made me nervous. "Okay. I won't case note it." On the standard document, anyway. "What's the next step, Edward?"

"I don't know," he admitted, sounding a little grim. "I need to do some work from my end. See what I can dig up. Can you keep your eyes open for now? And I'll touch base in the next week."

He wanted me to not report a bunch of violent lycans. If I didn't do this through the normal channels, going to the cops was totally out. But my broken hand said it was anyway. "Okay. I'll speak to you in a week."

"I appreciate your energies, Aurora, and your insight. Blessed be."

"Yeah, blessed be," I mumbled because I hated the traditional garbage. Hanging up on that conversation was a bloody relief.

Arthur. Fuck-knuckle Arthur. I should've known as soon as he told me he was a feminist and then looked at me waiting for praise.

Quietly, I tried to contact folks who knew anything about Jaye. A lot of messages were taken, a lot of handballing done. His pack was on a border between two districts. His Caretakers had left. He was passed back and forth like a hot potato, and his current Caretaker was temporary while they hired on someone to take the actual caseload left by Jaye's prior Caretaker.

Coincidence? I doubted it. I doubted Arthur would've missed the significance either.

By the end of the day, I was no wiser than I had been when I'd walked out of that garage.

I went back to Lilith's, we ate Chinese, and after venting about the day, we shared anything interesting that popped into our social media scrolling. She got me an ice pack for my fist and even had ice left over to make a pretty good scotch.

I worked Saturday, because I could. I stopped in to see Jeff, who worked at the bottle shop nearby, and picked up a few bottles of red wine for Dad and Oma's favorite dark ale. Jeff didn't look at all surprised to see me. He side-eyed the labels on the wine while ringing it up. "Witching doesn't pay well, hey?"

My brows rose. "Are you saying I'm cheap?" I asked, pretending to be affronted as I tapped my card.

He considered it, then me. "Yeah."

I held up the ale. "It's for my grandmother. Her favorite."

A small smile tugged at the corner of his mouth. "And the red? There's cask wine better'n that."

I feigned interest. "Really? These are for my dad. I figure if he buys it, he doesn't hate it. I don't know anything about wine. I'm a gin girl."

He grunted and eyed the purchases again, his expression a bit softer. "Two bottles for your dad?"

"One for the lasagna, one to drink." I picked up my purchases. "Next time, I'll hit you up for some wine advice, because my dad is absolutely a cheapskate, but I love him, so I could take him something a little nicer." I hesitated, thinking now of my wallet. "But maybe I'll get the cask wine for the lasagna."

He laughed at me, glancing guiltily at the customer who had just wandered over waiting to be served.

"See you at training, Rory," he said. "Hello, sir, can I help you?"

I let myself be moved along, pleased with the interaction and happy that I'd killed two birds with one stone.

The train ride home to Ballarat was long and lulling. I watched a show Lilith had recommended when I'd caught up with her the night before. Dad waited, sitting in his car listening to a podcast, when I arrived.

It was easy to slip into the pattern of being with him as the day eased into night, and the normality of it soothed me. We made the lasagna together. While it cooked, I sat beside him at the dining table, marking multiple-choice tests as he churned through a big pile of essays.

"One day, I'll quit teaching and get a nine-to-five job," he said, as he always did after a stint of marking, stretching his back. "Reports are coming up."

Ah, reports, marking, Beryl the humanities area leader. Smiling, I made him a coffee, poured him a wine, and set them before him while we worked. We didn't talk much, and it was perfectly safe, perfectly wonderful.

Aspen rocked up in time to steal some eggs and bacon the next morning. She looked the same as ever, blonde hair worn in a half shave, silver earrings, silver necklace, silver bangles, silver rings.

I'd become used to all that silver since Brandon's death. But now it struck me again, the depth of what Duke had cost us—had cost her.

"So," she said, refilling my coffee and loading a piece of toast with scrambled eggs as Dad smiled over at us from his spot by the stove. "Tell me. Are there like super bad arse witches in Melbourne?"

"Pretty much like here," I said, already done with my own breakfast but not unhappy to have more coffee. "In fact, my coven is probably less progressive, if anything. Pretty sure they all do kitchen magick."

"Don't underestimate kitchen magick," Dad said. "Okay. Sorry. Butting out now. I'm going to mow the lawn. You two shout at each other over the mower."

"Love you, Not-Dad," Aspen said with a wave. "Probably won't be here later!"

"Love you too, Not-Kid." He stopped to press a kiss to her head. "Give my best to your olds." I got a kiss, too, and he let himself out the sliding door, temporarily sending a blast of cold, wintery air over us.

"Okay, now he's gone"—she leaned forward—"spill."

"Spill?" I asked, raising my brows.

"Cute people. Melbourne's, like, an untapped pool of potential fun for us." She bit into the toast, waving a hand in a come-on motion.

"Well." I said, wary because my brain went straight to Beo, and Beo was a lycan. "There's a sexy detective."

"No. Way." Her eyes widened. "That's actually a thing?"

"In this case," I agreed, amused at her reaction. "He's got one of those raspy, up-all-night-catching-bad-guys voices. He's a bit of a hard arse."

"Oh, I love him." She sighed happily and picked up bacon with her fingers in a way she wouldn't have done if my dad were watching. "I assume hard arse in a good way."

I considered it. "I think so. He had his arm twisted by the district wizard and called me in to give him leverage to diffuse a shitty situation." At least, I was pretty sure that's what O'Malley had done. If not, well, it made a good story. "He's heading up a murder investigation into the witch I took over from, so I'm sure I'll have more to—"

"Wait," she said, her mouth still full. "Wait. What?"

"Oh." *Yeah, nice one, Rory.* "The witch I took over from was murdered."

"And you forgot to mention this?" she demanded, waving her bacon threateningly at me. "Rory! God!"

"Well." I cleared my throat, shifting. "Anyway, sexy detective. And the District High Wizard has personally asked me to dig up dirt on his nephew, who's the wizard of my coven."

She cringed. "Ew. Families are so fucked." She took another bite, and around toast and egg asked, "What's he done? Your wizard?"

"Aside from protecting systems of oppression while simultaneously declaring himself a feminist?" I asked, raising my brows. She snickered, wriggling in closer in her chair. "Could be covering up Betty's—my predecessor's—murder."

She paused mid-chew, her eyes going huge in her round face.

Before she could open her mouth again, I sighed and went on. "It's weird. I've got a lycan pack on my books." She choked and some of the glow faded from her cheeks. "Sorry. Look, they're okay. But the whole thing is weird."

"You're a witch," she managed, swallowing with a wince. "Shit is always weird, Sunshine."

"Yeah, but this is like," I wrinkled my nose. "Admin kind of weird. Like my pack. The way they've been managed is just so..."

"Weird?" she asked.

"Yeah."

"Okay," she said slowly. "So that was a super possessive 'my' you just dropped there."

I couldn't tell her about Beo and how he was probably related to Duke. I couldn't remind her of what Duke had done to Brandon.

Suddenly, the streaming sunlight was too warm, too familiar. *The smell of blood, the trees and earth of the bush.* I reached for my coffee and took a fortifying swallow. "I don't know, Aspen." No way was I going to admit I'd curled up against Beo and almost fallen asleep. No way was I going to tell her that I kind of wished I'd kissed him.

The guilt was too real—too huge.

I could've saved her brother.

I hadn't.

"Don't know what?" she asked, suddenly serious.

I sighed, scooped up my hair, and twisted it so it lay over my back.

"What I'm doing," I admitted, and the stark truth of the words made me feel hollow.

She reached out and wrapped a hand around mine. The silver of her rings and the small amount of bacon grease just added to the normality. "Look after you," she said, seriously. "That's what you have to do. Okay?"

"Yeah." I blew out a breath. "Yeah, I'm trying. It's hard, you know. I don't know the players. They've all got back stories, agendas."

She nodded, still regarding me. "And you don't play games well."

"I really don't," I admitted, chagrined. "Although, I did have a killer meeting with the High Wizard where I totally played him."

Her grin returned. She sat back and asked, "Was sexy detective there to admire?"

"No. I don't need a cheer squad. Oh, hey, there is one super cool witch. She's got amazing sapphire highlights in her hair."

"Sapphire? Like, blue. Say blue, Rory."

I rolled my eyes. "Anyway. She isn't in the office much, which is perfect because I'm getting to know local cafes and get out of there."

"What kind of magick does she do?"

I frowned. I hadn't seen Lilith do much magick. "Not sure. I'll get back to you. I think she's pretty good at staying low-key. Brain, not bang."

"Just like you," she said, sitting back and taking another bit of bacon. "Is she cute?"

I considered being upset at not having bang but didn't want to risk the conversation straying toward Beo. "Super cute. Tall, great hair, black nails, killer grin. Not sure if she's gay."

Aspen sighed. "I'm going to dream about a tall witch with blue hair and a great smile anyway. Don't tell her I'm totally objectifying her. Also, introduce us. I'll tell you if she's gay or not."

I wanted to laugh at her. "Okay. Sure. So, things with Greg didn't work?"

"Greg who?" she asked. "Oh, that dirtbag? No. He became super gross when he tried to bring in another woman for funsies and then was like totally not giving any fucks about her. Like he went deep into the 'I'm a stud in a porno.' Why are men, Rory? I'm giving up on them for a while. Women are hit and miss, sure, but at least the sex is better."

I could feel Beo's arms around me, cradling me. I was so glad my memory edited out the gear stick. *Hells.* "Mm."

"That was a very suspicious 'mm'," she said, narrowing her eyes. "Eat some bacon, bitch."

I took the bacon, and I also ate with my fingers, because I could hear Dad out the front and I wasn't likely to cop any flack for it. "Okay, okay, there's another bloke. He's a jitsu coach."

Her eyes widened. "And you mention this now? Jesus, Rory." She nudged me hard. "Spill."

So, I did, editing out any mention of lycans, and by the time I finished talking, she was all but moaning. "Do it. Do him. Oh, fuck, Rory, he sounds awesome."

He really did. When I edited.

ELEVEN

DAD DROPPED ME BACK AT THE STATION ON SUNDAY AFTERNOON, LOADED down with a cake and jam from Oma and a belly full of her cooking. I was home by nine, sending off texts to Oma, Dad, and Aspen so they wouldn't worry that I'd been stolen by faeries on the train. I made myself a hot chocolate before bed. Hot chocolate was fine for dinner when I'd had bacon and eggs for breakfast and stamppot for lunch.

Deirdre had her first day of work on Monday. When I stopped by mid-morning to see how she was doing, I only caught glimpses of her. She still looked pale and frail, but her movements held the grace of practice, and she conducted herself with the ease of someone comfortable in their role.

Some of the sadness that had sat so heavily in my chest lifted. I knew it was probably a mask—still, she could access it. I had to hope that was a good thing.

After going into the office and making sure my case notes were up-to-date and my emails and paperwork sorted, I went out again but arrived too late to check on Callie at her TAFE class. After a short internal debate, I headed to her workplace. I wasn't sure of her roster, but it was worth a go. Worst-case scenario, I wasted an extra half hour of my afternoon with the travel.

When I got to the little bakery, which was one of three jobs Callie held, I was pleased to see her standing behind the display serving a customer.

Thinking I'd just pick up a cinnamon scroll, I wandered over, hands in pockets. "Nice day," I said when her eyes fell on me. Because it was true.

Her expression went from retail-polite to pitifully grateful. "Rory! Help!"

Energy flooded my system. I took the keys from my pocket, my fingers tightening over them. "What's wrong?"

"My...niece." The hesitation was so brief I wasn't sure if I'd imagined it. "I need, I don't know—colouring books? Dolls? Valium? Something!"

I blinked. Could lycans take Valium? "Uh, sure." Would a coloring book be a work expense? Shit, I wished I'd listened to Janet a bit more about the art stuff she was forever organizing. "Is there something nearby?" Did lycans like coloring books? Was the kid even a lycan? "How old is she? Are"—I racked my brains—"like, unicorns, cool?"

She shuddered. "Don't even talk about those beasts near me. Something Sunwalker-y. Uh, human."

Unicorns were actually a thing? How had that not been mentioned? "Okay, human." I could do human. Sometimes. "Do you want me to like, take her to a park or something?"

She sent me a look that was both dismayed and wistful. "I'd be disembowelled if I let her out of my sight. No, just something for her to do so she doesn't just sit there."

I followed Callie's gaze. On a small, cracked table in the corner, a child sat lifelessly in the chair, her face downturned, her long hair hanging like curtains to disguise her face. The clothes she wore looked new; they were a bit big for her yet.

Silently, I weathered the questions that blew through my brain.

"Be right back," I promised, returning my keys to my pocket and weaving out of the little bakery, determined to get this right.

Also, since when were we Sunwalkers?

I glanced up and down the street but didn't see anything that screamed 'I can amuse kids'! I opened my phone and did a quick search while I strode to the nearest tram stop. I almost got on the wrong tram, caught myself in time, and made my way to an arts and crafts store where I gathered art stuff and a couple of mindful coloring books—one with Australian animals, the other with a variety of patterns that weren't recognizable as anything. No unicorns. I veered away from dragons, too, just in case.

Half an hour and forty bucks later, I was back at the bakery and second-guessing every choice I'd made. Callie was with a customer, and the girl didn't look like she'd moved at all in my absence. I sat at the table opposite her.

She flinched as I sat down, just a tiny movement. Unease became a dragging dread.

"You don't know me," I said, so quietly I couldn't even hear the words myself, "but I know Callie and Beo."

"You're the witch they're talking about," she said without looking up.

Well, that confirmed she was a lycan. No human child would've heard me.

I didn't ask her what they'd been saying. I wasn't sure I wanted to know. "Callie is worried you're bored." And possibly memorable, too, with that eerie stillness. "So, I got you some drawing stuff."

She didn't move. I lifted the bag, took out the pencils and the books, and arrayed them before her like I was dealing her into a card game. Her head lifted as she studied them. The noise of the bakery flowed around us like a wave and broke over our little pocket of quiet.

"What do you do with it?" she asked me.

My heart ached. I shook out the pencils, moved the book with the patterns into the middle of the table, and started to color. Every now and then, I'd switch pencils; the effect was eclectic and far from artistic.

"You can join in," I told her with studied nonchalance. "Or start your own."

She didn't move for so long I thought she might just leave me coloring all afternoon, but eventually, she reached over and hesitantly picked up a blue pencil in her left hand.

Without changing my pattern, I watched her clumsy movements from the corner of my eye. Now that she'd shifted her position, I could see the way her right shoulder dropped was unusual. I said nothing, but I couldn't help but wonder who had hurt this kid.

"My name's Rory," I said as I colored. Our pencils scratched back and forth. "What's yours?"

"I don't have a Sunwalker name yet," she said, the words raspy, quiet. "I'm not allowed to... I can't say what I was." And the numb acceptance in her words cut me to the quick. "Don't be sad, Rory."

She looked up at me for the first time, and I saw her eyes, the same brilliant, unforgettable true green as Beo's.

As Duke's.

And I saw the huge scar that carved her cheek in half and dragged her bottom lid downwards.

"I don't want to say that name. I want to be here. It's warm. I have a good pack. I have to learn new rules. They will keep me safe."

My heart broke at the almost puzzled look she sent me. I swallowed. "Yes," I agreed, because even though I knew the world wasn't that neat, I wanted—needed—it to be for her. With those eyes looking at me with such a horrifying scar of the violence she'd survived, I couldn't ask her what I so desperately wanted to know.

Is Duke your father? Uncle?

"It doesn't hurt."

I raised my brows, put my pencil down. There was no fooling this kid. I wasn't going to try. "It looks like it would've." She shrugged, looked back down at her coloring, and fell silent again. "I like the green, blue, and purple together, I think. I don't like black."

The words made my skin crawl. "The dark can be pretty terrifying. Especially when you know what's in it. Let's stick to the light until we're braver."

She nodded, a small movement. We colored together until the pattern was finished.

I should've left. My job was done, more than done. I'd seen Callie and interacted. I knew she worked where she said she did. I'd seen her with customers.

And damn it, I'd met her probably-illegally-migrated niece.

From the little she'd said, I'd bet that my pack weren't her tormentors; they were her protectors.

Despite all of that, I flipped a page and started anew, working in silence alongside the girl while trams dinged as they went past, the bell over the door rang, and people entered and left.

Callie brought us both a muffin and a lemonade. I didn't complain, but I did dig ten bucks out of my wallet and forced it onto her with a scowl.

The girl didn't use her right arm to eat or drink; it sat there against her side in a way that made alarm bells clang in the back of my mind. But she did eat and drink, completing the motions with an almost mechanical detachment. Not a drop was spilt, nor a crumb dropped.

By the time Callie's shift ended, we'd completed three full patterns and had made progress on a mandala. My hand ached, and the girl's pencil control suffered, but she didn't stop until Callie approached, the hoodie over her uniform shirt unable to hide the tired set to her shoulders. I was sent a wan smile, then watched as she injected some energy into the expression and swung her eyes to the girl.

"Let's go, shorty," Callie said, her hand skimming over the girl's hair.

The child leaned into the affection, and, for just a moment, there was a spark of warmth as she looked up at the woman. It didn't fade when she looked at me.

"Can you come, too?" she asked.

"Rory's got stuff to do, people to protect," Callie told her before I could figure out how to respond. "Don't you, Rory?"

My heart squeezed. I was a glorified box-ticker. "Yeah, I do." I had no idea what time it was, and I didn't even care. "But you can take this with you. Maybe next time I see you, you can show me one you've done."

"Tonight?" the girl asked Callie, her eyes big. "Everyone comes to eat. Rory eats, too. I saw her."

Callie shot me a quick look of apology. "Tell you what, I'll let Beo know you want Rory to come, okay? And he'll figure it all out. But he might say no, or she might say no. They've got a lot of stuff to juggle."

Shit, wasn't that the truth? I stood and walked out with the two of them, the child flanked by us. Callie looked at me over the girl's head, her expression sad, and mouthed 'sorry'.

I shook my head and shrugged. Kids invited people inappropriately all the time, didn't they? I didn't belong at a lycan family thing. There was no getting around that. It was sweet that the girl wanted to include me, but as much as I ached to grab her and protect her from the world, the reality was that I may end up on different sides of battle lines than her.

Especially if she'd come Overworld illegally.

By the time I made it to class—gi again—the warm-ups had already begun. Beo wandered over after I had my pants on, which I doubted was an accident.

When he looked at me, I saw, for a moment, the girl with the flat eyes and puzzled voice. It made me uneasy.

"Training one night a week won't do much more than keep you from backsliding," he said, arms folded as he watched the class doing lunges from one side of the room to the other.

Get your head in the game, Rory. "I missed you too," I told him, mock-sweetly.

The look he shot me was full of wry amusement. "Your squats need work."

The scowl that snapped onto my face was pure reflex. "I know." And the reminder meant he'd seen me blowing off steam last week and seen me with poor form, which made the reality even more irritating. I shrugged on my top and went down on one knee, quickly looping my belt.

"Double-time it. You don't want to go in cold."

I agreed with a nod and joined in, lunging faster, deeper, and coming up harder than the others. When they jogged, I lifted my knees and kept the pace. When they did push-ups, I went up on my fingertips. Or I did for the first five. I was human.

The session went without any need for me to put on my metaphorical witch hat, but a small part of my brain worried about what I'd seen that afternoon.

My job required I report any suspected illegal Overworld migration.

If I did, the girl would be taken into custody until the paperwork either went through or was denied.

I'd heard stories that the process could take more than two years. I'd heard rumors about the state of the supernatural camps. Considering the way the government treated minorities and human refugees, I had no trouble believing even the worst of those stories.

And if I didn't report the girl, not only was my job and my license on the line, but if it was discovered later, punishment would also include those who had harbored her.

I'd barely tied my belt at the end of the class when Beo appeared at my elbow. "Barbeque tonight. I hear you've been invited already."

My head spun. I let my mostly undone top fall. I was wearing a serious sports bra. No one would care. Besides, bigger problems.

"Is that wise?" I asked him quietly, dead serious. Maybe I could forget I'd seen her once—feign ignorance. But twice?

"Worried you'll end up on the menu?" he asked me as I reached for a hoodie to pull on. His brows rose and there was no suggestion or innuendo in the words.

With a jolt, I realized I hadn't been at all concerned about the idea of strolling into a gathering of lycans. There was something wholesome about these folks.

"I've got a line I have to walk with my job," I said honestly. "If I walk it wrong, it won't just impact me."

His expression hardened a little. "Yes. And we can talk."

Still, I hesitated. We could talk in a lot of places. But would he? "Hellfire," I muttered, tossing my gi top into my bag. "Fine. But first I have to go home."

"Need your wand, Caretaker?"

I shot him a pitying look. As if I didn't have it with me. "I need to cover my tracks, Alpha. I've got my work phone with me. If I go home as usual..." I shrugged, left that acknowledgement hanging. "I'll just go out to pick up some groceries. Maybe a salad. Something to go with a barbeque. Where should I bump into you?"

His expression softened fractionally, but the lines of worry around his mouth deepened. "You don't need to bring anything"—he paused a beat—"especially cheap wine."

"Ouch." I pretended to clutch my chest in pain. So what if I liked cheap wine just fine? It just meant I saved cash or drank more. Either way, it was a win. "Give me an address, I'll tell you how long it'll take me to get there."

Eighty minutes later, showered, changed, and armed with a tray of steaks and a fluffy toy axolotl, I ran into Jeff in the produce section of the grocery store Beo had pointed me towards.

He grinned at me, took the meat, and walked with me down the street towards an apartment building that had a slightly bigger fence and hedge than most others. I asked no questions, but I couldn't help noticing it wasn't any of the addresses I had on file.

He asked about the lasagna. We talked about wine. It was the weirdest conversation I never expected to have with a lycan.

Jeff shouldered open the first door on ground level. "Hey," he called. "Found her."

There was a smattering of laughter down the hall. I recognized Callie's face as she peered around the corner. "You brought red meat!" she said happily. "You didn't have to, but it'll be gratefully received."

Before I'd left the long, narrow corridor, the girl appeared at Callie's hip, her eyes too old in her pale face. Totally out of my depth and unsure about my choice, I passed her the stuffed toy.

"It's an axolotl." When she hesitantly took it with her left hand, I amended, "Well, it's a pretend one. The real ones aren't half as cute. You don't have to keep it if you don't like it. We can give it to a kid who doesn't have one. But if you do like it, it's yours."

Behind me, Jeff kept me moving when she withdrew, studying the light blue thing with its big, sparkly silver eyes. I was ushered out through a small dining area and into a courtyard. The blonde, shaggy guy who only owned a helmet when he went to the police station stood behind the barbeque, a few helpers around him. A lamp had been set up on a trestle table where salads were being prepared and Beo diced tomatoes.

Despite the pretty serious chill in the air, I pushed up my sleeves and reached for a bag of carrots and a peeler, fitting myself into the flow. I was welcomed with varying levels of wariness, but it was okay—kind of stilted, a bit uncomfortable, but okay.

"How's the hand, Rory?" Frankie asked me, coming over and taking some of the carrots I'd prepared.

"Better than it was. Did you get the eggs and bacon?"

He glanced up guiltily. "Not that morning, but I got wiser."

I figured he'd probably come charging in to rescue me rather than make breakfast for his friend. "Hellfire, if you screw up and learn, you're pretty set, I think. I hope. Because I'm screwing up plenty."

He laughed at me and shrugged. "Not too bad."

Not yet. But I didn't say it out loud.

"Bye!" Callie called, when I'd been there for about ten minutes.

"What?" Zane paused scooping lettuce into a huge bowl to scowl at her. "Where're you going?"

She scowled right back. "Got a two-hour shift. Hey, Rory, c'mere."

I set the carrot in my hand down, half-peeled. Someone else picked it up before I'd gone two steps. I felt Beo's eyes on my back the whole way.

"She's keen to talk to you. Wants to know about witches. Just wash your hands in the sink. She's coloring in the spare room." She touched me gently on the shoulder, her expression one of shared worry. "Thanks."

Every response seemed inappropriate. I went in the direction she'd indicated, bracing myself.

The girl sat with the book balanced on one knee. Not coloring but holding a pencil. "Hey," I said quietly. "Heard you wanted to talk about witches." I folded myself down on the ground in front of her with a sigh. I was tired. Physically, yeah, but my heart was tired. And I didn't even have to carry around all that trauma. What a lazy bitch I was.

She nodded. "I've heard the pack talking about you. They don't know what sort of witch you are. What sorts of witches are there? They won't say. They just say, 'Don't worry about it,' or 'We'll handle her.'"

I could very well imagine Beo saying both of those things. "There are a lot of types of magi," I said warily. Shit, I didn't have the university degrees, just what I'd picked up on the fly. What did I know? "And we use a lot of different names and spells. We all use words, though, and we all have different connections to magick." She just sat there, looking at me. Did she want to know about schools of magick? How we learned? "Um. Magick has been around forever. Everyone understands it differently, but a bit more than ten years ago, it was made legal because Samhain rifts basically led to…" Carnage. What was a kid-friendly word for a bloodbath? "A lot of problems." *Nice save.* "The short version is, our government didn't have a choice. Now they're trying to control it. Because that's what they do." *And fuck them.*

I had barely got into my monologue when a gentle tap sounded on the door. I glanced up and saw Beo, still in his gi pants, leaning against the doorframe, a smile tugging at one corner of his mouth. "I hear you two had a muffin for lunch. Come and eat."

Obediently, we both followed Beo out into the courtyard. The smell of blackened sausage, chicken skewers, and steak filled the air. Beo ushered us along the table where the food was laid out, making sure we both had plenty on our plates. She was set beside Zane and given a squirt of sauce; I was steered back into the kitchen.

How Beo managed all of that without ever touching me was a mystery of body language.

I fell into the seat Beo offered me at the small, empty bench. "It's too cold for you out there," he said, propping himself up on one elbow, and, without further ado, spearing a piece of capsicum with his fork.

A small, tired part of me enjoyed that sight in the strangest way. He was right, though, about the temperature. I went straight for the steak. It wasn't what I'd brought; this was rump, not T-bone. Whoever had made the marinade deserved a medal. I gave a sigh of appreciation and focused on the meal in front of me.

"If we declare her, get the paperwork done legally, she'll be killed."

I blinked, startled from my internal debate between cucumber and a piece of chicken. "I'm sorry?"

He shot me a look of disbelief. "I can't keep her safe in your" he paused, for a moment, "*camps*." The word held disgust. Hatred.

Neither could I. Which was why I hadn't already declared her. "What happened?"

He didn't blink. "War. Want a beer?"

It was tempting. And, curse it, so was he. Believing in him was far too easy. "Why am I here, Beo?"

He straightened, heading to the fridge. "Damage control."

TWELVE

"Bullshit. You could've spoken to me after class. Or anywhere." I eyed him warily. "You probably even know where I live."

He didn't deny it. "She wanted you here." He took two beers from the fridge, brought them over, and twisted off the caps. "I want you here."

I scowled at the salad on my plate. "I can't sleep with a client." I was pretty sure that was a rule.

"Fine. Then we won't sleep." He took a pull of the beer then picked up his fork again. "That's a separate issue. She's been through enough, Rory. She needs our protection."

Another sigh escaped me, and I reached for the beer, a headache starting above the bridge of my nose. "Can you get her papers?"

"Yes."

I closed my eyes. *Shit.* Helping supernaturals go Overworld was an unforgivable offence.

"How long?"

"Two weeks-ish."

"Two weeks?" I didn't know if I was horrified, impressed, or dismayed.

He shrugged. "Look, usually I'd—"

I held up a hand. "No. Don't tell me what you usually do, or don't do, or how often you do it. Please. I took a pull from the beer. The bubbles and bitterness danced in my mouth and down to my belly. "Arthur is coming on Wednesday. No mention of this. None. Can you"—I waved a hand at the house—"keep her out of sight or something?" She had been far too visible this afternoon with Callie.

He regarded me seriously. "I'm trying."

My belly sank. "How long has she been here?"

"Three weeks."

Betty had been killed three weeks ago. Shit. "Who brought her over?"

He filled his mouth, obviously stalling while he considered me. "A cousin."

"Did this cousin happen to chomp on a witch?" When anger flashed over his face, I raised my brows and said, "You and yours didn't do it. Someone did. This is your turf. You know what goes on."

"It wasn't us." The words were a low, furious rumble.

I rolled my eyes. "Yes. I just said that. So, who was it, Beo?"

"I don't know." But there was something there, a flicker across his face before he took a slice of the steak and filled his mouth again.

He might not, but he knew something. "I didn't see her. Okay? She isn't a bargaining chip in this. I'm not out to hurt the pack. Unless you're out to hurt others. Then I'll fuck you all up."

The flicker of mirth and disbelief on his face irritated me, but he grinned, considered me anew. "Maybe. Not if we take you to the ground. Your jiu-jitsu is good, but not that good."

Duke's snarl of pain echoed in my head. I remembered the way his form had warped, writhed, changed. I shifted, reassuring myself with my keys in the pocket of my jeans. The plate of food sat there. I ignored it. "I'm not playing games here, Beo."

"I know." He touched the edge of his beer to mine in a toast. "I like that about you. You're our Caretaker, right? That girl"—he lifted his beer in the direction of the lycans outside"she needs you a lot more than we do. So, thank you for doing your job."

"Fuck," I muttered furiously and stabbed a piece of tomato I didn't want. He raised his brows and I said, impatiently, "You're fucking welcome." I bit down on the tomato, but my appetite was ruined.

Hadn't I wanted a change of pace? I took a pull of the beer and thought about what a dramatic change of pace this really was.

I was trying to figure out how to lever the information about Betty's murder out of him when the girl appeared at my elbow, her eyes big, round, and worried. "I thought you might've gone."

"Just chatting with Beo," I told her, wondering why she cared so much. "Got some more questions?"

She stepped back and nodded. I put down my fork and followed her into what must be her room, for now. Who lived there? How long would she stay? I couldn't ask. I didn't want to know.

"My arm hurts," she said, sitting down matter-of-factly. "And people stare at my face. It makes them hurt to see."

I was not equipped to deal with this. I wished I could reach for my phone, make a note to chase up. *Look into trauma training.* "It's horrible that you have to live with that," I said, struggling to find the words she needed.

"You're our Caretaker. You look after us."

My mind skipped ahead through the line of questioning, and I felt my heart do a sick, slow roll in my chest.

"There are a lot of ways to look after people."

But there was some hope in her eyes, and fear. I understood both. They went hand in hand. "Witches can heal."

My heart had stopped its slow roll and started to run. My lungs tightened, the pressure of panic on my chest. I didn't dare look down at my hands for fear they'd be coated in blood.

"Some can." The words, somehow, made it out of my throat. I could feel the sun on my face. The reek of punctured bowels and piss and blood. I heard my own rasping breath and didn't know if it was just a memory.

"You're scared." She looked at me, the fragile hope in her eyes starting to ebb. I could see her, superimposed on Brandon's broken body, his lips moving, her voice spilling out. I pressed a hand to my chest and tried to breathe. "You're scared I'll ask you."

My heart roared in my ears. Scared didn't cover it. I looked down at the cheap, worn carpet under my knees.

Winter, Melbourne, Beo's lycans. They were my when, my where, my who.

And the why was this girl.

I breathed and felt the resistance in my chest—the panic. I didn't fight it, breathed again, held it, let it out.

The girl. That was why I was here, in this room as twilight fell, with the taste of beer in my mouth and my old jeans snug on my legs.

What had it cost her to voice her question? Was this what she'd been leading up to all afternoon, all evening?

"I'm not a good healer," I told her, and my voice was too low, too scratchy. "The last person I tried to heal—" I broke off, my throat closing completely over the words.

Brandon's broken body lay there between us, and the warmth of the sun made me want to weep.

"You failed." The words, so simple, so emotionless, were a knife in my belly.

I swallowed hard. "Yes." And I'd lost the man who'd been like a brother to me.

"That doesn't make you bad at something." She looked at me, and her face swam as tears blurred my vision. "If you try, and it doesn't work, it won't kill me. Will it?"

My hand went to my chest to hold in some of that pain. I felt the muscle, the bone and pressed hard.

"No."

It couldn't. I couldn't. But what I said no to—

"Then I want you to try. If you know how. And maybe you won't fail."

That did it. I put my face in my hands, sucking in air. I couldn't say no. I couldn't have said no to anything this kid asked, not with that fragile hope just blooming.

"Give me a minute," I asked her from far away. But even as I tried to gather myself, tried to sort my shit out, my brain was already offering up strategies, spells, herbs, foci. My heart hurt. My bones hurt.

When I lowered my hands from my face, she was still sitting there in front of me, cross-legged.

And the hope was in her eyes.

"Does that mean...you'll try?"

A tear overflowed. I swiped it away, furious with myself. "Yes. Yes, I'll try. It'll make you tired. Maybe for days." She nodded, the fear back in the unhappy curve of her lips. "Let me see your arm."

She took her jumper off. It had a zip; I expected it'd been bought with her injuries in mind. She wore a plain blue T-shirt, and I could instantly see the problem, even without x-rays. The whole thing was a twisted, scarred mass.

Terror roared through me. *Could* I make it worse?

"Can I touch you?" I asked her quietly. When she nodded, the hand I reached towards her shook.

I breathed deep, reached deeper, into the core of who I was, into the deep well of strength and the deeper, firmly guarded well of compassion.

Show to me these injuries. The words formed in my mind, firmed, and were infused with power.

The air around us stirred. I felt the whisper of my curls against my neck, my hoodie shifting against my belly. The bones weren't as terribly fragmented as I'd thought. They had been; I could feel the lines of old breaks and another's attempt to heal them. But they were in the wrong spot, and the scarring of flesh and sinew and tendon was horrific. Those in her face had pulled and ripped at muscle, dug into the bones in her jaw.

I wanted to weep, but I didn't. I could do this.

At least I could do some of it.

As I will, so shall it be. The power hummed back into me, left me feeling whole again and calmer without the detailed awareness of those horrifying injuries.

She sat before me, her eyes wide with fear and hope and, the thing that almost undid me all over again, a kernel of trust.

"I need to gather some things," I told her quietly. "Have a drink, go to the bathroom, brush your teeth, and get ready for bed. Make sure your pajamas leave your arm bare, though. I'll be back soon."

Had the supermarket up the road had fenugreek? Did they have comfrey in the courtyard? Was there a local garden I could raid? I straightened, running through my options rapidly. And saw Beo leaning on the bench again, his expression unreadable.

I narrowed my eyes then sniffed, furious at being caught vulnerable. A kid was one thing, this guy another.

"What do you need?" His gaze ran over me. "I could send someone to go get your wand."

"Do you have comfrey?" As I emerged, I saw the kitchen and dining area brimming with bristling lycans. Fine, I'd ask about that later, but for now, I pointed to the nearest one. "Fiona, I need gems. Anything that sparkles. I don't care how valuable. Zane, start cutting up onions. All of them."

He glanced over my shoulder at where I could feel Beo lurking. Whatever he saw there made him relax slightly. He ran a hand through his shaggy blonde mane. "How do I cut them?"

"I don't know. Circles. Doesn't matter. Skin them, and wash them, okay? Jeff, I want turmeric, fenugreek, and parsley." He blinked and turned to the pantry, looking somewhat lost. "Jordan, Chance, and Luke, I need comfrey. As much comfrey as you can get your hands on. The leaves, mind you. You might find it in a garden around, you might not, but try. Keep your eyes out for nettles, fresh parsley, and dandelions while you're out."

I eyed off the people remaining. "Frankie, if there are any oats in this place, I want them all in a pot and cooking. If there aren't any, go buy a bag. Cheapest, biggest bag you can get." He nodded and started happily opening cupboards.

"Who owns this place? Never mind. Raspberry leaf tea? Do we have any?" The blank male faces told me very clearly this wasn't in their normal drinking rotation. "Forget it. Someone go buy some. It'll be advertised for menstrual pain. Also, get me something with vitamin E in it. Capsules, face cream, I don't care." I grabbed my beer and took a long pull. How in the seven hells had I gotten myself here? "And Finn—" The lycan stopped on his way out the door, looking back to me. "Get me a bag of chips, too, yeah? Salt and vinegar."

It took me the better part of the evening to prepare the ingredients and the foci they'd scrounged up for me. It stank to high heaven and drank up the spells I held in my mind then poured into it. I made her an infusion to drink, then wrote out instructions for ongoing care while I finished my beer and polished off the chips.

No one questioned me. If they had, I'd probably have set them on fire. Maybe they could tell.

Callie returned and read my patient a bedtime story, something about wombats.

As it ended, I went into the room and laid a few towels beneath the child. She was pale and tight-jawed in an old superhero singlet that made her look as fragile as a bird.

I smoothed the salve on, murmuring information to her as I went. What I'd used, what it would do, how it would feel, what I would be doing, what she was likely to feel afterwards. It was background noise, though, as much part of the ritual as the ingredients themselves.

The gems that had been dug up were pretty lacklustre. When Beo mentioned getting my wand again, I speared him with a look and snapped, "Next time you mention it, I will ward you out of this room."

He was silent from then on.

When the girl's arm was smothered in the salve I'd made, I spread it over her face, too. "Ready?" I asked her as she stared at me from those heart-wrenching green eyes.

"Yes." She closed her eyes and let out a long breath. "You aren't scared now. You know what to do."

My breath caught and held.

I let it out deliberately and felt the way my chest moved, the fabric of my clothing, the slight shifting of my position.

I did know what to do. I just didn't know if it'd be enough.

THIRTEEN

By the time I was done, it was dark, and she was in a deep sleep.

I was tired. Not just physically tired, which I'd already been from the training, but magickally and emotionally spent too.

I sat back and stretched the kinks out of my neck. Maybe tomorrow was a good day to take off. I thought of my calendar and sighed. It would mean juggling the next week. More effort than just going in.

Beo unfolded himself from where he'd sprawled on the floor at the foot of the bed. I waved him off, but he followed anyway, a big, powerful shadow as I moved into the kitchen.

Zane sat up from the armchair in the corner. Was it his place? I didn't ask. Using one elbow, I turned on the sink and washed my hands.

"She might sleep for hours. Possibly all day tomorrow. If she hasn't woken by tomorrow evening, call me."

Zane's eyes flashed. "Is she in danger?"

"No. It would simply be a sign that her body is struggling. I could give her a boost." I didn't even care about him bristling, just scrubbed the mess off my hands and forearms. I was going to reek for days. I'd forgotten how messy kitchen healing was. "I'll show myself out," I told the two menacing men, waving them off. "I'm sure you'll hear me going."

"I'll take you home," Beo said, picking up some keys.

I thought of his motorcycle and the heat in his eyes. "No, thank you."

"You're done, Rory," he said, without any sting. "I'm not letting you catch public transport home. You couldn't fight off a fly right now."

The urge to argue was strong. "I appreciate it," I said, walking towards the door, "but I assure you—"

"Fine." He put the keys in his pocket. "Then I'll ride with you."

I blinked, looked around for a trick, but saw only Zane yawning. "You'll catch a tram with me? Home? And then back?"

"Yes."

My poor feelings couldn't take any more battering. I felt myself crumbling and stiffened my spine. "I'm not going to sleep with you."

A grin flickered over Zane's face. He clapped Beo on the back and said brightly, "I'll leave you two to sort out the details. I'm going to get some rest. See you when I see you, Beo."

"Yeah," Beo said, frowning at me as if I'd just insulted his favorite sports team. "We agreed on that already."

I rolled my eyes, let myself out the door, and huddled deeper into my hoodie. It was arse-bitingly cold. When I checked my phone, it informed me it was on the grisly side of one in the morning.

No wonder I was tired.

Beo fell in beside me and I stopped to put my hands on my hips. "This isn't necessary."

"You're tired," he said, quietly. "And you're hurting. You're both of those things because you helped us. I'm not going to leave you while you're vulnerable, Rory."

Tears burned my throat and nose. I turned away.

"Fine. Stay out late, get cold, and pay too much to sit on a tram that smells like body odor. I don't even care." I asked my legs for a longer stride, a faster pace. They obliged, though not without complaint.

Again, he fell in beside me. "You never spoke a single spell."

I said nothing, huddling into my hoodie once again. The chips were a long time ago. The steak even longer. I could've really gone for a hot, sizzling steak right then with horseradish and mashed potato. I began to consider the merits of fast food. I was in a city. Something would be open.

"I could smell you using magick, but you didn't speak the words or use a wand."

"Well, I did."

"I was in the room, Rory."

I shrugged. I wasn't going to tell him all my secrets. Why should I?

"Witches use words and wands to cast spells."

"There's more than one way to skin a cat, Coach," I muttered, annoyed. If he'd just left me alone, I wouldn't have to make nice. Not that making nice was something I was super good at.

He waited silently at the tram stop, his jacket open, arms folded, looking for all the world like he was out on an afternoon stroll. I shivered and refused to look at him, hunched down into the hoodie that had felt comfortably warm earlier and now felt uncomfortably threadbare.

I checked my phone. Checked it again. Two minutes had passed. I resisted the urge to triple-check the tram timetable. Still a fifteen-minute wait.

A group of men walked past, talking too loudly to each other. Beo straightened, wandered around a bit, then settled back beside me.

I remembered, all too well, the way he'd looked as he'd stalked into the auto garage, and I ached.

There was no pressure from him, none of the undercurrents I was so familiar with wading through. And no violence, no threat. If there had been, I wouldn't have ever come. No, I could trust my instincts, and they all said this man wasn't a danger. At least, not a physical one.

Maybe he was even an ally.

Bones crunched. I drew in a breath, reached up, and found I wasn't wearing my necklace. *The smell of blood. The heat of it on my hands as it dried in the sun.*

Bad things shouldn't happen on a bright, warm afternoon. It felt so wrong.

I paced away from Beo, chafing my hands together. Dry, not wet. But though the night was dark and moonless, I could still feel that sun.

Shit.

I pulled out my phone and shot Aspen a text. *You up?*

A moment later, it went from delivered to read, and I felt a trickle of relief. My phone rang, and I answered, still facing away from Beo. "You okay?" Aspen asked, her voice thick with sleep.

"Yeah." *No.* "Talk to me."

She did without any further questions, a ramble that started off slow and drowsy. Her work as a re-educator for violent men. A difficult client. A sweet old man and his wonderful grandson she'd spotted in the park role-playing a wedding between two action figures. A pair of shoes she'd found on sale online. And with every little bit of herself she shared, I felt more relaxed, more whole.

By the time she got onto a conversation about what she'd made for dinner, I was on the tram, Beo silent and opposite me, sprawled over technically more seat than he should've been.

"I'm good now," I told her, looking down at my battered, old runners. There was a fenugreek seed in the webbing. "Thanks, Aspen."

"Any time," she said, and I knew she meant it. "You safe, Sunshine?"

I glanced over at where Beo lounged as we rocked along. "Yeah." Because I believed him. He'd do what he could to keep me safe. Right then, I was all out of righteous indignation. And... "Just tired."

"Okay." She sounded like she didn't entirely believe me. "When's your next day off?"

"Um." My calendar swam in my head. "Sunday. Fuck working Sundays."

She laughed. I heard her kettle boiling in the background. "Maybe I'll come up one evening. You can take me to a cool city witch-club. Invite your cute witch friend."

"Go have your reishi and go to bed. Thanks for talking me down."

"No thanks needed. Keep looking after you. Call me."

I smiled when I disconnected and pocketed my phone. Beo might be hot, but he wasn't likely to take on a load-bearing role in my life.

Aside from anything else, there was the small issue of him being my client and the power imbalance that entailed.

I rested my head back and let my eyes drift closed, but I kept track of the stops and opened my eyes as Beo started to move.

He disembarked with me. I didn't tell him not to walk me to my door, and I did seriously consider asking him in.

He followed me up the stairs, saying nothing as I turned the torch on my phone because the entry light was out then juggled my keys until I found the right one and got it into the lock.

"Want to check my cupboards and under the bed for a lurking troll?" I asked him, raising my brows.

"No. There's no one in there." He stood in my doorway, looking as fresh as if he'd just rolled out of bed and downed a coffee. "What you did for her, Rory..."

Doubt wormed its way into my heart. "Wait and see. I'm making no promises."

"Even if you haven't made her any better, you did everything you could to help. You didn't have to."

Surely it had to be illegal for him to look so damn sweet when he was able to rip people apart with his bare hands.

"It's my job. I told you to call me."

He shook his head a little. "No. It's you. You just found the job."

My poor, exhausted heart quivered in my chest. "You want to come in?" I asked, because all that concern and tenderness shouldn't be kicked out at two in the morning.

"Pretty sure if I come in, there will be sleeping eventually. So no, I won't." He shifted forward a half step. I saw the move coming and didn't sidestep or counter it, lifting my face. "But I'd really like to kiss you, just once."

I raised my brows. "Once."

"Tonight." He leaned in until I could smell the sweat from training, the onions from the mix he'd helped me combine. "Is that what you want, Rory?"

A smile tugged at my lips. "Once, tonight?" I asked, deliberately misunderstanding him.

"I can catch a tram in an hour," he offered, still hovering there, waiting.

The idea of kicking him out at three was even worse than kicking him out at two. Also, "I'll be dead in an hour."

He let out a breath, his expression tender. "I know. I'm sorry." And he started to straighten away from me.

A sliver of alarm gave me strength. I reached out, grabbed the front of his jacket, my grips firm as I reeled him in.

His mouth met mine, not tentative or cautious, but soft and gentle.

The warmth of his hands enveloped my face, my jaw, as I was cradled. He tasted like darkness, and I felt my bones melting, like someone had pulled the plug out of my body and all the fear drained away.

I was caressed, treasured. When I opened my mouth in pure reflex, he fitted our bodies together and held me up when I would have been happy to turn into a puddle at his feet. One of his hands moved into my hair. From far away, I felt the tug of a curl caught and pulled, but it was small, unimportant.

Heat swept through me. I kept the fist I held in his jacket and hooked an arm under and around his back, anchoring him firmly to me. The heat of him, the hardness, made my body come alive in a rush. Every nerve ending sang, every sinew sighed.

I took a step back, further into the room. Vague ideas of closing the door behind him, getting out of clothes, swam through my head.

He sucked in a lungful of air. "You got an underhook."

I blinked, then tightened the grips I had him in. "Yeah. Yeah, I do."

"Going to take me down, Rory?" he asked, and there was a bit of worry in his eyes.

I leaned up, went in for one more quick taste. Warm and wet and soft. I shivered in delight.

"We can take turns," I suggested, which was very equitable of me.

The worry smoothed away, replaced by amusement. "You're home safe." His eyes dropped to my lips, then further down to where I was no longer plastered against him. "Go get into bed. Think of me." He swooped in, pressed another kiss to my lips, then took the door and closed it behind himself.

I stood there, scowling at it. "Fuck."

"I heard that," he said, from the other side of the door.

"It was a proposition," I said, hands on my hips.

"No, it wasn't. Lock this."

"I'm warded to Timbuktu." I reached forward anyway.

"I don't know where that is, or how it's warded, but lock the damn door." With a sigh, I flipped the snib. "Thank you."

There was a smile on my lips, but my heart was heavy as I turned and sought my bed.

I was in deep, way too deep.

Fuck, I hoped I could swim.

FOURTEEN

I TOOK A DAY TO RECOVER BUT WAS IN THE OFFICE EARLY THE NEXT, catching up on the admin I'd missed. Lilith floated over, and we chatted about clients and the changeling who'd vanished, and how she'd been alerted to their presence by the kitchen witch who ran the cafe we met at. We went back there for lunch. Work reasons, of course—not because of the food or coffee. We were professionals.

"Got some info on that lycan you wanted tracked," Lilith said while we waited for our order to arrive. "Duke. He mentioned in an interview, I may or may not have illegally accessed, that he had brothers who'd come after him and get revenge. I can give you the transcripts if you want, but that's the gist of it."

A chill went through me. "Names?"

"Nothing I can pronounce, and nothing like your friend's."

It was still more than I'd had. And it made me feel no better. I put it aside that afternoon, did the rounds, and went with Arthur to The Playground. He didn't have a gi, but he did have a cast.

He couldn't have trained anyway, although I suspected the cast was mostly for show. He was his usual too-pleasant, sickly-sweet self, which was better than his sulky-child self. I was even treated to some vague ideas of what he'd like to do with the coven one day—a Head Witch and Wizard to rule them all.

And the way his eyes lingered on me made me quite confident I could buy a lottery ticket into this nebulous future he was conjuring up.

Arthur was a dirtbag wizard who was mismanaging lycans. I thought of the way my whole body turned liquid when Beo had waited for me to take what he'd offered.

Arthur was nowhere in my future plans except, perhaps, SuperSec.

When we got to training, I was greeted warmly by the lycans. Arthur was completely ignored. I did as I always did, stripping out of my shoes and socks over my bag, pulling off my pants and rolling into my gi pants, and Arthur, on the chair beside me, half-choked.

I pretended not to notice, just did the tie at my waist and pulled off the knitted sweater I'd worn to work. He goggled at the sport bra I had on like he hadn't seen anything like it before. I was pretty sure that's what he goggled at, anyway, though my weird belly button could've been the target of that shock, too. Nope, definitely the bra, or its contents. I was tempted to ask him, 'Did I steal your breath, King?' But I kept it to myself, kept my face in its normal lines as I shrugged into my gi top, taking off my earrings and rings and stowing them.

"No knitting, Arthur?" Beo asked, wandering over. His expression said the question was an idle one. The furious look Arthur shot Beo, and the way his hand tightened on the messenger bag that held his wand, made my eyes narrow, but Beo had already turned to me. "Good to see you again, Rory," he said, perfectly friendly. "Save a roll for me."

Butterflies swarmed behind my ribs. "You're on," I promised, tying my hair back in a bun that wouldn't hold for long. I didn't ask him how the girl was doing, not with Arthur staring at us. But the thought was there, simmering in my heart.

"Hey," Zane called, from the other side of the mat. "Me, too!"

Before I could respond, Beo started the warm-ups. I paced myself throughout the class. Beo didn't get on the mat, but I rolled with Zane, got submitted half a dozen times in five minutes, and was pleased to have gotten him twice, too. "You're like a damn monkey or something, climbing all over me," he complained. "Ugh. I think I have a hair in my mouth."

I laughed at him and tied said hair back again. "Get your face out of my hair then."

With a clap on the back, I went to quickly grab a drink while partners were rotated. I fought a class regular—a human—and pushed them, encouraging them to practice the skills they'd been drilling. I let them get a submission when I saw them setting two up, though I made them work a bit for it. And so the pattern went until Beo got us to do the warm-downs and we bowed out for the night.

Arthur waited with my bag over his shoulder at the top of the stairs before I was even off the mat, clearly impatient to leave. "Hey, Rory," Jeff called. "We're getting ribs tonight from Luke's place. Want in?"

I saw the color that ran up Arthur's neck and didn't care. The offer wouldn't have been made without Beo's approval, so I didn't even bother glancing at him to double-check it was okay.

Besides, I'd promised him a roll.

"Ribs? Like, with chips?"

There was a smattering of laughter. Apparently, my request for chips before the healing was a talking point. "Beef or pork?" Jeff asked, shaking a set of keys in his hand casually.

"Beef. Pork. Oh, I can't choose. Can I split it with someone?"

He grinned, jogging past. "Only if you're fast."

I reached for my socks. "Done. At The Dancing Pig?" I asked, naming the place Luke worked a lot of evenings.

"You cannot be serious," Arthur hissed under his breath.

"I'm deadly serious about ribs and chips," I told him, hopping into first one shoe, then another. "I need my bag, Arthur."

His hand tightened on the strap, his eyes flashing dangerously. "I can't believe you. Eating with them. Flashing your arse around. What, are you fucking them all?"

I straightened, ice settling in my veins. "Don't you—"

He stepped in closer to me. We were equal in height, and I could take him apart physically, but obviously, he hadn't considered that. "You told me you couldn't heal, you damn liar. I thought you were just shy, but I read your fucking job application, you bitch, and—"

I reached out, grabbed my bag, and twisted it out of his hold forcibly, fury giving me strength. "I *can* heal. I *can* make you burn so hot that they won't even be able to ID you from dental. Maybe you should ask why I *don't*, King."

He swelled, and I could feel the power running through him, in him. My belly clenched. He was a wizard. They knew all the fucked-up curses. And I couldn't counter-curse my way out of a wet paper bag.

"Are you threatening me, Witch?"

"That was a question, fuckwad." I felt the protective wards swimming in my mind, kept them close. I doubted I'd win in a duel, and I wasn't here to find out. "This is a threat, right here." I pressed a finger to his throat, just lightly, meeting him stare for stare, spell in my mind that'd steal his air. Just for a second. "I." I pressed it a little firmer. "Am." His mouth opened, and I knew I was about to start casting. Panic rippled through me. *Breathe not through this ward.* The spell rushed through me in a flurry of fury. "Not." I held it as he gaped like a fish. "Your." *As I will, so shall it be.* The spell ended, and he gasped in a breath. "Property." I wiped my finger on my gi pants, disgusted with him.

"Problem?" Beo asked idly.

He'd appeared right beside us at some point. I flicked a glance at him, my heart still drumming as I waited to see if Arthur would hit back. "Yeah," I said, dropping my bag so I could put my belt away. "I need to know where these ribs are at."

His face impassive, Beo folded his arms. "Sure. I'll get Zane to go with you. You okay, Arthur?"

Arthur's face was redder than my two-second choking ward should account for. I figured it was mostly temper, and I was surprised to feel the slightest twinge of shame. Then I wondered if I'd be embarrassed if my Oma knew. Nope, no need to be ashamed. Screw him. "Yeah. I'll see you tomorrow, Aurora."

It was a threat. *Fuck.* Guess I'd have to call Edward about this.

"You can come, too, if you want some ribs," Beo offered, mildly.

Arthur shot me a look of disgust. "I don't want sloppy seconds, thanks." With that, he turned and walked away.

I grabbed my temper in a stranglehold, then double-checked he hadn't stolen my charmed jewellery or keys. When they were all present, I slid my ring on, put my earrings back in, and blew out a breath. That could've gone very, very wrong. "He's a feminist," I told Beo, with distaste.

A brow cocked. "I don't get it."

"I do," Callie said, from the other side of the mat, grinning. "You're not the target audience, Beo-Beo."

His eyes rolled over me, as if he'd spot a hex or curse and be able to intervene. "You did it again."

"Did what?" I asked, re-tying my hair. I was disgusted at Arthur, at myself for giving in to my temper, and at the laws that said it wasn't okay to just murder the scumbag.

"A spell without speaking."

"I spoke." I tossed my gi top into my bag. "I'm angry. I want carbs and salt. Doesn't have to be in that order."

"Is he going to come after you?"

The words were all but growled. "Probably. In a million tiny, shitty, micro-aggressive ways. If he comes at me head-on, I'll rip him apart." I didn't even care about the paperwork that'd come of it. But I did have to chat with Edward. "I'm going to find a kebab van if you don't take me to these promised ribs. That's a threat."

A hard smile tugged at the corner of Beo's mouth. "Fine. Ride with me."

I glanced over at Zane, who was suddenly very busy drinking from his water bottle. "Nope. No motorcycles without proper gear." I shook my head. "HSPs it is. Bye, awesome folks!"

I saw his green eyes flash with temper that sent me spinning back in time to another place. Another lycan. Was he Duke's brother?

Did it matter?

My feet found their way down the steps two at a time, my heart roaring in my chest. And still, when I went to open the door to escape, Beo was there beside me. "Callie'll take my bike," he snapped. "You and your rules, Rory."

"Mate," I said, irritated, "it's called self-preservation. Try it."

"I lived for six years in the Darklands." The words were snarled. He looked huge and threatening in the gathering twilight. "Don't talk to me about safety."

Ice settled in my bones. I had no idea what the Darklands was, but I recognized the fury in the planes of his face and the set of his shoulders. I held up a hand and he didn't get into my space.

"I'm sorry. I'm pissed off at Arthur. I don't want to talk. I just want to forget the whole thing. I bit your head off without explaining that. I can talk about Arthur later. I don't want to talk about magick, including the limitations and tools I use, at all. But if it's important, I can have an adult conversation with you about it later. And we can try to find a middle ground. Later."

The anger in him visibly ebbed away, left him...smaller. Still not small, but no longer so imposing. "Okay."

I nodded, let out a long breath, and glanced up towards the tram stop. "Where are we going?"

He let out a long sigh and ran a hand through his hair. "Same place as Monday. I didn't want to say so in front of Arthur."

I fell into step beside him, irritated with his reaction, but probably mostly as an overflow of my own fury. "I don't need you fighting my battles, Beo." Except that day with Jaye, I kind of had needed help. Fuck it, no woman was an island.

"I let you deal with him," he said, the words level as we waited for the tram together. "Even asked him over."

A snort escaped me. "Oh, come on. You knew he'd rather have crawled over hot coals."

"Sure. But I asked, didn't I?" He eyed me, speculation in his gaze. "What'd you do to him to shut him up like that?" Then, with a bit of a frown, he added, "Does that come under the category of stuff I need to ask about later?"

"Yeah."

A bit of a smile tugged at his mouth now. I let my eyes linger there, on that curve, and remembered how it felt to taste him, to melt against him. "What about the fire thing?"

"Mm, no, thanks. I have something much more fun in mind."

The smile widened a little more. He lifted an arm, offering a space to me. I hesitated for a moment before I stepped into the circle, letting his embrace settle over me like a mantle. It was grounding. Safe. "So. I missed you flashing your arse, I hear."

"That's the category of Arthur."

He sighed. "Okay. You hit a really nice armbar on Zane. You're pretty fast, considering how long those legs are."

I made a hum of approval. "He's strong, and he's got technique on me, no question, but he's not as fast as he could be."

"He's got a few old injuries," Beo said, glancing up as the tram dinged its approach. "He does well, considering."

It was nice. It was easy. He worked hard so it would be, and I appreciated it.

When I got there, I was greeted by one tired-looking but no longer deeply-scarred girl. She showed me her coloring, done right-handed, and my heart took wing.

It was Zane's place, and he didn't mind me using his bathroom, so I risked cold chips and not getting to try both beef and pork ribs to wash off the sweat of a whole class and the stink of the mats. It was almost a healing ritual. Arthur was banished from my mind.

I ate at the crowded table as we all sheltered from the rain that had settled in. At the end of the meal, I still didn't know which ribs were my favorite. It was all delicious. I managed not to eat enough to end up in a food coma, but it was a near thing.

The girl curled up in Beo's lap and listened to the back-and-forth in the tiny room overflowing with lycans. She fell asleep there, held protectively against his chest.

Though I wanted to stay and admire the sight of a big, burly, dangerous-looking man holding the child with open adoration, I stood, stretched, and thanked them all for dinner. Offers of repayment were brushed aside.

When I saw Beo gently shift the girl to Zane's lap and take his keys from Callie, I eyed him with distrust. "Hey, Zane," he said. "Rory's borrowing your helmet."

Zane scowled at me. "Keep the hair out of it."

I laughed it off and waved farewell. Beo got me out, got the helmet on, and even helped me adjust it. "I can catch the tram home," I told him, amused at the process. "It's not even ten and I'm juiced. I could fight off a whole horde of flies."

"Scared, Caretaker?" he asked me, climbing onto the bike and glancing over his shoulder.

My mouth went dry. "A little," I admitted, eyeing the bike. "I've got a friend who worked in the Emergency Department. I've heard stories." But at least the rain had stopped for a moment.

He settled himself and waited.

I threw the bag across my chest, watched his eyes dip down to my breasts as the thick, warm fabric was pulled against them. My bra had been soaked with sweat that had primarily not been my own. It was now in my bag. If he minded that I was free ranging, I sure couldn't tell.

"Stick to me," he said as I climbed on behind him. "Lean where I do. I'll take it easy." The bike started with a roar and a cloud of fumes he eased out of almost before they'd hit my nose. I wrapped my arms around him, feeling a thrill of terrified excitement as we rolled out into the traffic.

Protective wards floated in my mind, and I clutched tightly to him, but the fear eased with his obvious skill. I relaxed into it and felt the rumble of the bike beneath me, the heat of the man in my arms. There was no way he wasn't coming in tonight, and the memory of his kiss turned my bones to liquid again.

We were stopped at lights when I took the opportunity to let one of my hands wander down his thigh, exploring the densely muscled strength encased in the rough, heavy-duty fabric of his jeans.

He took my hand and lifted it back to his belt. I thought I'd been rebuffed for a horrible moment before he reached back and squeezed my knee. "Hold on," he said, over the noise of the engine.

I satisfied myself with plastering my breasts against his back, and when we got our green and he took off, the thrum of the bike between my legs was deep and heavy and so reminiscent of my vibrator that I happily leaned into it. I let those delicious sensations roll through me, the flowing, aching heat of it.

We stopped before I was at the panting stage, pulling up before the building I dimly recognized as mine. My knees didn't want to hold me, but I unlocked my limbs from around him and climbed down.

"You're coming inside tonight, right?" I asked him with lust a primal beat between my legs.

He stood and adjusted his pants with a quick flick of fabric and a roll. "Right."

I took the steps two at a time, gnawing desire driving me. The key fit neatly in the lock and turned. I dropped the bag then kicked it out of the way. He closed the door behind us, his eyes locked onto mine. By the time I grabbed the hem of my knitted sweater and pulled it off, his jacket was on the floor.

"I want to touch you."

The words were almost a growl. A small warning sounded somewhere in the back of my mind, half-hearted and weak. The thought of his hands on me was wonderful, but I wanted more.

"Yeah, sure," I said, impatiently pulling his shirt off, then pressing myself against him. *Heat. Skin.* Hellfire, it felt exactly right and not enough at the same time. I wanted so much it hurt, and I knew I was close, so close. "Touch me." I found his jaw, his ear. My hands skimmed over him, devouring. "Anywhere. Everywhere." My breath shook as I revelled in the contact, arching into him as he touched me with a fevered exploration. "Just get inside me."

His mouth was hungry on mine, and I opened myself fully as I fumbled with his pants. He spun me around, pressed me against the door, then dealt with the zipper himself. Anticipation clenched the muscles inside me, released, then clenched again, and the world outside of his arms ceased to exist.

His hand found my breast, his fingertips on my nipple. I shuddered as I undid the buttons on my slacks. He jerked off his pants, his mouth still on mine, consuming me. I kicked off a shoe and felt the scrape of his teeth, the caress on my breast.

Air was less important than more of him. His tongue stroked, and I sucked it deeper, wanting the hard thrust, the pillage. I got a leg free, banging one hip into the doorknob. Urgency made me clumsy, but the roaring fire kept those details at bay.

The door was cold against my back but the perfect base. He gripped my thighs, and, by the Elders, it felt good, and right, and good right now.

I wrapped my arms around his neck, buried my hands in his hair and fisted them. He shuddered in my arms, and, as he lifted me, I locked my legs around him. My hips tilted in a plea. I felt the hot hardness, the promise of him seeking, and couldn't breathe, let alone think or wait.

"Yes," I demanded. The word was almost a moan, almost an order, but all of my truth.

When he surged into me, the wonderful rush of sensation swept through my whole body. I moaned. I took, consumed, ravenous. Pleasure pulsed through me, bright and greedy—so good, so right it hurt. I gulped air, felt the movement press my breasts harder against him and moaned. I gulped in air again.

He let out a breath more growl than groan and moved in a sharp, hard rhythm that sent surges of heat through me.

Single-minded, I tried to move against him, demanding more, wanting the peak, the sharp jagged edges, wanting the rush and roar, wanting everything.

His breath washed over my neck in short, ragged bursts. My fingers dug to find traction. His hands bit into my thighs. I wanted him there—right there—fused, consumed. I lifted my head, tried to find him with teeth, with lips, and couldn't. My head fell back against the door, and it didn't matter, I didn't care. It was the bunch and release of muscles that was important, the tiny, hard circles that drove me closer, closer, until I felt the final swelling crescent of it and stopped fighting for more.

The orgasm ripped through me like lightning, bold and bright and beautiful. He drove into me harder. From far away, as I floated in a sea of contentment, enjoying those long, firm strokes, I heard the rattle and shake of the door behind me.

His breath caught, then held. He shuddered, his hands digging deeper into me as he lost himself for a few long moments that would've made me smile if I could get any muscle to move. And we stayed there, panting, as he held me pinned against the door, balanced by the remains of the fury of our lust. I tried, vaguely, to get my bearings.

At some point, I realized how incredibly uncomfortable I was. I gasped in some more air before pressing a quick kiss to his neck, gasping again. Maybe I hadn't breathed that whole time. It was worth it.

"Put me down," I managed, painfully aware of how much the angle and pressure hurt my back and hips.

His hands gentled swiftly. "Are you okay?"

My feet touched the ground. My legs gave out. He caught me as I threw an arm out and mostly steadied myself. I still had one shoe on.

Laughter crawled up into my chest and bubbled forth. "That was amazing. Infernal Hellfire, my hips hurt." His hands were gentle, his face soft with affection and worry. "Round two in bed."

He grinned, the worry replaced by mirth, and stepped back while I took off my remaining shoe and the pants bunched above it. Hands on my hips and face in my hair, he followed, close behind me, into the bedroom. I half fell onto the fresh sheets and felt the bed shifting under his weight as he joined me. I'd have to wash the sheets again, but if that minute against the door was any indication, it'd be more than worth it.

FIFTEEN

LILITH SAT BACK, NURSING HER COFFEE AND FROWNING. "I PICKED ARTHUR for the slut-shaming type, not direct conflict. You know you could've lost your license or ended up in SuperSec for that stunt."

The truth of her words shocked me. I hadn't even thought about it, and that told me how off the rails I was. That, and the fact I was about to have a muffin for lunch.

"I wonder if he'd be any good in a duel."

I broke the muffin in half, shrugged, and passed a chunk across. "I'm not scared of him." I was wary. That was different. But I was scared of SuperSec—very, very scared.

Her brows rose. One of her earrings glittered as the sun caught the light on the amethyst there. "Is that because you're as bad arse as you seem or because he's a High Dingleberry?"

"Both," I said with a grin, putting my doubts aside. He wouldn't rat me out. It would make him look like he'd been bested, and he would hate that. "Look, if I tell you something, will you take it to the grave?"

"Any grave in particular?" she asked thoughtfully, as she broke off a tiny piece of muffin from the chunk I'd shoved at her. At my pointed look, she laughed. "Yeah, yeah. But don't tell me. Let me guess. You cursed Arthur to suffer from ingrown toenails for the rest of his life."

What a fantastically horrible curse. "Not yet. But now that you mention it…"

"Okay." Her eyes narrowed a little as she considered me. "You're banging the lycan."

I glanced around, horrified at how loudly she'd said it, but the patrons of the cafe were absorbed in their own pursuits. "Yes!" I admitted in a low hiss. "Keep it down! Shit, Lilith."

She shrugged but leaned in and lowered her voice. "And?"

"Look, it was just last night. And let's just say he didn't need to do much. But he's thorough. And intuitive. And *properly* into consent, to the point where I was all but screaming out what I wanted."

Her expression was pained. "Does he have a brother? I can't believe thorough and into consent is even on my list. My younger self would be horrified. But, shit, Rory. That sounds amazing."

I made a mental note to tell Aspen that Lilith was into blokes. "It is." I sighed, looking at the muffin I'd shredded.

"But he's a lycan."

"But he's a client," I corrected, disgusted at myself and the situation. "It's almost as bad as a teacher dating a student."

"Oh, it's so not," she scoffed. "He's a grown-arse adult. Maybe more like boss and employee. And that happens all the time."

"'Does' and 'should' are different. Also, most bosses can't get your citizenship rescinded." She rolled her eyes at me, but I didn't wait for her counter argument. "And the brother you want? Might be in SuperSec because he eats people for shits and giggles."

"Yeah. Yeah, that's not on the list. Not that sort of eating, anyway."

I heard Brandon's bones breaking and shuddered, pushing away the muffin.

"So? What's your plan?"

With a sigh, I sipped my coffee. "See what happens. Play it by ear. The whole thing with Betty doesn't sit right. Something's off. I keep getting stonewalled at every turn. How is risk usually established?"

"Team decision," she said around some muffin. "We always have some data on the books when someone comes in. Sometimes, the meeting involves transfer folks, someone they've had dealings with. Otherwise, we do some data collection as a coven. Breeze in, breeze out, that sort of thing."

Betty's notes indicated Arthur had done all of that alone. "Always a coven discussion?"

She thought about it, frowning. "Yeah, pretty sure. Like, the hours needed to properly deal with a high-threat supernatural is a budget drain. They're usually sent to SuperSec if they're already committing a crime when they're first picked up, declared, or put on probation, then they work with the parole officers. We aren't supposed to get any actual high-threat folks."

"That wasn't what I was led to believe by Arthur," I said grimly. And the guy had almost literally thrown me to the wolves, too, although maybe not knowingly. Maybe Arthur had caught wind of Edward's suspicions. Maybe he knew I was helping Edward.

Was *that* why he was so pissy?

"When are you seeing him again?" Lilith asked me, drumming her silver nails with black cats on them idly against the side of her mug.

"Arthur?" I frowned. "Probably today, if I'm not super lucky."

She looked at me with pity. "Mr. Super-Thorough-Lycan."

"Oh. This afternoon." I sipped some of the coffee because it was there. "He wanted to do lunch."

"Well, joke's on him, because I booked you first." She looked quite pleased with that. "You know, I'd probably cancel on you for a juicy, enthusiastically consenting lycan."

"You're full of shit," I told her with no hesitation and was rewarded with her deep, rolling laugh and a playful flick of blue-streaked hair. "Maybe dinner?" I gave her, because it felt good to laugh, to share. Because I wanted to draw out the moments of connection and normality. "But even then—sisters before misters."

She winked at me and offered her fist. I bumped it, and our rings chimed together as they met lightly. "Want to come talk to my banshee client with me?"

"Banshee?" I frowned at her, transferring the coffee to settle it between both hands. "What's up?"

"Oh, she's got an interview at a retirement village." She glanced at her phone. "In about twenty minutes. Figured I'd catch her on the way. Have a conversation about suitable jobs where she can't get monetary kickbacks from sad families."

"Hm." Curiosity gnawed at me. I'd like to see Lilith at work, but... "I told Beo I'd catch up with him at Alfred Lake this afternoon, figured I'd swing by Dierdre's clinic before I went."

"The lake?" she raised her brows. "You into public sex or you getting some gooey feelings?"

The choices available made me wince. "If those are my options—Hellfire. I guess it's goo."

She didn't crack a joke or even raise her brows, just looked a bit concerned. "Well, that makes the situation a lot less funny and a lot more worrying. Keep me in the loop, okay, Roars?"

"Yeah. Yeah, I will." I blew out air and stood as she did.

"If the dude is meeting you to hold hands and wander around the lake in this weather," she glanced out at the clouds, looking unimpressed with the heavy load they carried and the speed in which they floated over the sky, "then he's pretty keen. As he should be. You're wonderful. Catch you tomorrow. I'll be in."

I wandered to the door with her. "Morning? Afternoon?"

"Morning," she confirmed. "Meeting at one. Going to smash out some paperwork, get Vince to look at my work phone. Latest update has done something screwy with my apps. They keep crashing. Anyway." She reached out, squeezing my shoulder. "Blessed be."

"Yeah, yeah." I put my hands in my pockets. Vince, the ICT guy? Was he in today? I had no idea. "See you soon."

The wind was cold and damp without a trace of the beautiful sun from the last few days. Getting onto the tram was a relief.

Deirdre spotted me in the clinic, giving me a quick wave without interrupting her conversation with a woman holding a floppy, hollow-eyed child. The mother looked like she hadn't slept for a week. No way was I interrupting *that*.

I wandered, browsing the remedies. They were a mix of pharmaceutical and magickal that made me smile. Gone were the days where we had to grow our own herbs or prepare our own tinctures. My thoughts circled back around to the little girl curled up in Beo's arms, sleeping peacefully. If a lycan walked in with the vague questions some customers had, would they be served?

If they were served, would they be tracked?

The prejudice I knew was very much alive and well punctured my levity. I slipped out, checked the time, and headed to the lake. I'd be early. Maybe I'd be able to shake my mood.

I clocked off again, as I had for lunch with Lilith, because I wasn't giving out ammunition in case someone I'd pissed off was looking for an excuse to throw the book at me. Someone like Arthur the arsehole who had already emailed me chasing a risk assessment that was literally half an hour late. Apparently, he called Lilith if her case notes weren't complete each day by five, which was bullshit because we worked flexible hours.

Box tickers.

I'd neglected practicing my craft, and I got off a stop early, considering that as I wandered. I'd neglected practicing my healthy wariness of rules.

Lots of people wanted to know our limitations. What could magick not do? Where did it end? And the answer was invariably with a public lynching.

Nowadays, it looked different than it had a few hundred years ago. Now it looked like charges of assault, murder, and practicing magick with intent to dominate. It took the guise of Retrieval teams, gags, and soundproof cells. But a cell in a prison with a bunch of supernaturals who'd been on the other side of the battle lines was every bit as lethal as a mob or a pyre.

"Not sure what's heavier," I heard Beo say from my shoulder. "Those clouds or your face."

I put it aside and turned to him, because I knew the risks and the costs. And when he offered his hand, I took it. The bastard threw out heat like a furnace, and I huddled a little closer to my personal windbreaker. "You're early. I was getting set to brood."

"Don't let me interrupt. We can brood together."

Under my lashes, I scanned him quickly. He didn't seem particularly broody. "Something going on?" he asked.

A shrug was my answer. We wandered along the walking track. Most of the ducks were settled in the reeds, but a few brave or desperate souls paddled close to the edge, hunting for bread or bugs.

"Thinking about whatever happened that made you scared to heal?" he asked me after a while.

"No." But now I was. I saw Brandon's face, with his eyes that laughed more often than they accused. "He loved Coke. Went nowhere without it, except a—" a Retrieval. "Delicate work thing." I let out a breath. I wasn't good at walking lines and holding stuff back. Okay, maybe I was when the situation called for it. *Like Arthur. Douche canoe.* But Beo wasn't a douche canoe. "I was thinking about the poor, cold ducks."

"They're fine." He dismissed them with a brief, amused glance. "He was in your bones? Your Coke-drinking patient?"

I tried to puzzle that out. "In my bones?" I asked because I must've misheard.

His eyes stayed on the lake. "Love. We don't say it the way you do. Sorry."

In my bones. I turned the idea around. "What's it mean?"

He was quiet for a little while, pondering reeds or ducks, or maybe trying to figure out if the big black waterbirds were swans or geese. Or maybe he knew. I didn't. "It means they're what holds you up. Where your strength is. I never liked your Sunwalker 'heart' thing. You can live after love ends. You can heal. It hurts, but it can happen." I let the ideas swirl. "But while they're there, with you, in your bones...you're stronger."

I felt the quiet words in my heart *and* my bones. And I ached. "Well, Brandon was in my bones then." Because it hadn't killed me when I lost him, had it? I took my hand back so I could bury it in my pockets, round my shoulders, and hold my blazer closer to me. I should've packed a proper coat and tissues. "I didn't have siblings. Brandon and Aspen were about my age and lived over the road. He was basically my big brother." I glanced up at the calm lines of Beo's face, realized he'd had his hair trimmed. Not as much as he should've, but some. It made me smile, that little thing. It was a sweet slice of normal. "Nice hair."

He made a noise in the back of his throat that could've meant anything, then shrugged off his jacket.

I scowled as he held it up for me. "No. You wear it. It's, like, five degrees."

"Twelve," he corrected, apparently amused. "I'm fine. You need it, so wear it."

I let him bundle me into the big, worn jacket that still held his body heat. I folded it around myself with a sigh. My nose was still cold, but it helped. And the look he sent me did too.

"You tried to distract me. You're pretty good at that." There was little evidence of that being true, but I sent him a quick wink and a grin, which made him smile. His arm lifted, and I stepped into it, letting him loop it around my waist. The heat still rolled off of him. Our pace was unhurried, our path directionless. It felt so good my heart ached.

"You must've been young when it happened."

"Oh?" I asked, raising my brows.

"Yeah. You're a fighter. You've seen shit." Before I could deflect or deny, he pulled me a little closer, rubbed his lips over my hair. "Like recognizes like, Rory. Maybe that's why we get on so well." My poor heart shivered in my chest. Probably not from the cold. "So tell me. What happened to Brandon that made you doubt yourself so much?"

"I don't—" I cut off the denial, then blew out a long breath. "Okay, shit." Honesty was a bitch. Luckily, so was I. "Maybe I do. He was important—to me, to Aspen, to Dad, to his parents, to his partner—and I screwed up." The sudden, shocking sound of bones crunching. No shout of warning. No snap of twigs or pulse of magick. I felt sick. "I go to Christmas dinner, to birthdays, and he isn't there. That's on me, Beo. I could've done something."

"So you didn't heal him."

"I tried." I remembered all too clearly the ward I couldn't hold while also trying to stem the spurting blood that had pulsed with his heartbeat. First brilliant crimson arcs, hard jets of lifeblood. Then a sad bubble, like school drink taps. Then nothing. "It was chaos. We were at work. Routine job. We'd had the training, done the work, but it didn't really prepare us. It couldn't. We had no idea what we were up against."

"Yeah." We stopped walking in front of a bench. He tugged me down. "Yeah, I know how that feels. Come on."

I folded down beside him, glad of the company, of his solidarity and his gentleness. "I'm done. I don't want to talk anymore about him. It was a long time ago." And it was yesterday.

"Okay." He pressed his lips to my temple. "I get that too. Callie got another distinction in class."

Relieved, I latched onto the gambit. "She'll be a good accountant. She'll be good at anything she sets her mind to." He nodded his agreement. "How she works all those jobs and studies and seems like a relatively put-together person—" The word person wasn't technically correct, but I didn't bother trying to find the right word. "You do good."

"Someone needed to look after them," he said, the words a deep rumble in his chest, full of pleasure and worry. "I've had some sleepless nights."

I'd bet he had. "You're not what I expected of an Alpha."

"Oh?" I glanced up to see the amused twist of his lips and the glitter of mirth in his eyes. "I know how your men use it, you know. I'm not that out of touch. In my world, it just means leader. Much like your Caretaker."

But it wasn't just leader, or even Caretaker. "You're almost their dad."

"Most of their parents are dead, fighting, or enslaved. They need safety and hope."

"Love," I offered, remembering how he'd cradled the girl who hadn't yet chosen a name and couldn't speak hers for fear of it being overheard. "Or...someone to hold in their bones. Someone to strengthen them." Had Beo been there, done that, with all of those young folks in the pack? "Why did you settle here? There are quieter places to raise a—" *Family*, I wanted to say. "Pack."

"Easier to blend in." I looked up with disbelief and he sighed. "There are...rifts. I can grab those of us who make it through and help them out. You don't want to hear that."

Rumors of riftrunners scampered in the back of my mind. "No, I don't." Not in my official role. "But I kind of need to, Beo." And I regretted it.

He shifted a little beside me. "Yeah. I guess you do." He let out a breath. "We're tracking them, okay? As much as we can. Fae, lycan, and human involvement make it messy."

A chill ran up my spine. "Human." Like the police?

"Yeah. Someone's covering their tracks with magick."

Fuck. I closed my eyes. *One of us.* O'Malley was right. "Any idea who?"

"Can't identify the human's scent," he admitted grimly. "Yet."

"Okay." I supposed it was information, of a type. "And the lycans? Know them?"

He paused for a moment. "They're not mine, if that's what you're asking."

It wasn't. We'd established that. "I know it's not your pack. But do you know who it is?"

He rubbed his jaw against my head, and my damned heart melted. "I know. But their names won't mean anything to you. They aren't legal here."

Hellfire, that didn't make me feel better, but it did give me a lot to go on. Magick to cover up crimes meant magi working with them in a serious fashion, not just peripheral involvement. And if Beo said they weren't from here, well… I had to trust him, didn't I? And right then, it was easy. "Okay. I'll take off my Caretaker hat now." I glanced up at him, surprised at the darkness on his face. "I'm sorry."

"It's fine. Risk of dating a witch, I suppose."

But it wasn't fine. "I'll try to separate them better. And for now, I'm a woman, not a Caretaker." There was just the tiniest hint of relief on his face, and it made me wonder. "You must've come from a pretty horrible place." I'd heard stories, of course, but who could trust them? Going Overworld wasn't just a mess of paperwork, fees, and tests, it was also physically demanding. And our presence there was as closely monitored as theirs was here—except the people we sent Overworld had nothing but their wits and the few draw cards humanity held in terms of trade.

We couldn't compete with the faeries, the trolls, the vampires, or the rest that we were still figuring out. Those who wanted to come home again knew it and didn't try. The others… Well, it wasn't considered a low-risk field of employment.

"It was a place," he said, with acceptance. "Good and bad. In a lot of ways, your world is almost as dangerous for us. But we're making a home, working hard to do the right thing."

"Even when it's illegal?" I grumbled because I couldn't help it.

"Yeah," he agreed with no hesitation.

"Is that why you all work multiple jobs?" I asked because my melting heart didn't affect my curiosity in the least. He shrugged, silent for a while. "Don't tell me you send money home." Quickly, I did the mental math, judged average wages. I didn't know much about unskilled labour rates, though, and they were all technically unskilled, with Callie being the first to go through higher education. This huge gap in access that I'd overlooked horrified me.

"No. Not exactly. But…" He hesitated again. "Some things are useful to our packs back home. Critical."

The way he said it, the slow, almost painfully offered up words, made wariness trickle down my spine. I was shit at not being a Caretaker, apparently. "Not weapons?" I asked, wondering if I could blame him for arming his friends against his foes.

I was sent an irritated look. "No. Medicines."

Guilt tugged at me. "I haven't heard of that. I know about some drugs and weapons, but…"

"Yeah, most of the official channels are controlled by the old vamp families or the fae royalty." He had withdrawn a little. I felt it and I didn't like it. But I didn't push. He'd let me have my omissions with Brandon. I'd give him the same benefit of the doubt. Even if I did want to crack his head open and peer at his thoughts. "It's nothing illegal in this world."

"Probably would be if they knew," I admitted, tiredly. Steroidal creams had been available over the counter until we'd found out they were being bought and sold as anti-troll weapons. Gingko biloba, which hadn't had a lot of mainstream uses, was now a government-controlled substance. Apparently, it was some sort of performance-enhancing drug for vamps. There had been a lot of deaths before someone had gotten to the bottom of that.

I expected there was a very unhealthy black market going on.

"What do you need?"

"Why?" he asked, raising his brows. "Want to be a supplier?"

Though the question was flippant, I couldn't tell if he was serious or not. "I know some healers," I said warily. "If it's a medicinal substance, and for an actual good cause…"

He leaned down and kissed me. "No. I don't want or need that. I was teasing." He sighed. "You should get back."

So, that was that. "You know I'm going to snoop, right?"

He stuffed his hands in the pockets of his jeans, frowning at me. "Why?"

"Because that's how I'm built."

He made a noise low in his throat that sounded like approval. "I like the way you're built."

As I stood, my mind spun over possibilities. Medicines, he'd said. Against diseases? War wounds? Some sort of strange, magickal parasites? "Tell me what the medicines are for, at least," I asked, because it felt like that was probably more important than knowing what it was.

He hesitated, looping an arm around my shoulders. "Mostly for the kids. The vamps have messed with the sun. They found ways of blocking it for weeks, sometimes months. The little ones don't get enough. You saw how small"—he paused then said carefully—"my niece is."

I pictured her. Tiny, delicate. "Sure. She's a kid."

"She's ten. We don't age quite the same way, but it's close enough."

I stopped, shocked. "No way. She's, like, five."

"Kids are like flowers," he murmured quietly. "They don't do well without sun. They're small. Sick."

"So, you're sending them vitamin D?" I asked, horrified at this thought. "What about the adults? Wouldn't it mess with their bones, too?" Then I eyed him. "How come you're so huge?"

"It happened after I'd almost finished growing, and I've been Sunside for more'n a decade. But, yeah, it's impacting adults, too." He shrugged, looking resigned. "The kids are the ones who suffer the most. And we don't make vitamin D from the sun the way you Sunwalkers do."

The name suddenly made sense. I fell in beside him, trying to figure out what their bodies would get from the light. Trying not to imagine children suffering, their bones growing with agonizing slowness. I couldn't help but wonder if it impacted their understanding of love since they used bones instead of hearts as the metaphor. The idea was achingly sad.

"You know I came here thinking I could talk you into coming straight back to my place tonight," he said darkly. "Or yours. Or a dark, quiet corner somewhere out of the wind. I'm not picky."

I laughed at the sudden change of topic, the image of him scouting for some conveniently sheltered shadows. "I like meals with your pack." Then, as the reality dawned, I added, "They need you."

"They'd be fine." He took us down another path, and I could see the tram stop up ahead, past some parked cars, some artfully planted trees, and a small, sad playground. "But I guess we can eat first too."

My mind went back to my lack of magick practice, and I sighed. It would keep for another night. "I've got my bag at work because I was going to come straight from the office." He waited, brows raised, for the problem. "I don't have much in the way of a change of clothes." I'd been pretty tired and humming on pleasure when I'd gotten ready that morning. "And they do need you, Beo. You're their rock. You go. You can come by my place after, or I can come to yours." I marvelled at how wonderful that sounded. How grown up. *Look at me, Dad, juggling a career, a lycan pack's needs, and a love life.*

"I'll come to you."

I remembered the way he'd escorted me in the middle of the night. The way he'd made it easy. Like he did now.

"You're a big sweetheart, you know that?"

His eyes glittered at me in amusement. "I know what I am." He didn't agree or disagree, so I couldn't rib him anymore. I took off his jacket with regret once we reached the tram stop. He took it, pulled it on, and his smile widened. "I like you smelling like me, Rory. I like smelling you on me."

I blinked. I didn't think he meant the faint scent of whatever soaps and deodorants we used. "Um?"

"Maybe you ought to leave some of those very sensible work clothes at my house. In case you run into any other lycans."

The thought sent ice down my spine. "Am I likely to?"

"You're looking into Betty's murder, aren't you?" he asked, raising his brows. "Safer if they know you're with me."

"Like, what kind of distance are we talking, for this scent stuff?" I asked, uneasily.

He sent me an unimpressed look. "Well, before you get to asking distance questions, it'll give you a bit of protection." He glanced up as the tram rumbled to a stop beside me. "This is you. See you tonight. No-gi." I bounced up on my toes, planted a quick kiss on his lips, and jumped in, out of the cold.

I knew there was suspicion about their sense of smell, but was it *that* keen? Was I some sort of scent post now for every passing lycan? *Hey, I'm screwing an Alpha, get back!*

It was definitely another complicating factor. Because I didn't have enough of those already.

SIXTEEN

MY HEAD WAS FULL OF SUSPICIONS ABOUT MY SIREN CLIENT AS I CLIMBED
the stairs to the mats at The Playground. I finished off the email about her
recent questionable activities, checked I'd cc'd the relevant parties, and
dropped my bag as I hit send, then realized I hadn't included a signature.
And, damn it, I'd forgotten to call detective Sexy-Voice O'Malley.

Jeff swaggered over as I unbuttoned my shirt. "Hey. Got a good special
on some wine your dad might like."

"Oh yeah?" I shrugged out of the shirt and jacket simultaneously. "Is it
cheap?"

He grinned at me. "It is. Cheap enough to use in a lasagna, good
enough to drink."

"You're talking my language." I kneeled and dug out my rashie. "How
long is it on sale for?"

The flow and rhythm of it felt like coming home. It helped that Beo
was hands-off, treating me the same as ever. We hadn't talked about that ,
but we both knew our personal relationship was a secret we'd have to
keep, at least in these public places.

Anticipation sang in my blood on the way home. I rode the tram in my
compression leggings and soaked rashie, getting a few glances from other
commuters that I ignored.

When I got back to my building, I already had my keys in my hand when I spotted three young women loitering out the front, scrolling on phones, huddled down in lightweight, fashionable cardigans.

They were definitely up to something. A low-grade warning tugged at the back of my brain, but I shrugged it off. I had been up to something, too, at their age—every chance I got. I didn't pay them any mind, letting myself in and going up the stairs, trying to remember what I had in the fridge that would be edible. I was pretty sure I had a bag of chips, if all else failed.

"Excuse me," one of the girls said as I reached for my doorknob. I glanced up, struck by how damned slight and pretty she was. Her eyes were huge in her heart-shaped face. The beanie over her head allowed artfully arranged waves of ash blonde hair to tumble around her shoulders.

Hellfire, I felt old.

The kid must've been fifteen, and her friends, the same. They were all gorgeous. One of them held a scarf, a pretty swirl of blues, greens, and golds. She twisted it anxiously between her hands, shifting from foot to foot.

The speaker's lips moved. I knew there were words, but I couldn't hear them. The other two girls were moving. The words, their passage, was lost in a blur of static as the speaker's eyes became bigger, deeper, like some sort of secret pools. My world shrank.

The ring on my finger burned.

Adrenaline shot through me, even as her eyes narrowed. My hand on my keys shifted until my fingers coiled around the wand I kept on my keyring. The hiss she let out was pure fury. Power thrummed through me. Time slowed.

A weight landed on my back as the spell coalesced in my mind, infused with power, long practice, and adrenaline. *Through this dome none shall leave or come.* Pain across my mouth. The scarf. I didn't reach up, didn't react. Movement, around me. More than three—*unless it is with me.*

The ward leaped up and I held it, in my mind, in the depths of my heart, as one of the creatures before me was sheared in two. The wall beside me, solid brick, exploded outwards. The creature behind me screamed in fury, and I tasted blood as my head was yanked back, twisted off-balance.

Faeries.

The sound of something striking my ward rang like a bell. Again. My heart hammered in my chest, and I could feel the blood pounding through my veins. I reached up with my wand-free hand, grabbed hold of my attacker by the hair, and felt teeth, hot and sharp. I threw myself backwards against the ward, knocking the faerie off me and ripping the scarf out of my mouth.

It leaped at me again, using the ward like a trampoline. I ducked, felt the rake of its claws over my back.

Claws, fangs, hypnosis, ridiculous strength, speed, and agility. A complete and utter refusal to quit. These were the faeries' weapons.

She had already spun as I straightened, feeling like my limbs were weighed down. Like molasses in the winter, Oma would say. Her voice and the smell of her kitchen enveloped me in the strangest way.

The faerie inside my ward moved too fast for me to cast anything and expect to hit it, even if I could have mustered up a second spell.

It kicked off the ward like a swimmer off the side of the pool, and I felt my body respond out of habit and survival.

I raised a forearm, felt the bite of its claws as I deflected it away from my throat, and drove my fist forward.

Bones crunched. It spun, graceless, hurdled against the ward.

Bird bones—the main weakness of the fae.

Five more faeries—six? four?—swarmed against the edges, pounding furiously, climbing, ripping up carpet to try to get in. When they'd arrived didn't matter—they had. Fury throbbed through me, burning me. I lifted an arm, smeared in my own blood, and levelled my wand at them, paperwork be damned.

One of them met my eyes. Not the blonde who'd tried to hypnotise me, the third from the original three, the one who hadn't been sheared by the ward, hadn't been caught inside, and her expression was one of horror.

Recognition flashed over her painfully beautiful features, and she froze, her mouth an O of shock.

Then the group moved so fast it was a blur of fleeing, pounding feet with long, gazelle-like strides, and they were gone.

In the beats of silence that followed, I stood there, letting my arm fall to my side and my brain scramble to catch up with my body.

I had no idea who they were. They couldn't have known me.

What could scare off a faerie in full attack?

The faerie I'd punched lay crumpled against the edge of my ward, its jaw halfway up its cheek as a pool of its brilliantly blue blood oozed out of its broken shell. The faerie's head was bowed in a way that made my belly roll. "Are you okay?" Someone shouted, the sound semi-hysterical. "Oh my God, are you okay?"

Down on the street, a woman, probably my age, stared up at me, her eyes huge. A bag had spilled a box onto the street. One new shoe poked out drunkenly. Behind her, a couple of teenagers had their phones pointed directly at me.

I spun and hid my face.

Fuck. Fucking fuck.

I didn't drop the ward because there was no way those faeries should've run. Instead, I rummaged through my bag, found my work phone, and, with hands that had begun to shake, called the police.

This was now *their* shitshow.

SEVENTEEN

DETECTIVE TAIG O'MALLEY STOOD BESIDE ME, HANDS ON HIS HIPS, AS THE last of the debris was cleared from the road below. The door to my apartment had been blown in by the ward. I hadn't noticed at the time. But it didn't bode well for a good night's sleep.

"You've given us enough to go off," he told me, his gaze on the brilliant blue pools of blood. "You'll need to come in tomorrow, make a formal statement, of course. But first you'll need to get medical attention and find somewhere to sleep tonight."

That much I'd figured out. The "why" I was still getting to. "Any reports of suspicious fae activity in the area recently? Any jewellery stores, antique shops, hardware stores robbed?" They went after anything shiny with a ferocious single-mindedness; this and their indomitable attitude made them excellent thugs.

"No faeries on our beat. Plenty of crime, I'm sure, but nothing that's passed my desk that fits." He smiled at me and jerked his head at my apartment. "Pack a bag. You got somewhere to be tonight?"

What he didn't say: somewhere safe.

Almost on cue, the rumble of a motorcycle met my ears. I didn't glance over. "I need to take a few minutes," I said slowly. "Figure that out."

He nodded, unsurprised. "Whoever it was didn't know you could cast without speaking."

The rumble of the cycle had slowed. I still didn't look. My heart ached. *Beo.*

How many times had he asked about that? Three? Four? Most witches, gagged as I had been, would've been torn to shreds. Most witches would've fallen to the hypnosis.

Would Beo send a swarm of faeries after me? Why? I'd kept my mouth shut, honoured my part of the bargain. It didn't fit.

My mind swam. My arms felt like I'd reached into a bin of broken glass and rummaged around. My face was a ball of fire from the force the creature had used to yank my head back with the gag, but I was pretty sure I wouldn't need to see a dentist.

I was in no state to be figuring out anything, except how fast I could get to the bottom of a bag of chips.

Would Beo come up?

The thought made fear dance in the bottom of my belly, but imagining his arms around me felt so good I ignored it. The thought of trying to explain the situation to the detective made exhaustion pull at me.

"I'll pack," I said, shaking my head, trying to clear it and focus on what needed to be done. "The cuts aren't that bad." *Were they? No. Maybe.*

"I'll stick close," he said, almost lazily, as the sound of the bike faded into the distance. My heart fell. I turned into my apartment where crime scene helpers had picked up the slivers of the door, leaving little behind but dust and police tape.

"Yeah. Thanks." I took a deep breath. "I'm crashing. Haven't had an adrenaline spike like that in a while."

"No worries." He wandered in, impersonal. "Got a friend? Family? Partner? Colleague? Someone you trust?"

My heart squeezed. My core people weren't in Melbourne. I didn't trust myself right then. So that pretty much left only one choice. "Yeah." I pulled out my personal phone, opened the recent calls, and clicked on the second name from the top.

"Hey, Roars," Lilith said on the other end. "Don't tell me your evening got as dull as mine."

I closed my eyes and let some of the tension ebb out. "Sure hasn't been dull. I need a place to crash. You've got a couch, right?"

"What? Shit. Are you—"

"Long story. Cops here. Got no door to my apartment right now. I think it's a crime scene. Is it a crime scene?" Taig nodded. "Yeah. Is it okay if I crash with you?"

"Yeah," she said, worry coming across loud and clear. I walked into my room, looked at my cupboard, then my drawers. "Of course! Shit, Rory. Want me to come get you? Do you need a healer?"

"No healer." I tried to remember where my gym bag had ended up but couldn't. I dug out a bigger travel bag. It'd do. "I'll come to you. Thanks, Lilith."

"Yeah, of course," she said impatiently. "I'll see you soon, okay?"

I grabbed some clothes and realized I was still in my no-gi gear and covered in lycan sweat.

Was that why the faeries had fled? I remembered the look on the faerie's face—horror, recognition, and shock.

Was that really what I'd seen in that split second?

"You all good, Rory?" Taig called.

"Yeah." How long had I been standing there? It felt like ten seconds. "What's the weather tomorrow?"

"Sunny, I think. A bit warmer than today but not much." I grabbed a pair of flats I wore to work. The style that was totally fine for strolling through an office and wouldn't give me problems in a sprint.

"Where'd my bag go? I dropped it in my ward. I'm pretty sure I saw it after the dust settled."

"Evidence," he called back. "Sorry. Anything you need?"

"Work phone. All of it, eventually, but by tomorrow? Just the phone."

"I'll get on it." A moment later, I heard him talking and assumed he'd made a call.

A toothbrush, hairbrush. I went back to my bedroom and remembered bras and underwear—three of each, just in case. Did I need three bras? I didn't try to answer that question, just grabbed. Cozy jumper, scarf, socks... *Stop it, Rory. It's for a few days, max.* A charger, headphones, my entire selection of jewelery because it all doubled as weapons...

Fuck. Weapons.

I opened the bottom drawer, hauled out the black tote I still kept loaded and ready to go with my Retrievals kit. It hadn't seemed worth unpacking it, not when I still got the occasional contract even after I'd left the team's full-time roster. And when I'd moved to Melbourne, well, it kept it all together in one neat spot, didn't it?

I shouldered it, the weight and drag familiar. "Okay." I stepped out and frowned. My wallet was in my bag. "I don't have a Myki for public transport. You've taken my wallet into evidence."

Taig tossed his keys, caught them. "Got you covered, Caretaker."

"Huh. Isn't that beneath your pay scale?"

"Duty of care," he told me, reaching out and taking the bag I held in my left arm, where bite wounds still oozed. "Those look sore. Sure you don't want a hospital? They've got some awesome drugs."

"Drugs schmugs." I put my hand firmly on my old kit and he eyed it but didn't reach for it. "I have herbs." At his raised brows, I scowled. "My friend will have herbs. What kind of witch doesn't have yarrow?"

Turned out city witches didn't have yarrow.

I explained the situation as Lilith washed the wounds in warm, salty, spelled water, and slathered them in antiseptic. By the time I'd eaten half a tub of ice cream, my vision blurred. My brain had well and truly shut down. I curled up in a ball on Lilith's couch, grateful for the quiet sounds of her moving around doing everyday chores as I let myself drift into sleep.

I woke to the incessant ringing of my phone. I dragged myself up from sleep, took the phone Lilith passed me, and struggled to coordinate my brain and my hand enough to accept the call. "Hello?"

"Aurora." I shook my head a little, regretted it instantly. "I heard you'd been hurt. Are you okay?"

Fuck. Who was this? I held the phone away from my ear and didn't recognize the number. "Sorry," I said, feeling fuzzy. "Who's this?"

"Edward Van Der Holst," he said, and there was a trace of irritation in the words.

I tried to rouse myself a bit more. "Sorry, Edward, I don't have your number saved in my personal phone." Lilith, in the chair beside me, lifted her brows. I shrugged in answer and regretted that, too. "Yeah. I'm okay. A bit torn up, but okay."

"You don't know how pleased I am to hear it." He didn't sound it. "What happened?"

"Faeries." I tried to prop myself upright. "Hit me after class."

He was quiet for a moment. "Faeries."

And then I remembered... "Faeries are working with the lycans. Riftrunning pixie dust." And then another blinding memory. Beo's information, confirming what O'Malley suspected. "They're being protected by a magi."

"What?" he asked, the word a low warning. "How did you learn this?"

I blinked. "Contacts. Anonymous ones."

"Aurora," he said, frustrated.

I just let my head fall back and shut my eyes. I hurt. Everywhere. And there was no way I was giving up Beo. Even if I was a bit concerned about how tonight had panned out.

He let out a long sigh. "Your integrity is one of the things I value about you. Okay. I'll let it go, for now. Did this contact know where you'd be?"

He had. "Anyone who has access to the tracking app would know where I was."

Silence. Then, quietly; "Arthur collates all that data."

My head pounded. Of course, he did. Why hadn't I considered that? He'd been tracking my movements. Probably getting his jocks in a knot because I was spending so much time with the lycans.

Probably worried he'd be found out.

"I need to investigate further," Edward was saying. "I'll stay in the background, but keep me abreast of information, please. If I'd known this afternoon what you just told me now..."

He couldn't have done shit unless he'd seen Arthur hand over some shinies to a bunch of faerie thugs and smacked them all with a sleep charm on the spot.

"Sorry, Edward. I feel dreadful. I'll talk to you soon."

"Yes. Yes, and please, Aurora. Take care. Blessed be."

I hung up and curled into myself with the phone still in my hand. "What was that?" Lilith asked, her brows raised.

I yawned. "Later. Please. So sore."

She stood and vanished. After a moment I felt warm softness draping over me. "Go to sleep," she sighed.

And I did.

It felt like I'd only just closed my eyes when the phone in my hand screamed at me. I lurched up, feeling sick. The lights were off. Disorientation, pain. And on the phone screen: Detective O'Malley.

I hit answer. "Yeah."

"Caretaker Aurora." The voice swam through my head. I sat up, pounded by pain from my arms, my back, my face. "It's Detective O'Malley." I knew that. "I have a wizard here, a Gerrard Gold, inquiring as to your whereabouts."

The carefully neutral way he said it sent ripples of wakefulness through my body. "A wizard? My dad? What's he—" I felt the ring on my finger, the cool weight of it. The way the faeries' hypnosis had made the world smaller, blurry—but, ultimately, failed. "Yes. Yeah, sure. Um." My mouth tasted like sour milk and salted caramel. Dad's protective spell had been triggered, of course he knew. "You need permission to tell him where I am?" Why hadn't he just called me?

"I do."

"Oh. Yeah. Sure. Do you have the address still?" Then I blinked as Lilith appeared from the direction of her room wearing an old T-shirt with a faded rock band logo. "Can my dad come over?" I asked her.

She rolled her eyes. "No." And she headed towards the kitchen.

"Yes, I have the address," Taig said on the other end. "You're happy for me to send him over?"

"Sure. Yes. Oh, Taig. Can you get him to pick up some chips?"

"Give me a moment." There was a muffled conversation before Taig returned. "He's on his way. He said to tell you he already has chips and coffee for you."

I sighed. I loved my dad. "Thanks, Detective."

He sounded amused when he said, "Anytime, Caretaker. How're you feeling?"

"Like shit," I said with no ado. "But I have coffee and chips on the way, so things are looking up. Any decent leads?"

"Lots of questions right now. One thing that might be of interest, though. Give me a moment." I heard murmurs, doors shutting. There was less background noise when he said, "You there still?"

"Not moving too fast right now," I admitted.

"Yeah. Going a round with a faerie isn't something I've seen any person do without serious armor and no better options." The admiration in his voice didn't hurt me at all. I let myself bask in it and told the niggling guilt to go fuck itself. "I'd say you're lucky, but I think it's a bit more than that."

Sometimes a woman just needed to be told she kicked arse while she wore sweatpants and hid under a fluffy blanket. And, okay, if it was said in that smoky voice, it didn't make it any harder to hear.

Smiling, I said, "That's very sweet of you." The sound of a kettle boiling drifted from the kitchen. I heard Lilith moving around in her cozy apartment and enjoyed my little cocoon. "But be careful, Detective; I'll think you like me. Aren't you supposed to be super neutral when it comes to all us loose-cannon magi?"

"I can admire good work when I see it," he said. "Anyway, I thought I ought to mention, just quietly, that those fae arrived in an area we suspect holds an Overworld rift, where two lycans were seen a few weeks ago."

The heavy inference there wasn't lost on me. The riftrunners he'd mentioned; now these faeries? My belly did a slow roll.

"I'm assuming I know what you're not saying there, Detective."

"What you assume can't get my badge rescinded, can it?" he asked mildly.

I stretched my legs out in front of me. Why did *they* ache? "I'm not keen to find out," I admitted. "I'm also going to assume the fact that two groups travelled through a rift means that they could be being sent by a similar person, or at least have some sort of link."

There was amusement in his voice when he said, "That isn't a question."

"No, it isn't. Just, you know, thinking out loud."

"With the holes in your face, I'm not surprised your brain is leaking a bit," he said, and there was definitely a light teasing note to his voice. Was he flirting with me? Had I flirted back? I shook myself. *You're adrenaline drunk, Rory.* "Rifts don't move much. Usually, they're made and then defended. The parties at both ends control the flow of traffic. We have no idea who controls either end."

"Suspicions, though?"

"None that we've been able to dig into very far. And even if I had, I couldn't have told you any names, so it's moot."

Maybe. But knowing they had nothing was still information. "Is the suspected address something else that's classified?"

"Highly."

"Figures." I leaned back in my little cocoon. "So, I've worried whoever actually did take out Betty. Well, shit, at least I'm on the right track." And if this track led to Arthur, he was in for a world of hurt.

Taig cleared his throat. "Caretaker, I need to remind you that your job is to—"

"I know my job," I cut in, my tone as mild as his. "Just like you know yours. The lines seem really clean on paper, don't they?"

"They do," he admitted with a sigh. "Maybe we should sit down, have a chat off the books. You can catch me up with what you've been doing."

Lilith set a coffee on the little, cluttered table near my knee. I mouthed "thank you" and she gave a brief nod, raised her brows, and shot her eyes towards the phone. I held up a finger to her, asking her to wait a moment.

"Is this a back-and-forth sort of deal, Taig?" I asked, curious to see what he was willing to offer. Hells, I could play along. At least he didn't have some relative in SuperSec I'd thrown in myself. As far as I knew. "Because I'm really good at reciprocity, but, you know, ladies first."

He laughed, a deep, inviting sound. "I've always worked on that theory, too."

Still smiling, but not keen to lead him on too far, I admitted, "I don't have my calendar to try to book you in."

Another laugh. "I'm glad you've got your priorities, Rory. I'm off soon, but I suspect you feel like death warmed. How about breakfast? I can shout."

Right then, I had no idea what I was doing tomorrow, but this was important. And he'd hinted at an information exchange, not just an interrogation. "Yeah, okay. Where?"

He gave me an address on the other side of town—something I appreciated. We were less likely to be seen. "See you there," he said, once I confirmed I had it. "Eight okay for you?"

"Eight works. Thanks, Taig."

"Anytime. Be safe."

"Yeah. You, too." I hung up and, at Lilith's expectant look, felt laughter bubble up in my chest. "Oh, shit. I think I just flirted with the detective who's heading up the investigation into Betty's murder and the attack on me."

Her expression was one of bemused awe. "Okay. Why?"

"Because he started it," I admitted with a shrug. "And, he's hardly terrible company. Also, looks like there's a link between Betty's murder and the attack on me."

"Which was, absolutely, attempted murder," she pointed out. "Your dad is coming over, I gather?"

"Yeah." I shook my head and stood. "I need to get my brain into gear. It's just revving wildly and getting no traction."

"Brains," she said with an understanding sigh.

I stretched, rotated my hips, and pulled a face. "Shit is fucked."

"You know," Lilith mused as she wandered ahead of me into the little kitchen, "you have a real way with words."

"I have been told that," I agreed, taking my coffee and following after her. A knock on the door had me glancing in that direction, wincing.

"No." Lilith stepped between me and the door. "The target of faeries can stay right here, thank you." She swept past me, regal in her rock shirt and old sweats in a way that I hoped to be when I grew up. "Hi, Rory's dad," I heard her say brightly. "I'm Rory's friend, Lilith. You can come in."

I hovered at the end of the hall and felt a rush of relief I hadn't expected and wasn't prepared for as he stepped in, carrying a bag of shopping in one hand and his staff in the other. Opening his arms, he headed straight for me.

I let him enfold me, breathing in the smell of the same cologne he'd worn since forever and the faint, lingering hint of coffee. "Why didn't you call?" I asked, burrowed deep into the spot that had always been mine, the point under his chin where it met with his shoulder.

He rocked me. "And distract you? Warn them? Sure, Sunshine, great plan." He pressed a kiss to my head. "Now I can see you're whole, what the hell happened?"

I sighed, ran through the attack in vague terms, and let him inspect my wounds. "Huh. You always did throw a mean punch," he mused.

"Coffee, Mr. Rory?" Lilith asked.

"Gerrard," my dad said with a smile in his voice. "I've got a thermos in the bag, don't worry about me. Came prepared."

"For war," I muttered, straightening and giving his staff a disapproving look. "You've got to be licensed to carry that shit around, Dad."

"Cops didn't stop me." He kissed my head and let me go, worry still on his face.

I thought of my dad when he was in Full Wizard Mode. The man could fire off curses like an automatic weapon could fire rounds, even if he *was* just a hobbyist.

"They wouldn't dare." But Taig had still flirted with me. I was pretty sure he had, anyway. Maybe my brain was just too fuzzy. "Make with the chips."

His expression softened. "Ultimate comfort food," he told Lilith, who, with an expression of deep confusion, watched him take not one, but four bags of chips from the little bag he carried. "So, faerie thugs, huh? Any idea who paid them?"

The question was a little too casual. I blinked as my brain finally started to whir. He'd spelled a lot of jewelery for me in my life, but there was only one item he'd drummed into me to never remove.

I took it off, of course, but always put it back on as soon as I could. And now here he was, openly carrying a staff despite being quite protective of his normal life and Regular Joe status. It was a good two-hour drive. I glanced at the time. Factoring in the delay at the police station and finding a place to park... "You left immediately."

He thanked Lilith for a cup and took out the thermos. "Did you want some?" he offered her.

"Dad."

"Oh, sorry. I didn't realize there was a question mark at the end of that statement."

I blew out air. Teachers. "What's going on?"

"You just got your head half ripped off by a bunch of tiny, gorgeous bullies," he said patiently as he poured some coffee for Lilith.

"Yeah. And when I had a vampire give me a love-bite six months ago, you called to check in and brought Oma to the hospital to heal me on the low. No staff was hauled in, no war drums beaten."

He tossed me a bag of chips, sat at the counter. "Yeah. But the vamp had already been Jesus'd by that point."

Lilith looked at me with raised brows. "You got bit by a vampire?"

I sighed, sitting. His excuse didn't fly, but that was a later problem. "Long story." I opened the chips, offering some to Lilith. She grabbed a few and nibbled. "So, the witch I took over for was killed by a lycan." I caught him up with the clusterfuck I'd found myself in—Arthur's suspicion of Beo, High Wanker Edward's reaction; Beo's relationship with Duke.

"This Alpha, this..."

"Beo."

"Yeah. Beo." He paused for a moment. "As in Beowulf?" I shrugged. "Lycanthropes that read classic lit? Who knew. Anyway, has he got any reason to want you out of the picture? Have you found any dirt, aside from the link to another lycan already in the lockup?"

I glanced at Lilith, who nibbled on a chip, waiting.

Damn it. I scowled, stuffed my face full of salty, carby deliciousness, and crunched. I'd promised. I was pretty sure I had, anyway. Right then, I couldn't remember the exact phrasing I'd used. But I knew I'd made a deal. I'd also almost been faerie food.

I knew I'd waited too long to answer when Dad set down his mug firmly. "They didn't know you were protected against hypnosis or that you can cast without speaking. Doesn't seem beyond belief that the lycans could pay someone and make it look like it wasn't related to them."

And Beo had inferred he knew the lycans riftrunning. And he had asked about my ability to cast.

I hated doubting him.

"Yeah. Yeah, I know some stuff that could get them all in a lot of hot water."

"How much hot water?" Dad asked, his eyes narrowing. "Why haven't you told anyone?"

I sighed, thinking of the girl. "Because. There's a kid involved illegally. They're protecting her."

"You're sure?" he pressed.

My gut wanted me to say "Yes. He's a good guy." Instead, I admitted, "No solid proof." I hated it. And, damn it, they didn't tell me who from. There could be a turf war or something. But I'd already signed on, so to speak, to keep their secrets. "I—" I hesitated, scowling at the chips. "I'm sort of seeing Beo. He hugged me while we looked at ducks. He rescued me from a touch-and-go situation with another lycan pack. I can't see why he'd..."

"Well." He let out an unimpressed huff. "First, I want to meet him." I opened my mouth. "Don't you 'Dad' me, young lady. You seeing anyone and breaking rules to protect them means you care about them, and I want to know them." I shut my mouth, sent Lilith a quick look of supplication. She hid a grin, nibbled some more chips. Traitor. "Second, did he know where you'd be tonight? And when?"

I felt a tug of worry, my hand halfway to the bag. He did. He'd even said making plans tonight had been at the top of his agenda. "Yes."

"Faeries wouldn't want to linger too long," Dad said ruthlessly. "Whoever sent them knew, roughly, when you'd be there. Anyone else know your movements tonight?"

I sat back, feeling sick. "Arthur."

"Who's worthy of suspicion, but"—Lilith sighed—"more likely to act out of fury or self-interest." I nodded my agreement, but I didn't like it. Not with all the stuff from Edward simmering around in my brain.

"Tech guy?"

"Don't assume gender, Dad," I muttered, despite the fact that he was, in fact, masculine presenting. "No. Doesn't fit."

"Great." He threw his hands up, sat back. "The obvious answer here, Rory, is the lycan. You know that."

"Sure, I know that," I snapped. "Obvious doesn't mean right."

"Why?" he asked, narrowing his eyes at me. "Because he's cute?"

I choked on a sip of coffee. "Cute" and "Beo" did not belong on the same continent.

"Do you love him? What's going on?"

"Holy Hellfire, Dad." I buried my face in my hands. It hurt, so I sat up straight. "I don't love him. It doesn't fit. Look, he told me shit he shouldn't have today, not to get out of trouble, but because we talked. We shared." I winced. "Not...not the spell. Like. A good chat. The guy escorted me home after I healed, when I was wiped out—"

"You *healed* someone for him?" Dad demanded, setting down his cup with a clatter.

"I didn't heal for *him*," I said, furious. "Why are you twisting everything! She was hurt. She needed help, I could help."

His eyes narrowed dangerously. "Fine. Let's play it out. He takes you back to your place. I'm assuming he was a perfect gentleman."

"He was," I agreed, irritated. "Even when I would've gone in for more."

"He found out where you live," Lilith pointed out.

I levelled a finger at her. "You're on my side, damn it!"

"Yeah," she agreed, obviously not worried about my pointing finger. "The side that wants to keep you alive, not the side that's being controlled by ovaries."

"Nice," Dad murmured, brows lifted as he looked at her with some admiration.

Silently, she offered him a fist. He lifted his. I watched them, furious, as they celebrated their teamwork with a bump.

"All right, fine." I hated it. I hated the whole thing. But maybe they were right. "How do I figure out if it was him?"

"Meet up with him on a dark night somewhere isolated," Lilith suggested thoughtfully. "You'll sure know at the end. Risky, though."

"I retract my fist bump," my dad said disapprovingly. "That's a terrible idea."

Lilith shrugged. "I can deal. You could dob him in, let the cops sort it out. This is their job."

I rolled my eyes. So did my dad.

"Fine." She stole another chip, leaning forward. "Ask Duke."

Everything inside of me froze. "What?"

"Ask him." She shrugged, nibbling a corner of crinkle-cut perfection. "He can't get out, so Mr. Thorough won't know. He might not say anything useful, but who knows? People do weird shit for family."

"Mr. Thorough?" Dad asked. "No. I don't need to know."

"You don't," Lilith agreed with dark delight.

Okay. She was allowed back on my team. "Duke won't talk. First rule of lycan club."

That was met with silence. I sipped my coffee, my face hurting. I touched the side of my tender mouth, wondering if I looked like some sort of clown.

"What if you used Beo as leverage?" Dad asked slowly. "Like, 'ha-ha, you killed my brother, now I'll nail your's sort of thing. See if he takes the bait. If he doesn't react…'"

I shook my head, a headache starting behind my eyes. "That might work." But I felt dirty even considering it.

"He might not believe you," Dad said, frowning. "Otherwise, it's probably the safest way we have of knowing if they were allies when Duke got put away. Which doesn't rule out Beo becoming a bad guy in the meantime."

The memory of the warmth of Beo's jacket felt almost like a hug. I breathed deeply. "He'll believe me."

"Please tell me he's got a birthmark on his dick that's super distinctive and that no one else would know about," Lilith said, her eyes big and bright.

Dad winced.

I ignored their by-play, feeling sick. "Better. I'll smell like Beo when I visit Duke."

EIGHTEEN

Taig wasn't there yet when I arrived at the designated coffee shop at not-quite eight.

I'd left Dad in Lilith's hands since he'd insisted on taking the day off work. I still had no idea how I was going to contact Beo or what I was going to do. Maybe just rock up to training without a jacket and wait for him to do his caring routine. But I wasn't in any shape to train, and I didn't know if the smell would linger.

I figured I'd go into work because I hadn't read the policy on leave. Did I get to take paid leave if I was injured? What happened to my clients if I was down and out for a week, a month? I wasn't, but I sat there and wondered about it while I scrolled through social media without seeing it.

I needed to post something on my work account, send off a few requests. The Siren was at the top of my list. I hadn't wanted to move on her too fast, but time was ticking.

Taig slid into a chair opposite me, and I put my phone down. His hair was still wet, but he was buttoned up in his suit for work. I could smell one of the products he'd used, something with a hint of sandalwood. "You look better than I expected," he said, his eyes lingering on the bruises on my mouth—or my lips, but I was pretty sure it was the bruises.

Which was another concern. If I went to Duke with such obvious marks, would that impact the whole situation? Could he smell the wounds that were covered by every bandage Lilith owned and some torn-up lengths of old T-shirt?

"I don't know if that's a compliment," I mused, because I had to make a comment back, and I didn't want to tell him that he looked okay. Not great. The suit didn't quite look right on him. The blue was wrong. His eyes, a pale grey or light blue, looked lacklustre with all that navy.

"Don't know that it isn't," he said nonchalantly. "What'll you have?"

The menu was printed above the counter. I'd already skimmed it. "Coffee."

"And?"

"More coffee."

He raised his brows. "Aren't I buying?"

"Already eaten." He didn't know I'd been up until the wee hours of the morning, hammering out details with Lilith and Dad and eating my way through all the chips.

I had a carb hangover. It was a thing.

"But you go ahead. Long black, please."

He stood and went to order, returning after a moment with a numbered sign that he sat on the table between us. "So, you show me yours, Caretaker."

I sighed, leaned back, then sat forward with a wince when it pulled at the claw marks on my back. They probably should've been stitched up. Or at least butterflied.

"Okay. I'm bending confidentiality pretty far here, though, so this is very, very strictly off record." He nodded, so I explained the strange way the lycans had been designated as high-risk, the way the Van Der Holsts had been quick to blame them, the refusal to consider further, the way I'd been making myself very present in the pack's space, and how Arthur was pretty pissed about it and had thrown around some nastiness.

I told him about how Edward had passed on limited information about Jaye and how it had all gone down; we had some conversation about that, but the bottom line was if I didn't want to press charges, it was good information for him but officially useless.

I didn't mention Duke's possible relationship with Beo or anything to do with Beo's less-than-legal activities.

Taig's breakfast was delivered while I talked, a huge plate of eggs, bacon, sausage, hash browns, avocado, and some token wilted spinach on the side. I eyed off his hash browns. He had three. Who needed three hash browns all to themselves with that much protein already on their plate?

He kept eating for a while after I fell silent, his eyes unfocused. I could almost hear his mind whirring. I drank my coffee and reminded myself I had already eaten half of a potato farm. I didn't need a hash brown. Even if it did look crispy and golden.

"Okay," he said, pushing the plate into the middle of the table. "Eat them. You've been eyeing them the whole time. And it'll make me feel better. I did promise you breakfast." Caught, I reached over and lifted the top hash brown off the pile with pleasure. "I'm not going to tell you that we've recently got some information from Betty's phone. The telecommunications company didn't like being subpoenaed, but tough shit." I bit into the potato, listening closely. With carbs, fat, and salt, I felt better almost instantly. "She met with a new client we were investigating for the distribution of pixie dust." I raised my brows because that hadn't been anywhere in her case notes. "The client wasn't officially on the books yet, and they've since gone missing. I only know they exist because they cropped up on our list with the drug squad. We suspect Betty went to the meeting with a third party, though her vague calendar notes didn't indicate anyone would be there."

Though I didn't think that was standard procedure, I waited for the interesting part, licking some grease off my finger. His gaze flickered down to my thumb, then back up to my face. I waved a hand in a keep-going movement, impatient.

"We haven't identified the third party," he admitted. "We're reasonably sure there is one, though it looks doubtful they were linked to the coven. But we've got a line on someone who can give us a description." He paused for a moment, leaning in a little bit closer. "They were carrying a staff."

I paused, flicking through options in my mind. I hadn't known the woman, didn't know her circles, but there weren't many people who carried a staff. That shit was illegal unless you were licensed. And not everyone could get away with as much as my dad did.

"Arthur could mess with her calendar. A few people could," I offered.

Taig obviously didn't love the idea. He skewered a mushroom with his fork.

"But there's no motive," I added.

"Money is always a motive," Taig disagreed. "Our working theory, which you don't know, is that the client or third party recognized the wizard with Betty. Once she knew the truth, she was a liability."

I put the last of the hash brown in my mouth, chewed, and considered. "Was the client a lycan?" I asked before licking my fingers clean and reaching for a napkin.

He hesitated then shrugged. "It's a possibility. I've got a description, but none of it makes it clear what sort of supernatural they are."

"Hit me."

He took out his phone, tapped on a few things, then turned it to me. "Artist's rendition. Witness insisted on the coloration."

The man had a square jaw, some stubble, and brown hair. He looked young, maybe eighteen. Three parallel scars severed his eyebrow and carved a line down his cheek.

And his eyes were brilliant, kick-you-in-the-guts green.

The hash brown in my belly writhed. I reached for my coffee and drank. "Shit."

"Recognize him?" Taig asked, eyes narrowing.

"No."

The coffee in my hand trembled. I drank again. I couldn't keep it to myself.

"Look. We're both breaking rules here, right?"

He shrugged, but his lips had thinned a little. "Yeah."

"Great. So, if I tell you, I'm going to break a few more, but I need you to trust me, to give me time. Will you do that?"

He furrowed his brow. "You're planning something." Then his expression cleared, and he looked almost amused as he shook his head. "Of course, you're planning something. Go on. Tell me. If you wind up dead, I'll at least know where to look."

I blew out air. "Wow, Detective, your bedside manner is really top notch."

"I'm better in it than beside it," he said, then winced. "I'm sorry. I take that back. It was inappropriate, and I don't want to make you uncomfortable."

The joke would've amused me, but also, yes, it crossed that fine line between harmless fun and serious flirtation. The apology stopped it from being uncomfortable.

I settled deeper in the chair and felt myself relaxing. "I appreciate it," I admitted ruefully. "All of it. Thanks. So"—I cleared my throat—"I was on Retrievals." He nodded, holding his coffee like a shield. "I met a lycan called Duke." I breathed deeply, then took a swallow of coffee. Half of it was grounds and I didn't even care. "No, I didn't just meet him, I nailed him." But, Hellfire, the cost of that victory still haunted me. "He had those eyes. I've had a witch in the coven who's good at genealogies do some work. We didn't get far, but we know Duke has brothers."

"Okay." He frowned, studying my expression. "Link?"

I pressed my fingers, warmed from the coffee cup, to the aching bite on my forearm. "Beo's eyes are that exact green, too."

"Beo Velvela. The Alpha?" He sat back and whistled. "You're thinking they're family? The rift is in Beo's pack's turf. You think there's a wizard cutting deals with them, getting them to move the pixie dust?"

I glanced around, but no one seemed to care. "No. No, I don't think that. I think Beo's being set up or given the runaround. Families aren't all happy-go-lucky, no matter which world you're from, and Beo strikes me as someone who's worked bloody hard to get clean." Well, he was as clean as morality let him be anyway.

Taig agreed with a nod, then nudged his plate closer to me. "And?"

"And I don't know if he might have a name for that person." I nodded to the picture. "But I don't think they're friends. I don't know if he'd report it or deal with it himself, though. I suspect the latter."

"Agreed." Taig leaned one elbow on the table and drummed a beat with his fingertips. "So, what part of this were you worried about sharing?"

"The part where I'm going to go hang out with Beo, get myself covered in his scent, then visit Duke and rattle his chain."

Taig's eyes narrowed and, this time, his lips did, too. "You're very confident Beo isn't our guy."

"Yes."

"So am I." He nodded, frowning. "None of it will be admissible in court."

"That's your problem, not mine."

"Actually," his expression softened a bit, "it's the prosecutor's. What're you hoping to prove?"

"That there's no love lost between Beo and Duke," I said without hesitation.

Taig shrugged, still looking worried. "Would it matter?"

"Process of elimination. From there, I've got Arthur. The only other candidate is Edward Van Der Holst. But I've got nothing on him, no leverage, no information."

"The District High Wizard?" His focus sharpened. "What makes you suspect him?"

"He's a player." I lifted my hand and started counting off points. "He's very good at dodging questions. He didn't follow policy when managing Beo and their pack, and he weasels out when you ask him why. He is all guns-blazing after Beo. The guy was planning on getting Retrievals in to mop them up." So many fingers for this guy. "Everything that applies to Arthur—the access to files and information—apply to him. That's more than a high-five worth of suss."

"You think he wants to use them as scapegoats."

"Not really." I put my fingers away. My poor arm didn't need the abuse. "But I don't know that Arthur fits for it, either, much as he's a fuck-knuckle. They both would've known where I was last night, because I log my movements in the tracking app when I'm working. I clocked off after class, but it's not that hard to figure out I'd be going home." Although I'd nearly gone to dinner with the pack.

"That's a whole lot of circumstantial and nowhere near enough for me to get a warrant." But he considered me, cool and calculating. "When are you going to Duke?"

I shrugged. "Depends. Got to marinate myself in some Beo first."

He tried to hide a smile, sipping coffee. "I assume you mean like you had last night?"

"Yeah. BJJ." I'd explained where I'd been and why I'd been wearing compression gear that reeked of a dozen people's body odor. "What did you think I meant?"

"It was an interesting turn of phrase," he said, sidestepping the question. "So, I'm going to turn over some rocks, see what I can find on Edward and Arthur Van Der Holst. You do the same for Duke. We'll contact each other if anything comes up. Your work phone and wallet will need to be signed out, but I can hand them over." I nodded, unfolded my legs, and picked up my phone. "Tell the office you want to talk to me about Betty, if you need to call me," he said, standing.

"Sure. You've got my personal number, so no need to dance with me."

"Maybe another time," he agreed lightly. "I'll see you when you come in to give your statement. In fact, I'm looking forward to seeing you." He paused then shot me a very loaded look. "For the first time today."

I rolled my eyes and nudged him lightly with my shoulder. "Give me some credit. You gave me a hash brown. I'm pretty much your snitch now."

"Noted. Witches will work for breakfast."

"Fried potato," I supplied helpfully. "Don't care what time of day it is."

NINETEEN

AT WORK, I WAS FUSSED OVER BY ALL AND SUNDRY. BERNIE, WITH A WICKED gleam in her eyes, had me stripped to the waist and smeared my wounds in an ointment she just happened to have with her, bickering with Janet about the best herbs to use. Almost instantly, they felt better. "You can't heal me," I told them as Bernie started to murmur a rhyme that I recognized. "I'll sleep for the rest of the day. I have things to do."

"Quiet," Cici told me with a forbidding scowl that made me feel like I was six again. "Nothing gets accomplished when—"

"Rory," I heard Lilith call warily. "You've a client here to see you."

Bernie cut off mid-spell and swore a blue streak. "You keep them out there," Cici snapped. "The girl's hurt. She needs mending. They can just come on back tomorrow."

"Her body, her rules," Lilith said, my stalwart defender. "Want me to take a... Hellfire, Bernie, right here? *Right here?*" Lilith spluttered.

I looked over my shoulder, feeling like I was about to get my ears blistered for my carelessness. Lilith blocked most of the doorway. "Out!" Cici bustled forward. "I don't care who you are or how scary you think you can be. I can be scarier. Now. Out!"

It was Beo. It had to be. I closed my eyes, humiliation complete.

"You," Janet said, indicating which grown-arse woman she meant with a levelled finger that made me quake, "Get yourself healed."

I groaned, then reached for my shirt. "I can't, Janet. I have to—"

"Fine," she said stiffly. "If you're so important you can't possibly let us help you for one day, that's just great."

Refusing to cower, I picked up my shirt.

Bernie stepped in then. "But I'm going to burn out that infection, whether you like it or not, miss."

I hesitated. That probably wouldn't wipe me out for a whole day. And it did sound smart. "Okay," I said grudgingly, setting the shirt back down.

"Pardon?"

I cleared my throat. "Thank you, Janet and Bernie."

Janet muttered about gratitude and folks not knowing what's good for them. I stayed still while I felt them both start the spells. The familiar trickle of power through my system made me relax, sent me drifting into a calm, restful half-sleep.

When the process was done, I swam back into my own skin. I felt dramatically better and couldn't remember for the life of me why I'd resisted having this done.

Janet moved around me, smoothing fresh gauze over the wounds and taping them down. I sat, drifting still, and pulled on my shirt when she gave me a firm nod. "Better. Still terrible, mind you, but better." She shot Bernie a somewhat disapproving look. I didn't wonder why. Bernie was just one of those people.

Feeling fuzzy-headed, I made my way out of the room, pulling my hair out of my shirt and blinking as light speared my eyes.

Beo sat in the kitchen, a tiny cup of tea dwarfed in his big hands, Lilith on one side and Cici on the other. "Oh." I blinked. "Hi. Yes. Client."

"He didn't see anything," Cici told me firmly. "Now, you sit him here and talk to him, and we'll just scoot him along. You're in no state to be"—she waved a hand—"bad-arseing around."

I squinted at her, trying to figure out if bad-arseing was a verbal phrase, verb, or just some sort of backyard concoction I needed the recipe for immediately.

"Okay. Wait. No." I shook my head, trying to clear it. "He can walk me to the station. I need to talk to Taig. Detective O'Malley. Today." For the first time. I gave myself a little pat on the back. "Is that okay?" I asked Beo, peering at him. He was underwater.

He stood. I couldn't make out his expression, but I could tell Lilith wasn't enthusiastic about the idea from the way she wandered over and put herself beside me.

"Should you be walking, Caretaker?" he asked me, cautiously.

My mouth opened then closed. I shook my head and cleared my throat. "Yes. But I'm going to need coffee." When Cici reached for the tin that contained the coffee brick, I flinched. "From somewhere else."

She clucked her tongue. "That'll send you broke. No wonder young people nowadays can't afford to buy homes—Splurging on coffee at every opportunity."

"Yes. Yes, that's absolutely why I'm not a homeowner," I agreed, happy to seize that excuse. "I also eat avocados. Smashed. I'll be renting forever. Let's go. Wait. My bag."

"I'll get your bag," Lilith said with a sigh. "Text me when you get there."

"Yeah. Yeah. If I forget, call me." But she was gone. I shook myself again. "Coffee." I managed to walk under my own steam towards the door. Lilith caught up to me and passed me my personal phone, pressing it into my hand. "Cops have your bag," she reminded me when I looked at the phone, puzzled. "Shit, Roars, maybe you should…"

"No. I have to give my statement. And…" I shook my head. "Maybe I'll crash after I've done that."

"Sure." She eyed me warily again. "Get the detective to call me. I'll come pick you up and take you home."

"I can work a phone," I protested, and I avoided tripping over my feet as I made my way out the door.

Beo appeared at my shoulder, close enough that I could see the hard set of his mouth, the tightness in his shoulders.

"You were healed, but you're still hurt."

"Yeah. Can't go all-in on the healing. That shit knocks you out." The wind picked up my hair, sending it spinning around me wildly. I held it down with two hands. "Fuck today in particular."

"What if I take you back to mine, let you sleep it off?" He put a hand on my back as if to steady me. I was perfectly steady. "I can wake you in an hour, take you in."

"What if you come pick me up," I suggested, anticipation coiling in my belly, "and then take me back to yours, and fuck me until I can't stand straight."

He let out a long breath. "Are you drunk?"

"It's like ten in the morning," I objected. "It's a good plan!"

"Yeah. Which you just announced to everyone on the block when we're supposed to be keeping things quiet."

I peered around. The trees swayed. His hand firmed on my back, his other going to my waist. Maybe it was me that swayed. I leaned into him, a feeling of wellbeing tugging at me. It was like being enveloped in the warmest, coziest blanket. And I didn't hurt. I was so tired, and now I didn't hurt, and he was so warm.

We walked. Or he walked, and I leaned against him, vaguely annoyed with the jolting, but happy enough to just be there, to exist. At some point, he put a hot cup of coffee in my hands. I passed it back, curling my nose. "I'm sleepy."

He pushed it back. "Rory. You asked for this. You want to give a statement."

I shook my head and blinked. "Shit." He was right. I had to give this statement. I had to keep some very specific cards close. I pulled the lid off the cup, sat on a bench, and leaned forward. Some of the pain was back, niggling at the edges of the spell. "Shit. Bernie hit me with a numbing spell!" I shook my head. No wonder I was fuzzy. No wonder Janet had been annoyed with her. She'd done more than she'd said she would. "Fucking witches. You can't trust them."

He sat beside me. "I know one who's okay."

"No. I'm a fucking bitch of a witch too." I closed my eyes and groaned. "I'm sorry. You should call Lilith, get her to scrape me up."

He nudged me gently with his leg. "Drink," he said. "I'm not calling anyone. You said you can work a phone."

"I'm a liar," I admitted tiredly, but I managed to lift it to my lips and take a sip of the dark, rich brew. "But I really like you."

"I really like you, too." He nudged me again. "Come on. Another sip.

Then you can tell me what you like about me."

"Mmm." I sipped. The warmth felt good, so I repeated the action. Whether it was the coffee or just time, I did start to feel a little less like I was half a bottle of vodka into a very hard evening. "At least I won't have a hangover," I said, reflecting on the similarities.

"I was worried about you," he said, quietly. "I didn't want to complicate things last night. I thought you'd call, once you could."

Without being overheard, he meant. Without the cops knowing we were climbing into bed together. We had once. Twice? Once—there had only been a bed involved once. The other time had involved the door.

"My door is toothpicks," I told him sadly. That door had good memories. "My door are toothpicks? My door was turned into toothpicks." That sounded better.

"You'll get a new one." He nudged me and I sighed, sipped, and stood. "I can help break it in, if you want."

I sighed again, but happily this time. "You're my hero. I'm a bit worried you might be too good, Beo." And maybe he was bad. Very, very bad. I kept that inside my head by filling my mouth with coffee.

"No fear of that," he told me dryly. "We're almost there. You up to this?"

"Yeah." I downed the last of the coffee. "Taig will look after me."

"Taig?" he raised his brows.

"Yeah. Detective. He was there when you drove past last night. Handled Frankie when Arthur accused him." I frowned. "Does he do everything supernatural in this hellhole? Anyway, he's a good sort. I'll just" —I reached into my pocket, fished out my phone—"let Lilith know not to send the cavalry."

"Let her know you'll get yourself home, too."

"Home's a crime scene." Another trickle of alertness wormed into my brain. "Fucking faeries." I took a deep breath, then looked at the glass-and-brick towering monstrosity before me. "Wish me luck."

"Always." He opened the door, and I pushed my hair back into some semblance of order before navigating my way to the desk. I was reasonably confident I'd managed to walk a straight line all by myself.

I introduced myself, waited for about thirty seconds, and was shown in.

Confronted with questions, I felt adrenaline trickle through me. There was some important stuff going on. I couldn't screw this up. I focused hard, until my head ached, until the relentless pounding behind my eyes sounded like my ward being struck by faerie claws.

Taig walked me out, his expression worried. "You sure you're okay?" he asked, for what was approximately the gajillionth time.

"Yes." I squeezed the hand that hovered near my elbow. "Big girl, here. Got it covered. Good night, I mean, good-bye."

"You definitely should go to bed," he said, frowning. "Should I get a squad car?"

The thought of holding in all the things I couldn't say just made my head hurt more. "Got a friend coming to pick me up," I lied. Or exaggerated. "Bye."

He responded, but I could barely hear it. Keeping my eyes open became harder and harder. I walked out into the waiting area, then out the front. The sun was warm, far away.

"How'd it go?"

I looked over to see Beo's face swim in and out of focus. "Good. I think. I need to sleep. Very badly."

"Yes. I wish I'd mentioned that an hour ago." He put a hand on my waist, steering me towards a tram stop. "Where are you staying?"

Lilith's address shimmied across my brain. I shook my head, took out my phone. "I'll call someone." I found Lilith's number, hit call, then listened to it ring. And ring. And ring. Her voicemail picked up and told me to leave a message. "Hey, it's Rory. Just finished with the detectives. I suppose you're doing things. Chat soon." I hung up and looked at the phone in my hand. "I am not sleeping at the office. They'll hit me with more healing, and I'll be out for tomorrow, too."

He sighed and put a hand under my elbow. "Come on."

I followed because there wasn't exactly an option. "Did you reconsider my offer?" I asked brightly.

"Don't recall ever refusing it." He glanced around, then pulled us to a sheltered spot at the tram stop. "But I think there's probably an order of priorities here."

"A what?"

He shot me a quick, searching look. I closed my eyes, let my head fall back, then shifted with a hiss when pain erupted across my back. Grey descended. I let him steer me. I couldn't have told you how far we went, which stop we got off at, even whether there were stairs to his place.

But I remembered the bed. The big, soft warmth of it, the smell of Beo in the comfortably worn-in sheets. I groaned in pleasure, not sure how I'd gotten there and not caring at all.

He said something. I know, because there was a deep rumble, the lift and fall of speech. But it all blurred together, indistinct. I felt tugging at my feet and made an unhappy noise and tried to nudge it away. And then my feet were cold. I tucked them up and hissed as the wounds on my back screamed at me.

Rolling onto my stomach ended most of the sharp pain. The dark, aching throb was far enough away I could ignore it as a weight settled over me and warmth encased me totally.

When I woke up, it was dark, and I was too warm in my cocoon. Rather than just kick off a blanket, I crawled out, a move mostly driven by a full bladder rather than excessive energy. The apartment stood empty, but a light was on in the kitchen.

On the bench, a bag of chips sat unopened in a bowl. Beside it was a mug with some instant coffee grains in the bottom, and a note:

Rory,

Gone to run the class. Will be back before 8:30. There are more chips in the cupboard and some gin if you feel it. Tonic in the fridge.

Your Dad visited and dropped off a bag. It's at the foot of the bed.

See you soon.

I glanced at the clock. A solid three hours before he was due back.

The man had bought chips. And gin. Before I got too warm and fuzzy about that, I double-checked the gin in question wasn't half gone.

The bottle was at the front of a collection of bottles, unopened, new, sloe. *Nice.* Damn it, how sweet could he get? He'd stocked this shit for me.

I let it go with a sigh. I needed something to do, and the obvious thing was cooking. He had herbs on his windowsill that looked healthy enough. Basil, thyme, oregano, and chives. His spice rack was well stocked and overflowed into some tubs in his pantry. I cracked the fridge and eyeballed the contents. What did a single guy do with two heads of cauliflower? Still, I had something to work with.

My body reminded me why I'd gotten up in the first place. I closed the fridge and hunted down the bathroom. A towel had been placed on the vanity. And, while I used the toilet, I spotted shampoo, conditioner, and detangler the exact same as what I had at my place.

My heart shivered. I washed my hands and peered at myself in the mirror. Big, dark bruises spread out on either side of my mouth, and I looked pale. My hair excitedly explored every possible angle it could. I finger-combed it as well as I could as I went back into the kitchen to re-read the note.

What in the seven hells had my dad been doing here? How had he known where to go? I thought of him walking in with his staff and that hard look in his eyes at Lilith's place, and I knew he'd been warning Beo.

Fucking shit-balls. A lycanthrope buying me my favorite snacks, my hair products, my drink of choice...my dad threatening him with generational curses. Not to mention a possible link to a killer.

I groaned, grabbed my phone, and called my dad.

It rang out.

If Beo had murdered him, I'd have to murder Beo. But damn it, I'd bet Dad had asked for it.

I checked the fridge again. I wanted real food. I could've done something with chicken and bacon, but I wanted comfort food—something hot that didn't involve potato. I eyed off the basil, and double-checked Beo's pantry. No wine. The bottles were mostly fizzy drinks or sports drinks. There was a six-pack of beer, but I couldn't make lasagna with beer. Could I? No.

My phone map told me there was a grocery store just over a block away. I debated whether I should go, since I didn't like leaving the place unlocked, but really, I'd be what, twenty minutes? Thirty?

Fuck it, if someone rolled a lycan's place, they'd get what they deserved.

Once I set out, I scrolled through my missed calls: six from Lilith, two from Dad, a text from Oma, all in caps, asking what was going on, and a meme from Aspen. I glanced at it, then glanced again. It was me. *When you set healthy boundaries and they cross them* was the caption, and the picture was a grainy one of me having punched the faerie. She was in flight backwards, her limbs trailing along like streamers from her body.

You're viral. Call me.

Fuck.

I sent a quick message to both Aspen and Oma: *I'm okay. Will call in a few.* First priority: Lilith.

She answered straight away. The darkness of the city streets was broken by the hard wash of streetlights, the glow from behind curtains, and headlights from cars as they passed.

"Hey," she said, and the single word held a lot of questions.

"You can talk," I told her, spotting the grocery store ahead. "He's taking a class and I'm about to buy some groceries. But first"—I crossed a side-street quickly—"I am so sorry for doing that to you this morning. I know you were worried, and I'm pretty sure I agreed to do things and didn't follow through and—"

"Yeah, you're a jerk," Lilith cut in. "But I get it. Tell me about now. What's your plan? Are you getting all covered in Beo's scent tonight?"

I tried to remember what I'd said to him. "Maybe. I'm not sure how far my mouth ran while I was punch-drunk from that healing. Did you know Bernie did a numbing spell, too?"

She sighed. "Yeah. After you left, she told us all about it, very smug. Obviously, autonomy isn't something she gets. If it makes you feel better, Janet almost ripped her head off over it."

Frustration gnawed at me. "I know it was helpful, but…"

"But she made you vulnerable when you couldn't afford to be," Lilith finished for me. "Which is why you didn't go get healed immediately."

Relieved that she understood, I turned into the little grocer and went hunting for minced meat. "Yes. I'm not just being ridiculously stubborn, am I?"

"I mean," she sounded amused, "that's definitely part of it. But really, we don't know who sent those faeries after you. We don't know what they'll do now. You need to be on your toes. You'll do better uninjured, but if you're wiped out from a healing and you're hit…"

I blew out a breath, grabbed a big bundle of mince, turned to the fresh veg section, and found some zucchinis. "Yeah. Thank you."

She grunted. "Don't make a habit of getting almost killed, yeah?"

"I'll do my best." I tried to remember what salad stuff Beo had, couldn't, and grabbed a bag of spinach leaves. Salad or breakfast, it did double duty. Not like lettuce, can't do that for breakfast. Did he have baking trays? "I'm making a lasagna for him."

There was laughter in her voice when she said, "Your dad made one here before he left as a thank-you. He's cool. For a wizard."

"Yeah, he's okay." Trays. There was cheese, but it hadn't been a lot. I grabbed more and some pasta sheets, just in case. "He rocked up at Beo's place, dropped off my bag."

"He…" She laughed, then said with admiration, "Oh, shit. How'd that go?"

"Don't know. I was asleep. He hasn't answered his phone this evening, so it's entirely possible he's dead and I'll need to murder Beo in retribution and eat the lasagna myself." Ricotta, to speed up the white sauce and tomatoes…fresh? No, some jars would do. Wine would be next door at the adjacent bottle shop. "Unless you want in."

"Hell yes, I'd help you deal with a dead body for lasagna. I'd do it for free, but lasagna is awesome. Your dad's is in the oven. I'm having a food-gasm just smelling it. You know he's kind of cute, for an old guy."

"Nope." I dumped my purchases at the small bench beside the register. "No, I did not hear that. I will not consider this. Do not. I *will* vomit."

She laughed at me. "Okay, okay, I won't." My groceries beeped in the long pause following this. "Tell you about it. Bye!"

"You—" Sudden silence made me pull the phone away to look at the screen. She'd hung up on me.

I bought a bag and some wine and hauled my purchases back to Beo's. It took me a bit of time to figure out which building, and then which number, he was. In the end, the open door helped a lot. I just jiggled every doorhandle on what I thought was the appropriate floor until one opened.

Garlic. Shit, how could I forget garlic?

Resigned to a sub-par lasagna, I got the meat browning. I did find a jar of garlic buried at the back of a bunch of condiments that didn't look like they were used regularly. I dumped it in and called Aspen, then gave her the summary of what had happened.

"You're supposed to be in a safer line of work!" she half-shouted down the phone. "This is not okay! Rory!"

I loved Aspen.

Once I ended the conversation, I took one of Beo's kitchen knives and considered the zucchini. I should grate it, so it cooked down in with the meat. Stealth vegetables were my favorite type. But I also needed to brush up on my craft a bit, and, really, what better time than the present?

So, vegetables washed, I lay them on a chopping board, held the knife at the ready, and breathed in deeply. The spell swam in my head, fragmented, grudging. I pushed back my curls, avoided stabbing myself, and breathed in again. *With this blade I cut you three by three from top to tail.*

The zucchini sat on the chopping board. I stepped closer, peered at it, then gave it a poke. A chunk slid off drunkenly.

Pleasure hummed through me. I repeated the spell, over and over, until the words coalesced in my mind even as I drew in the breath. I gathered my power and felt it sing down into the knife. By the end, I had a few diced zucchinis, some shredded basil, and was pleasantly tired.

While the sauce reduced, I climbed into the shower. I couldn't have said anything too terrible to piss Beo off, otherwise, he wouldn't have left all the stuff out for me. Right?

TWENTY

I'D STOLEN ONE OF HIS SHIRTS, PUT MY CLOTHES INTO HIS TINY EXCUSE OF A washing machine, built the lasagna, popped it into the oven, and started washing up after myself when I heard the front door open. The knife was by my elbow, and the spell still hummed around in my head like a song on repeat, so I wasn't concerned.

But it was Beo who walked in, in his no-gi shorts and shirt, smelling vaguely like bleach and a lot like sweat. "I could smell whatever you've made from more than two blocks away," he told me as a greeting while he crossed the kitchen, expression soft, hands reaching for me. "I was very much hoping the smell was coming from my place." He buried his face in my hair and wrapped his arms around my waist. I leaned back into him with a sigh. *Warm and fuzzy. So much warm and fuzzy.* "I'm glad you're looking brighter. You're hilarious when you're drunk, but you had me worried."

"Thank you for looking after me," I said, and I meant it. "I don't remember a bunch of it. Bernie—one of the witches who healed me—did more than I thought."

"I gathered." He stepped back with a sigh. "I'll shower and be right out. Leave them," he said about the dishes. "I've got them."

Of course, I ignored him. I was already sudsy, so why worry? I considered going and climbing in the shower with him, but he was out so fast I hadn't even finished with the dishes before he was back, poking his nose into the oven and running his hand up my thigh.

"So, my dad visited."

His fingers crept up under the edge of the shirt I'd stolen, then smoothed the curve of my still-naked butt. "Yes. You've been using magick. Is that why the food smells so good? Did you hex it?"

I clucked my tongue in disapproval and let the water out of the sink. "A hex is a bad thing. I didn't hex the lasagna. That's just the magick of garlic, basil, and cheap wine you smell. What did my dad want?"

"Coffee." He turned me around and pressed his lips to mine. "To arm you, and to suss me out. What's in that bag? It reeks like death."

I pulled back, shocked. "It does?" I shook my head. "I'll move it. Sorry. I don't want to...stink up your room, or whatever."

He caught me before I could go. "Your dad wanted it close to you. Weapons and armor I'm guessing, whatever they look like for witches. He wouldn't settle down until he'd seen you and dropped off the bag. He's an okay guy."

Water dripped from his hair onto his clean shirt. Apparently, drying was for Sunwalkers. "Yeah. He is. I'm sorry to spring him on you. That would've been a lot."

He shrugged. "I kinda like that your dad, at least, knows we're a thing." His hand splayed over my butt, lazy, comforting, while my heart warmed. "I see where you get your confidence from. You're better at jiu-jitsu than he is, by a long shot."

Again, I pulled back, horrified. "He went to training?"

"Yeah. Held up okay, too. You're not wearing underwear."

With an arch of my brows, I said, "I didn't want to overdress."

He leaned down a little and waited. I met him halfway and felt the softness of lips, a fleeting show of what felt more like affection than lust. "I think you hit the balance just right. Can I take you to bed, Rory?"

The melty feeling was there, and a jangle of nerves, too. "Is anyone else coming over tonight? Where's my dad?" I reached past him to turn down the oven.

"He headed home. You're visiting him tomorrow?"

Shit. Duke. I nodded, but the subterfuge sat ill. "No one else. Just us. Barring emergencies."

"Okay."

I twisted my arms around his neck and planted a kiss on his mouth. "Bed."

"Hooks," he murmured, reaching for my backside, lifting me. The reflexive sliver of alarm faded as I wrapped my legs around him, framed his face in my hands, stared into that bright, pure green, and let him carry me down the short hallway while his hands kneaded my backside. "I have condoms," he told me. "This time. I figured you have some sort of magickal morning-after. I'm sorry about last time. I wasn't thinking."

I shook my hair back, making my earrings dance. "I'm set. Got wards in place. Pregnancy, diseases, and viruses all covered."

His weight shifted as he kneeled on the bed, lowering us gently. "I still should've asked."

I lay back, happy to watch as he pulled off his shirt and pushed the sweatpants down his hips. Those hard lines, the evidence of all that strength, made my mouth water.

"Forgiven." His eyes trailed over me, and I felt like a delicacy there in his bed wearing his shirt and nothing else. "I'm not here to be coddled."

"That's a shame," he said, kneeling between my open legs, trailing his hands up over my knees. Heat pooled in my belly as his eyes followed the path of his hands, his expression one of intense focus. "Because I want to look after you. I expected you to knock on my door last night, after the dust had settled. Or call."

Guilt tugged at me. "My work phone was taken into evidence. I don't have your number on my personal phone. Seems like a bad idea, in case..." Come to think of it, had I got it back? Yes. Yes, I had. Good, good for me. His hands felt amazing.

"You know how to get to Zane's," he said, still stroking my thighs.

"I do." But I hadn't known who'd paid those faeries. I still couldn't be sure. Even if my gut—or my ovaries—told me it wasn't Beo, I had to be sure. "I wasn't in any shape to be with you anyway."

He paused, hands settled comfortably on the tops of my thighs, and he met my gaze, his expression growing even more intense, if it was possible. "I can be with you and not take you to bed."

My heart trembled. I looked up at the ceiling because I couldn't meet his eyes right then with the guilt and the hope all wrapped up in a messy knot in my chest. "I'm sorry."

"Why?" he pressed.

"Because I didn't come, didn't call, left you to worry, and—" I broke off. He'd come to the office. "Why did you come to the office?" I asked, alarm lancing through me. "Is the pack okay?"

He shot me an irritated look. "To find you. Too injured to make it to me, but well enough to make it to work."

"Okay. Shit." I nudged him aside and sat up, scrubbing at my face. "Look." I blew out a breath. Prepared to dance on a line between truth and lie. "The faeries that attacked me travelled through the same rift that the lycans who killed Betty used. And it's on your turf, Beo."

He sat back, too, face unreadable. "You thought it was me who sent them."

"No." That I didn't have to lie about. I met his gaze and didn't pretend I wasn't angry too. "No, I never thought it was you. But I do think someone's setting you up. I don't want to make you an easy target, Beo."

His eyes narrowed slightly as he studied my expression. Traffic noise filtered through, making the silence between us seem louder.

"You were trying to protect me?"

I stood, frustrated. "No. Yes. I crashed hard. Adrenaline and aftereffects of magick use. I'm not used to that stuff anymore. And I think that wound on my back—" I shook my head and waved my hand. It didn't matter. "I was a mess. I couldn't think straight. I knew other people were worried. I knew it was big, and I knew I couldn't do it myself. I crashed with a friend I trust, who isn't involved, because it was all I could do." Why had I been so wiped out? "I don't know why it all went down the way it did. My body—my brain—didn't respond right. I don't get it. I'm sorry I worried you. I never meant to. I could've gotten your number from a colleague, if I'd stopped to think about it, but I didn't stop to think. Or I couldn't. I don't know."

He stood, too, but without that sharp, almost judgemental, focus. "Next time, put me at the top of your list."

My poor heart trembled again. I folded my arms to hold the hope in, to crush the fear. Not because he was thinking about me being attacked again. Because he was planning a future. And I couldn't have a future with a lycan who was my client. Not until I'd definitely crossed Duke's name off my list of worries, and even then...

"Have you tracked down the lycans who are riftrunning on your turf?" I asked, keeping the question as neutral as I could.

His jaw tightened. "Not yet. They're very smart. And they've got help."

I sat there, in his bed, with him naked and me almost so, and turned that over in my head. I'd known he'd been trying, of course. He met my eyes and said quietly, "If it comes to it, Rory, I'm going to deal with them first and call you second."

Righteous indignation flooded me. "Yes, please protect me, the helpless, little woman." I climbed off the bed, disgusted. "That's all I ever wanted, Beo, was a man to swoop in and rescue me. Pray tell, do you have a castle we can return to once you're done slaying the foul beast, so I can have happily ever after, too?"

He shifted, and somehow, in that one move, managed to block the door. I folded my arms, anger hot and bright in my veins. "Rory, that isn't an insult. I know you can handle yourself. But there are faeries and lycans —who would you set on fire when there's fur flying everywhere? And they'd all go for you, thinking you're an easy target."

"Is that supposed to make me feel better?" I demanded, throwing my arms up. "Wow, Beo!"

His jaw worked some more. "I know one of the lycans." The words fell grudgingly from his mouth. "And he wants to hurt me."

My arms dropped, forgotten, while my heart did a long, slow roll, then dived straight into a warm pool of adoration. Hurting me would hurt him. That was what he meant, because he cared about me. What a fucked-up way to be told that.

"Beo." The word was too thick. I stopped and cleared my throat. This was all wrong. "Look, I am not a liability."

He stepped forward hesitantly, and reached out his big, blunt fingers.

"I know." They lingered, offered, checked, and I turned my face into his hand, feeling sick. "If it's important to you…"

"It is. It's my job. They're your pack, Beo," I told him seriously, "but they're mine, too. You all are."

He drew in a deep breath and stepped closer to me. "Going to fight me for my title, Caretaker?"

The jest fell flat. Aside from anything else, I doubted that Alphas fought for their role. Their turf, maybe, but not their role. "Never picked you as someone who couldn't share their power."

He looked worried. I understood perfectly. This wasn't a simple set up. I wondered if he knew exactly how complex it would become if someone discovered I was sleeping with him—the investigations, the transfers, the fine-tooth combs. "This could get messy, Beo. If there's an 'us.'"

"Seems to me like there is an 'us,'" he said slowly. "And it's already messy. And we're dealing with it." He cupped my face tenderly and swept his thumb over my cheekbone in a caress that made my heart roll over and wallow in all that affection. "I'm not scared of a bit of mess."

Gratitude, worry, compassion, affection… I drew it all in, drew it deep and lifted my hands to his chest. I felt the resilience in his flesh, the heat of him, the curve and dip of the muscles there. This man—this lycan—was good where it counted. "So, am I forgiven for not calling last night?" I asked him as his hand drifted up to tangle in my hair.

"This time." His eyes scoured the marks on my face. "They would've killed you if you weren't the only witch alive who can cast without speaking."

"I am not the—" I broke off, because suddenly words became really hard. He was right about my ability to cast—not that I was the only one. It was highly unusual and took intensive training, but it was possible. Avoiding those sorts of pitfalls was one of the reasons I'd had to learn to cast without speaking. It wasn't the main reason, but it was one of them.

He cradled my skull in his hand, tipped my face back and whispered his lips over the bruises on my face. "I don't care," he told me quietly. "I'm just glad, Rory. I knew you were okay. I saw you standing up, talking to the police. I knew you were alive."

The warmth in my chest spread until it was the sweetest ache between my legs and in my breasts. "I think I'm overdressed after all."

"Let me help you with that." His hands slid down my waist, found the hem of the shirt and lifted. My body eased out gently, no earrings catching, no hair pulling. "Can I do anything else?" he asked me softly.

With a nod, I let myself fall back into his bed. "Be gentle with me. And slow. I need slow and gentle."

His hand found my knee again, then trailed upwards. "You want me to make love to you."

It wasn't the words I would've chosen, but I shivered all the same. I felt agonizingly vulnerable and wonderfully cherished. "Yes."

He eased down beside me, turned my face, lingered, and found my lips. The kiss was languid and sweet, and the ache became a simmering want. "You liked me stroking the undersides of your breasts last time. Maybe I should do that again."

Impatience tugged at me. It had been so sexy last time as he'd explored, checked-in, explored further. But right now, I just wanted simple and easy and right. Maybe that wasn't fair. But I wasn't feeling fair. I was feeling fragile.

"Beo, I'm fully consenting. If there's something I do or don't want, I'll tell you as it comes to me, I promise. Just"—I hooked an arm around his neck, pulled him down—"just do. Don't ask. I'm done with words."

"I don't want to hurt you," he said against my lips. "I don't want you to have to say no. 'Yes' is easier. 'Yes' comes before things go wrong."

I held him close, cuddled into him, wondered who the hell I was and what was wrong with me. "Yes. Yes, to anything you want."

He nibbled at my ear. "Cheating." But his lips found my jaw and neck while one hand skimmed down my body. Relief rolled through me, and I turned my head, offering him more. Teeth skimmed the muscle where my neck joined my shoulder and sent sudden shocks of wanting through me.

Gentle touches on the underside of my breast made me sigh. I'd coiled my hands around his shoulders when I felt the teeth on my neck joined with hard suction. My mind blanked for a blissful moment as arcs of sensation bounced around my body. I moaned, trying to pull him closer.

"Again." The word was a mewl, not the demand I felt. "Beo."

I pressed him closer, shifting so I was further under him. He repeated it. Teeth, heat, the flick of his tongue. Air whistled as I drew it in. The muscles in his back bunched under my hand, and I felt my breath shake, every part of me waiting, anticipating, poised. He shifted, moving to the other side of my neck, then repeated, until I was breathing in short, sharp gasps. I rubbed myself against him, mindless, hungry.

He kissed and nibbled on my collarbone. I wrapped my legs around his hips, needing more. One hand knocked my knee down. He shifted his weight, trapping my leg between both of his. I snarled and shifted, but I didn't risk injuring any important parts of him by wriggling that leg. "You said slow," he reminded me, cruising down my body. "You said what I want."

"Fuck." The word was a sob, a plea. I sank my hands into his hair, forcing myself to lie back as he rubbed his cheek against the side of my breast. Warm, wet heat beside my nipple made my hands tighten in his hair. I shuddered, waiting, holding my breath.

He lifted his head a little, nuzzled at the spot with his lips then the tip of his nose. "The skin right here. So soft, so sweet."

I felt him turn his head millimetre by millimetre, felt the brush of his breath against my nipple. Desperate for more, for the flood of sensation to widen and deepen, I arched, half expecting him to pull back, to moderate what I got.

Instead, he took me in his mouth and enveloped me, sending my instincts clamouring for more. My hands flexed and fisted. I twisted, moaning, seeking. His weight shifted, and before I'd even felt his hand between my legs, they'd fallen open in anticipation.

I knew those hands, trusted them. I knew how he'd touch me, and I knew it'd be just right.

Oh, fuck.

I was all but in love with him.

I fell back, and all urgency flooded out of my muscles as I stared at the ceiling. I couldn't love a lycan. I could enjoy, appreciate, respect, even care about one.

But I couldn't love one.

That wasn't messy. It was catastrophic.

With something that sounded like a cross between a growl and a purr, his fingers traced my opening, slipped firmly over my clitoris. I felt my hips arch, fall back, my legs spread further, and I was suddenly very scared.

I couldn't do this. I couldn't give him all the trust, all my hopes and dreams. I didn't even know what my dreams were yet. I had life to live, fuckery to commit, adventures to have. It wouldn't work. I had to... I had to...

I had to figure out if he'd worked with Duke in the past. If he could still be, somehow, working with him.

I couldn't sneak around for the rest of my life, not calling him, not texting him, for fear of my phone records being pulled. I couldn't pretend I had no plans, no partner, when people talked, asked, joked.

Damn it. I was in way too deep, way too fast, and this was not the plan.

He changed the angle, kept my pace. His hands gripped, flexed on my hips, and I felt the familiar arc of hunger. I could've changed my angle, taken him in then. But I wasn't ready. Not for any of it.

Fingers firm and sure, he traced my opening again, dipped inside just a little, just enough to catch my breath and send shivers up my spine before he found my clitoris and pressed one fingertip to the side, rocking back and forth.

The pleasure rolled through me, but it felt hollow, almost performative. I closed my eyes, better to focus on my body, on the edge, getting closer. It felt wrong, though.

"Stop." I sighed, frustrated with myself, with my heart and with my brain. "I'm scared, okay?" I took his face in my hands, looking into his eyes. "And overwhelmed."

"Okay," he said quietly, resting his forehead against mine. "This isn't sexual overwhelm."

Insightful. Did I put insightful on a list of good traits, or irritating ones? "Now I am super turned on and also super frustrated and scared and worried and..." Excited. Desperate. Hopeful. "Please, Mr. Perfect, show me how to fix this conundrum."

"More sex, or less," he said, no hesitation. "Those are our options. I'm cool with either."

I believed him, though I could very much feel his preference. And it was mine, too. "More."

"You want to set the pace?"

My goddamn traitorous heart shivered. I could rub myself against him and get off. I could rub myself without him and get off faster. But that wasn't the point. "No. I like you all over me."

"I like being all over you. And under you. And in you." He pressed his lips to mine, leaned back so he knelt between my legs, and slid down to press a kiss to my belly, short and hungry. "I want to taste you again."

My brain just gave up at those words. I arching my back a little to make it easier and faster.

He nuzzled his mouth into just the right spot, and I sighed, long and deep. *Just right.* That was what I could deal with now.

I took. His mouth was warm and firm and the purrs, or growls, or whatever it was he did, vibrated ever so gently. Gratitude rushed through me with wanting, hot and sweet, flooding my system. Overwhelm, I'd said. I was on the mark. And it felt so good to be overwhelmed—to be undone by him. Rhythmically. Firmly.

The hunger in me was a beast, but it whimpered rather than snarled. The tide ebbed and flowed, ebbed and flowed, carrying me higher until I gasped, until I was boneless with it. And when he stopped, I shuddered and sat up, desperate for more. For everything.

His hands on my hips lifted, and my arms gave way, sending me falling back. I barely noticed, didn't care. He sealed us together with a hard thrust, and it was exactly what I wanted and still not enough, not nearly enough.

With a flex of my muscles, I drew him deeper. Further. I heard his breath catch and shake in response and then he moved, and I could've just dangled there, pummelled by sensation, drinking it up. The tide stopped ebbing. It flowed higher and higher until I thought my heart would burst, until my whole world was the thrust and sway of the rhythm he set, the stroke of heat inside me.

More, I wanted to say, but the word was too far away. *Please don't stop.* I heard his rasping breath, felt terror splash through me at the idea that this could end. That he might be further along than me.

His fingers tightened on my hips, the flesh of my thighs. His strokes became slower. The angle changed slightly, until all that was left of me on the bed was my shoulders. I felt the build of heat and hunger hit fever pitch and, no longer worried, just gave myself over to him.

The ripples of pleasure started deep inside. They grew, and I was carried along, drinking it up, lost to it.

I gasped for breath, still feeling the aftershocks, when he shoved me further up the bed and fell on me, hammering into me deep and fast. I wound my arms around his neck and locked my legs, then flexed my internal muscles, holding him clamped tightly.

The growl was half shocked, half exultant as he shuddered, driving himself home.

He held himself there, arms locked on either side of me, panting. Sweat dripped from his nose onto my forehead, and I wiggled, warm, sated, and content. I kissed him, languishing in that expression of utter bliss he wore. I probably did, too.

"Sorry for overthinking," I said. I felt foolish.

"I forgive you," he said, panting. "I don't know what you did, but I forgive you." He shifted, moved, and stretched out beside me. "Have I told you how good you smell?"

Taken by surprise, I blinked. "I don't think so."

"You smell real good, Rory. And now you smell like I've been at you, which just proves there is hope for this world yet."

My out-of-touch heart bumped against my ribs. I shook myself, got up, felt pure agony from my back, and caught my breath as it washed over me.

"Rory!" The word was quick, urgent. "Why didn't you say?" The accusation held more guilt than anger, but it was all I could do to stand.

A curse, something guttural and growling in a language I didn't know or couldn't recognize, met my ears as the pain began to ebb. I breathed shallowly, carefully. Beo took my arm. "Come on." He was coaxing, gentle now. I shook my head but let myself be towed along.

My back. Had it opened up again? Hellfire, it felt like it had, all the way to the bone. "I didn't feel it. Well, maybe I did it when I got up."

His expression said he didn't believe me, but he pulled off the gauze from my back, tossed it in the sink, and opened his cabinets. I stared at the blood-soaked wad of fabric. No wonder it hurt. "If this is after a healing, what was it like before?"

I didn't argue while he cleaned the wound and sealed it closed with a series of butterfly strips that I wasn't at all surprised to see in his very well stocked first—and second—aid kit.

Once I was patched up, he sat me in a chair, checked on our dinner, threw together a salad, and kept a weathered eye on me. As if I was going to combust or something.

Silence reigned until he slid a plate of lasagna in front of me and heaped some salad beside it. "It smells amazing."

It did smell good, and I realized I was ravenous. I'd just loaded my mouth when he said, from the bench beside me, "Do you want kids?"

The food turned into a giant lump, and I coughed, choking on it. It traveled down my throat in a ball of pure agony.

Wordlessly, he got up and disappeared. Breathing through the horrible sensation helped me avoid thinking about his question.

He set a glass of water in front of me. It didn't soothe the hurt. "So," he said, pulling up his chair again. "Do you?"

Shit. Did I? "I don't know. Everyone tells me I do."

"But?"

I couldn't look at him. I focused on my food. "No 'but,' I just really am on the fence. I don't know what I want yet." I forked up more food, then inspiration struck. "What's your family like?"

He finished his mouthful before saying, "Some good, some bad, like any. Big. I have a lot of half siblings, some step." He shrugged. "We don't all get along. We didn't all end up fighting for the same cause. What about you? You've got your dad. The children you grew up with."

I nodded, a bit more comfortable with this topic. "And my Oma. That was it for me." I ate a bit more, my mind whirring. He hadn't mentioned a specific sibling he was close to. "Aspen was like my sister. Almost like a twin because we did everything at the same time. We even came after one another on the role at school. Oma taught her a little magick, but her parents are pretty cut and dried, so she didn't practice much. What about you? Was there anyone you traveled Overworld with? Or were close to?"

"No one I'll be asking you to meet, so you don't have to worry about that." He somehow managed to load his fork with both lasagna and salad in a balancing act that deeply impressed me.

And totally avoided answering that desperate attempt to get information, to avoid tomorrow.

To avoid Duke.

"The pack is my family now." He considered his full fork, then said, "I wonder if Aspen would be happy to meet me, considering."

A chill crept up my spine. "Considering what?"

He sent me a droll look. "Considering a lycan killed Brandon."

I put down my fork. My silver knife was so close, in the bag at the foot of his bed. And it may as well have been on the other side of the moon for all the good it would do me. With my heart in my throat, I said, carefully, "I never told you that."

"Yes, you did." He reached over, brushed a hand lightly over my shoulder. "Just not with words. I'm sorry, Rory. I wish I..." I looked at him, waiting, feeling sick. "I wish I could have been there. When we're Shifted, there isn't much that'll stop us."

I knew I definitely hadn't told him that. I hadn't talked about that to anyone except Oma. Even Aspen didn't need those details. "How do you know the lycan was Shifted? The angle of my hip, Beo?"

He shot me an irritated look. "I assumed what form he'd wear. We wouldn't go up against a witch, her friend, and whoever else in our vulnerable form, would we? Sit down and eat. I'm not going to jump down your throat about it. Good and bad isn't based on where you were born or how. It's based on the choices you make as you go."

I hadn't noticed myself standing, putting some distance between us. Believing him was all too easy. Within moments, I was picking up the fork, chasing around a slice of carrot.

"This is why I don't want kids. Things are too hard to figure out for myself, much less to guide someone else through."

He chewed quietly for a while. "Maybe. It could be simple, though. Let others figure out right and wrong. Just find somewhere quiet, do what makes you happy." He stood and pressed a kiss to my head that made my heart whimper. "It's a nice dream."

Twenty-One

It was time to come clean.

"I'm still not certain they're related," I said to Edward, sitting in my car at SuperSec, on my phone like a dirty snitch, and feeling so wrong.

"It's a strong link," Edward said, the words crackling through the poor connection. "You've done good work, Aurora."

The praise didn't help. "They have nothing to do with Arthur."

"Maybe. Maybe not. I do hope not. Coincidences keep stacking up, though," he said. "Go. See what you can find out and report back. Blessed be."

I shoved my phone in my pocket and got out of the car. It was surreal to be back at SuperSec. To see everything exactly the way it was when I'd left my work years ago. Plenty of people still recognized me, though a lot of the entry-level personnel had changed.

I made my way through the visitor's corridors, escorted, double-checked, then cleared.

I waited as high-powered, reinforced doors whooshed open, as security codes were entered, as passes were scanned. I thought of Beo as he'd been last night, fast asleep with his leg thrown over my hip, his hand curled up against my jaw. I'd lain there worrying while he dreamt. And for some reason, that, too, had felt right.

I wanted him to dream. I wanted it for him, his pack, and the little girl he'd taken in.

Maybe if he dreamed hard enough, we could make something work somehow.

The light above the door went green, and the automatic lock opened with a hiss. I walked into the room, the last check before I'd be face-to-face with Duke.

My heart beat a slow, heavy rhythm. I suspected Beo could hear my heart rate; I was confident now that was how the girl had read me so easily when she'd asked about healing—not magick, just senses that worked differently.

For that reason, I stopped, centered myself, and breathed. Spells swam in my head like schools of fish, calming and strong. I went through one last metal detector, was patted down once more and then cleared to go ahead.

I hadn't showered before I left. I'd woken Beo up and had my way with him. I'd done it deliberately, manipulatively, and it made me feel ill to think about it.

The guards left, closing the airlock behind them. The final door opened.

My Oma always told me that if I was ashamed of something, I probably shouldn't do it. When I looked at Duke, chained to the wall, his hands clasped together and the silver collar that connected to a hard silver harness across his chest, I was ashamed.

If I'd told Beo what I was doing, maybe it would've made a difference. The man wasn't a threat to me. Maybe he was to others, but no others that I considered a loss to the world.

Duke's eyes glittered. He was clean shaven, but his brown hair was a little long, and, in that moment, the resemblance to Beo was enough to make my legs go to jelly. But at least Brandon's ghost was silent.

Over the intercom, the recorded message informed me I had seven minutes.

"Do you remember me?" I asked him, pleased at how regular my heart was. I wasn't scared. I was heartsick.

His answer was to bare his teeth.

I walked further into the room. It held nothing. Cameras were protected behind warded bulletproof glass. It was just Duke, his restraints, and me. "And how is good old…" He said a word that was part snarl and sounded something like *hrrrughwoophe*.

If I could ever replicate that, I suspected I'd have Beo's lycan name. "Oh, you can ask him when you see him." And, feeling ill, I didn't try to chase the bluff down with a smile. I just raised my eyebrows and folded my arms.

"If you came here to gloat that you've been wallowing in my brother's cum, you've got my condolences, Witch," he said with another toothy snarl. And, though I was braced for it, I didn't go back in time, didn't see him coated in blood over the broken body of my friend. "I couldn't care less if—" He froze then, his chest heaving as he took a deep breath, then another.

Unease crawled down my back as I watched the skin beneath his silver collar go red, then white, his smile turning into a huge, furious snarl.

"He has her," he said, the words shuddering with pure, undiluted rage that turned the unease into full-blown terror in a moment. "You tell my brother, next time he's between your legs, that I will take what is mine!" And he began to thrash, to ripple in a sickening, unnatural way that made the hair stand up on my arms and spells swarm in my head like hornets. I stared, my mouth dry. Still, I saw Beo, not Duke. "I will take her!" he screamed, as his restraints bulged and creaked. Alarms sounded. In the room, they were muffled, but I recognized them all the same. "She is *mine!*"

Without haste, I walked back to the door and stepped through it the moment it opened. I'd been there less than two minutes. I could hear his screams as I walked out, as the door shut behind me. The sound of metal tearing and breaking made my heart stumble in my chest.

Something heavy hit the door behind me. I glanced over my shoulder and saw the faintest of dents there. My heart rate tripled. Those doors were ten-centimeter steel with wood and silver reinforcements to hold the strongest, most dangerous prisoners.

Howls, furious howls, shouts, and then screams of pain. Human screams.

Death screams.

My hands shook as I held out my temporary clearance card. Every instinct told me not to turn my back. Told me to run as hard and as fast as I could.

I was whisked out through layers of doors. Alarms beeped on watches and radios wailed. Four people ran past me in full combat gear. The wizard of the group shot me a quick, unreadable look. He was so young that he still hadn't grown into his staff.

Nausea rose like a hot fist of sickness in my throat.

Something crashed behind me, and I heard tearing metal, snarling, howls, shouts, then chanting, cut off by a high-pitched scream that ended so fast I couldn't help but look over my shoulder again, couldn't help the cold spurt of terror.

That poor wizard.

What had I done?

I was hustled out, whisked through the exit procedure that usually took a good half hour in less than two minutes. I barely drew breath the whole time. I couldn't hear the words people said to me. Duke's threats rang in my head, screaming in my heart. It didn't matter.

They got me out, as I'd gotten out plenty of people in my time.

It brought me no comfort to be out in the sun, crossing the parking lot with wings on my feet. Bad things happened in the sun just the same as they did in the dark.

Not only was he not friendly with Beo, they were enemies. And Beo sheltered Duke's daughter against Duke's will.

Now, because of me, Duke knew it.

TWENTY-TWO

I DIDN'T SLOW DOWN FOR A SOLID HALF HOUR. TWO EMERGENCY VEHICLES screamed past me within minutes. I sucked in air like a drowning woman and put the pedal to the floor until the shaking of my hands made steering impossible and I pulled over into an emergency stopping lane.

He couldn't get out. There was no way. He'd done it once, yeah, but we'd learned a lot since then. The security measures—the silver! He was kept in the highest of high security.

Surely they knew better than to give him an inch. But if he hadn't broken free in that room, I'd eat my wand.

Supernatural prison worked similarly to our regular prisons. Word could get out. Allies could get in. Would Duke have enough friends, enough leverage?

Shit, he would be able to get word out if he wanted it badly enough, if he was connected.

The pack needed to leave and go into hiding somewhere. Now. Anywhere. That girl couldn't be hurt again. I wouldn't let it happen.

I picked up my work phone, struggling to make my fingers do their job. I slammed my palm on the steering wheel. "Get it together!" I shouted at myself, furious.

I'd never been good at taking advice, and I'd always been shit at taking orders. I opened the door and slammed it. Walked off the freeway in the sun and the wind. The cold cut through me, and I welcomed it. Shivering, I sat, put my head between my knees, and breathed.

I made a list in my head, things I needed to check, people I needed to contact. Before I'd finished, my phone went off. I glanced at the display. *Dad.*

I let it ring out, pushing it away. I'd call him later and make plans when a kid's life didn't hang in the balance. It stopped then started again.

Furious, I answered. "Hi Dad. Can I call you back?"

"Are you at SuperSec?" he demanded.

My heart jumped back into my throat. "Not anymore."

"Good. Word is some serious shit is going down. How far off are you?" The force behind the words very clearly said, *so I can keep you safe.*

"I'm going straight back to Melbourne. Driving." I hadn't thought it through. But it fit. It worked. I got up and walked back to my car. A truck went past pushing the speed limit and made my little hatch rock in the emergency lane. I waited for the cars following it to pass before I climbed in and did my belt.

"Aurora?" Dad said, and I realized I'd missed something. I hadn't heard, hadn't noticed.

Why hadn't it occurred to me that he could smell more than just Beo? How could I have known that Beo would carry traces of her, though?

How could I know it mattered?

"I just fucked up, Dad," I admitted, feeling sick. "With Duke. I think I've put some of the lycans in danger. I need to do some damage control, okay?"

"Do you need help?"

I closed my eyes, my heart drumming in my ears. "I love you, Dad."

"I love you, too, Sunshine." He sounded even more worried. "I'll come pick you up. You don't sound good. We'll go together. There's—"

"No." I swallowed down the lump in my throat. "No. I'm in no danger. And, honestly, I think at this point, I'll be doing a lot of emergency paperwork." *Transfers. Secure lodgings. A car. Groceries. Name changes.* Hellfire, was there budget for all of this support?

Had Duke gotten out? What could one lycan do against a pack?

But he didn't want the pack, just the girl.

And she didn't have legal support.

She didn't exist.

She couldn't exist in our system until Beo got her paperwork.

"I need to go, Dad," I said, drawing in a deep breath. "Please, don't come rushing out playing hero. I've got this. I'm shaken because it got ugly in there with Duke. But I've got this."

He didn't sound convinced when he said, "Okay. But call me. Or your Oma. She can't wait to meet Beo."

I closed my eyes. He'd have to leave, and I couldn't, not at first, not without being obvious, and not without questions. "Sure," I agreed because I didn't have the strength to do more. "Bye, Dad."

I didn't hear his sign off, just hit disconnect, tossed my personal phone aside, and grabbed my work one.

I scrolled past Beo in my contacts, though my chest burned. Instead, I went to the end, to Vince the ICT guy.

He picked up right when I dreaded talking to voicemail. "Hey, Rory," he said, clearing his throat. "You're in the field today, right?"

"Right." I glanced at the acres of farmland spreading out to my left as another truck roared past on the freeway beside me. "I need a solid, Vince. A quiet solid."

"Hey, they're my specialty," he said brightly. "Actually, I haven't done many. But I can learn, right? Hit me. Oh. Wait. I'll just, uh, duck outside, shall I?"

I closed my eyes. How dodgy was what I was asking, really? "No, it's fine. I just need to know if there are any new or pending clients on my list."

He cleared his throat. "That's, um, that's it?"

"Yeah." I drew in a deep breath. "Yeah, that's it."

That's the difference between the full force of governmental support and a rogue lycan pack: a piece of paper, a box with a tick.

From the other end of the phone, I heard some clicking, the satisfying clacks of a mechanical keyboard. "Your day going okay? You sound pretty wrung out."

I blew out a breath and leaned my head back. "Could've been worse," I admitted, feeling sick. I could be dead and unable to send up the alarm.

"You aren't selling it," he said warily. "I'm looking while I'm talking, by the way. Nothing so far."

"That's cool. I'm pretty shit company right now, Vince. I might pass on the small talk."

"Sure," he said, then cleared his throat. "But I could get Lilith to call. I know you two are tight."

"Not yet." I turned on my car and started to move. "I've got a lot of calls to make."

"Oh. One of those days." He was quiet for a moment, and I put on my indicator, watching traffic, waiting for a good, long break before getting the car rolling, then merging. "You're hands-free right, Rory?"

"Right."

"Good. Not that, you know, I'm a cop or whatever. Sorry. I'm sorry. You said no small talk. Um. I can't see anything. Oh, wait." Hope exploded, made my hands tighten on the wheel. "You've got a witch coming from, um, Germany? Yeah, Germany. Super secret, from the look of it. Van Der Holst is managing it. Must be another protective custody deal."

The hope rushed out of me, leaving me hollow and light-headed. "Thanks, Vince, for looking."

"Hey, that's okay. It's kind of my job anyway, to make sure that's all synced, so it's not even really a solid. It's just an everyday."

I glued my eyes to the road. "That's cool. Look, I'll see you when I'm in the office."

"Yeah, yeah that'd be good. Maybe we could get coffee or something."

"I like coffee. But maybe give me a few, okay? I think my brain's going to be a bit full for people."

"Yeah, sure, no worries, of course." He cleared his throat again.

"Have a good one, Vince."

"Oh. Yeah. You, too."

I hung up and drove with just road noise to keep me company for a while. It wasn't enough to drown out Duke's roars as they bounced around in my head.

Two options: go official and get the girl put in a camp where she'd be even less protected, or go rogue and risk her life, my license, my freedom, and the pack's lives.

Fuck.

It wasn't even my decision to make.

I scrolled back up through my contacts and hit Beo's number. "Hello, Caretaker," he said, the words warm, quiet, and welcoming.

I felt so sick. Why hadn't I listened to my Oma? "Hey. I need to see you. It's urgent."

His voice changed, became lower, harder. "Are you safe?"

A hysterical laugh bubbled in my throat. "Yeah. But we need to talk."

"Okay." The word was cool, clipped. "Where? When?"

"I'm"—I looked at the turn-off I was approaching—"about forty minutes out of Melbourne. Somewhere we won't be overheard."

"I've got a one o'clock private tuition. Can it wait until two? Say so if it can't, Rory. I can reschedule."

Fuck. What was an extra hour? "Two. Your place?"

He hesitated. "If it's pack-related trouble, Zane's is more defensible."

"Not today." Please, not today. "Not as far as I know." And I didn't want Zane to be there, or the girl. I glanced in my rearview. Nothing except the person who'd been tailgating me since...I couldn't remember since when. The exits blurred past me, jumbled. "Look, I'm probably freaking out over nothing. It can wait until tonight."

"It'll make you feel better to talk soon, so we'll talk soon. And I'll have my phone on, okay? Keep in contact."

I let out a long breath. Could I go underground with this man, give up everything? Would he even want me to? "Yeah, sure. Take care."

"You, too," he murmured, his voice dipping again in worry and affection. "You've got the death bag, don't you?"

And it struck me as a little sad that I knew exactly what he meant without needing clarification. "Yeah." I wouldn't have gone near Duke without my Retrievals gear.

"Good. I feel better knowing you have some tricks on you. I've got to go. Be safe."

I hung up, stress churning in my gut. I hadn't handled that well. But I couldn't tell him over the phone. Could I?

I should have. What did a face matter, a body? It was the exchange of information. I wasn't calling him back. So, I was a coward. If I was doing this, I'd do it properly. "Like a proper coward," I muttered to myself, rolling my head on my shoulders, feeling them pop and twang as some of the tension was released.

I turned on the radio, listened for any mention of an escape from SuperSec, and heard nothing about it. There was plenty about property prices, a flood up north, and a serial killer on the peninsula. Not my circus, not my monkeys. I turned it off when some cheerful pop song played. Fuck cheer.

I watched the minutes crawl by. When I got to the city, I picked up a drive-thru coffee using the cafe's app, navigated traffic, and executed a bullshit hook-turn—only in Melbourne did you have to turn right from the lefthand lane. And to make it worse, I was watched by a bemused gaggle of international students. By the time I'd somehow survived that shitfuckery of a road rule, I had to circle around trying to find a park near Beo's place. Urgency drummed at my breast, and I ignored it as best as I could. When I did get a space, it took all my rusty parallel parking skills to get my little hatch into it. *One-thirty.* Half an hour. I downloaded the parking app and tried not to worry, not to think. I failed, saved my car, logged my park, and didn't close the app so I'd remember to exit the park and not be overcharged.

Then I punched in the numbers for SuperSec, listened to the automated message directing me to the correct person to answer my questions, and followed the instructions. *One thirty-nine.* I got through to inquiries and sat on hold. *One fifty.* Eventually I spoke to a person. "Sorry for the wait," she said in a sorry-not-sorry sort of way. "You've reached SuperSec Inquiries and you're speaking to Jen. Just to let you know, our call might be monitored for quality and training purposes. Do you consent to this?"

"Hi, Jen. That's fine." I didn't have my wallet. The realization struck me like a blow. "I'm Caretaker Aurora Gold, working out of Melbourne. Today I was at your facility making inquiries regarding one of my clients. I was hoping for an update on the status of a particular prisoner, as it relates to my clients."

"Have you got your license number, Caretaker?" Jen asked me.

"Not on me, no." *Because of fucking course not.*

She paused. "Hold on, I'll see if I can find you in the system."

I closed my eyes. Please, let the paperwork have gone through. She was silent, tapping away. "Can you spell your surname, Caretaker?"

"G-O-L-D, like the metal."

A pause then more clicking. I opened my eyes, glanced at the clock on the dash. Two. I hadn't heard Beo arrive. Would I? I peered in the side mirror. I could see his building from where I'd parked. But if he had a one o'clock, he'd be tied up for an hour. Ten minutes travel, give or take the time to get out. Small talk. He could be another twenty minutes yet. "I can't see you. Can I have your date of birth, Caretaker?"

I wanted to beat my head against the steering wheel. "Sure." I rattled off the date mechanically, heard more clicking, a puzzled noise. It didn't sound like it meant "Yeah, sure, ask me anything."

"I've got you as contract Retrievals, not currently contracted, no longer allocated to a team," she said, still clicking. "Your clearances don't cover information for inmates as far as I can see. I'm sorry, Aurora."

Fuck. "Look," I began, turning on what charm I could, "I'm new in the role, and it must not have gone through yet. Perhaps—"

"I'm sure you understand, Aurora. We can't give out information on inmates without proper clearance," she said in that sorry-not-sorry tone.

"Yeah, I get it." I blew out air. Edward could get me the info. "Thanks for trying, Jen."

"You're welcome. Can I help you with anything else today, Aurora?"

"No, no, that's it. Thanks."

"No problems at all. If you could complete a short, thirty-second survey about the quality of our service, it will help us to assist others in the future. You have a good day."

I hung up on the automated message that played, because right then I didn't think I was a fair judge of anyone's service. *Two-ten.* I got out of the car, glanced at my Retrievals bag, hesitated, and left it. But I kept my keys in my pocket as I locked my car. I loitered, checked my phone, and considered calling Edward. But I didn't want to be talking to him when Beo arrived. *Two-fifteen.* I scrolled through some messages. *Two-sixteen.*

Apparently, this afternoon was a small-talk day. I went over to the gutter, balanced on the balls of my feet, dropped my heels, and stretched out my calves. I stretched out my hip flexors and felt the wind pick up, tugging my hair across my face. Surely he was almost here. I glanced at my phone. *Two twenty-six.* Shit. Not only was he taking forever, but my flexors were a mess.

I'd stretched out my neck and had moved on to my shoulders before I heard the rumble of his bike. I pulled out my phone as he guided the bike into a parking bay marked for residents only. *Two thirty-three.*

He climbed off, pulled off the helmet, and took out his keys. I felt sick as I looked at his face and saw the resemblance. With Duke's current hair cut, they were all but mirror images. "Sorry. She was late to start." The wind tugged at my hair again. I dashed it back and headed towards him. "Let's go in and…" he stopped, turning slowly to face me.

The hard set of his shoulders, the way the hand on his keys went white-knuckled would've told me, even if his face hadn't fallen into hard, unreadable lines.

"I saw Duke today," I said exhausted. "And I need to talk to you. In private."

His lips thinned. "Duke."

"I assume you know him by another name. Private?" I prompted.

He nodded curtly and led me into the building, no more apologies, no gentle looks or offers of hospitality. He shut the door behind us and turned on me. The darkness of the small entry room made it feel close, crowded, and I wasn't taken any further in.

"Talk."

The fury in him made the nausea churn higher. "He smelled her. The girl you're hiding."

His eyes flashed. "Of course, he did," he said softly. "Is there anything else, Caretaker?"

The coldness of those words, the harshness, made my heart shrivel in my breast. *This is what you get,* I told it ruthlessly.

"He wants her back."

"He wants her dead," he corrected, the words precise, cold.

The fury in him made me want to shudder. I refused to let the weakness show. "Her paperwork hasn't gone through yet. I checked on the way back this afternoon. Legally, if I alert the police, she'll be taken from your care and be more vulnerable."

"Your system looks after you," he said, the words still soft and all the more hurtful because of it. "Not us. We look after us. And we will. Is there anything else?"

My heart bled. "I'm on your side, Beo."

He opened his door, silent and dismissive.

An apology felt weak, pointless. I took a deep breath and nodded. "I mean it. Call me. Above board or not. If I can help, I will." But I didn't wait for a response. If I was in his shoes…

The sun glared into my eyes, so I glanced at my phone. *Two thirty-eight.*

I climbed behind the wheel and pulled into traffic, stopping somewhere where I didn't have to parallel park.

Could I go home yet? I so badly wanted to go home, to curl up in my bed to hide, weep, and mourn. The thought gave me a purpose. *My wallet.* I navigated to the police station, avoiding any more hook-turns, my heart beating. Time dripped by as I let myself get lost in the traffic.

Had I said this could get messy? What I had meant was colossally fucked up.

TWENTY-THREE

WHILE I WAS AT THE POLICE STATION, I ASKED IF DETECTIVE TAIG O'MALLEY was in. When he was, I figured I may as well wait. Time had stopped mattering to me.

Would I ever see the lycans again?

Taig showed me in and offered me coffee. I waved it off. "What can I do for you?" he asked me, closing the door on a small meeting room.

"I've got information on an active case I thought might interest you," I said, somehow managing to sound professional. "Beo and Duke are brothers. Whether they're half or full, I can't say for sure, but Duke referred to him as his brother when I saw him today."

He wore a much more suitable charcoal suit today, and it made his eyes gleam silver and brought out the grey in his hair in a way that made it look sexy. The information was small, unimportant. There wasn't enough ice cream or chips in the world to fill the hole in my heart.

I just needed to curl up somewhere dark, somewhere quiet. But I didn't have anywhere of my own. Could life have been any more shit?

"They're at odds," I said, hoping it sounded calm. "Significantly. I can't speak for Duke, but I doubt Beo would provide any information on Duke, and, to be honest, Duke's got more than a life sentence. We don't need any more dirt."

"No." He nodded slowly. "Well, it's not surprising, I suppose. It would've been neat if it had been him, but…" He shrugged. "You look like you've had a long one, Rory."

I nodded and stood. I needed a shower, too. Hellfire, what had I done? "Was in the precinct, thought I'd see if I could catch you. No news is still news, right?"

"It's not no news," he said, standing too. "I appreciate it."

I shrugged. "Don't stress, Taig. I can find my way out."

"I need to stretch my legs anyway." He walked with me, matching his stride to mine. "How're the wounds?"

"Yeah." I could hardly feel them. Everything else hurt a lot more than my body. "Yeah, they'll get there. Had some healing done. If I was really spaced out during the interview, that's why."

He made a noise of understanding. "I wondered if you were a bit shocked. I almost called in your coven but figured you had it covered."

"Just suffering from a dose of overly wand-happy witch and not enough sleep." I touched his sleeve, grateful for his kindness. "Thanks, Taig."

"Anytime." He put his hand over mine and squeezed lightly. "I'll be in touch. We're circling closer."

I went out into the precinct waiting area and headed back to my car with my wallet. I looked at it, wondering even with my license number if they'd have me in the system yet. What bullshit.

Helpless fury pounded at my temples. I didn't have the energy to call Edward. I just didn't.

I made my way to the office. Did Lilith have car parking attached to her place? Shit, I needed to contact her and check if I could crash at hers again. I pulled into a serendipitous car park, sent her off a quick text, and climbed out. The afternoon, the night, the week, stretched out bleak before me.

My phone rang—my work phone. My heart leaped for just a moment, but it was Taig, not Beo.

"Rory."

"Hey. So, I'm alerting you, in an official capacity as Caretaker of the lycan pack led by Beo Velvela, that the pack have been spotted in pursuit of another lycan who is wanted for questioning in regard to Elizabeth 'Betty' Brown's murder, headed westbound out of the city." Sirens in the background half drowned out the last few words. There was a muffled apology, barely audible.

My heart drummed again, adrenaline rushing through me. I opened the back door to my car and reached for my Retrievals bag. "This lycan," I said, grabbing the bag. "Is he the green-eyed, scarred one?"

"Correct." Taig said something to whoever was driving, and I turned and jogged into the office. "As Caretaker, I thought you may want to be present for whatever goes down. I've asked for you to be brought on in an official capacity as Retrievals. It'll take a few minutes to get the green light."

Those green eyes, so like Duke's, so like Beo's. I could almost hear him telling me *they want to hurt me.*

"Got it." *Fucking fuck.* I rushed past Cici as Janet pulled her out of the way, saving me jostling her. They stared at me with shock as I went into the tiny bathroom and threw the lock. "I'm kitting up now. Tell me more."

"Suspect is riding a motorcycle, was spotted outside of," he paused then read an address that I recognized. *Zane's.* I put him on speaker as I began to strip. "Mean anything to you?"

"Yeah." I took out the leggings and shirt made of a lightweight, tough fabric that looked a little like a wetsuit and could protect better than Kevlar. It wouldn't stop a lycan's teeth—I'd seen that firsthand—but it might lessen a sideswipe. A benefit of Overworld trade, Lupetec kept us alive and kept the government crying poor. "Anything else?"

"Not much. Appears the suspect is leading the pack away. Feels like a trap. You got a line to them?"

"Not anymore," I said grimly, tugging on the pants. They slithered over my skin without resistance, warming quickly. I barely felt it. "Thanks, Taig. Send me updates on locations. I'll be on the road in five."

"I'll look for you."

The line went dead as I pulled on the boots, the vest, and belted my weapons. The familiarity of it, the rush of urgency, was second nature—clip and pull, tug and tighten.

Beo was being led into a trap.

I was lacing the boots when I shook my head. Lycans did nothing alone. Surely the pack knew that. Why follow a lone rider when…

The girl.

Were they being led *towards* a trap, or led *away* from the target?

I threw my clothes in the bag without folding or neatening anything and double-checked my silver knife at my hip. I dialed Taig, sick to my stomach, as I strode out into the hall.

It felt like the whole office was there as I ran out, listening to the phone ring in my ear. Vince grabbed the door for me, and I didn't spare him a glance. "Taig," he said, the word hard and tight.

"Rory here. How many lycans? My lycans?"

"Best count, nine. Could be more, could be less. They're on bikes, splitting lanes." Tension made his voice hard. "I've got a squad kitting up in Melton, but we don't know that's where he's headed. Contacted Retrievals, who're sending a team via chopper, but it'll be a while yet for them to get up and running. Got the green light for you to be legally involved. Paperwork is pending, of course, but it'll go through. You want to quibble about rates?"

I was in the car and made an illegal U-turn, ignoring the blast of horns. Paperwork took time. I'd do what I needed to, hazard pay, legal support, or not.

"No."

"Figured."

Urgency fluttered at my breast, a caged bird that wanted to fly. "Taig. Any children present? With my lycans?"

"Children?" he repeated. "Clint, any kids? No, none reported. Why?"

"A hunch," I said, feeling sick, running an orange light and ignoring more horns as I blocked an intersection, waiting impatiently for pedestrians to move their arses. "I'm going to check something out here before I head across." Hellfire, people were slow! Why didn't I get a siren, too?

"Keep me posted."

They couldn't have left her alone. They wouldn't.

It took me eleven excruciating minutes and a thrice-cursed hook-turn to get to Zane's place. I double-parked, climbed out of the car, and was running towards the entry when glass and bricks exploded across the pavement and a huge, furry, golden body was flung, yelping, onto the road.

Spells swam. My heart hammered. I drew my silver knife and felt its reassuring weight. "Retrievals!" I shouted as someone up the road screamed, and my throat tightened. "Come out in your skin form!" The golden lycan on the road struggled up, whining and blurring sickeningly. With its gorgeous yellow coat, it looked more oversized lion than oversized wolf.

The girl shot out from beside the house, blurring before my eyes. I ripped my gaze away as she Shifted to avoid the reflexive nausea.

She landed beside the form on the road and began to tug at the wounded lycan's golden, bloodied scruff. A car braked hard, followed by a car behind it. Metal twisted, crunching, glass smashing. People everywhere fled in panic. "Get clear!" I shouted, not taking my eyes off the building.

Determination and loyalty warred with self-preservation. I steadied the knife and my wand. *Too late, self-preservation.*

I planted myself firmly between the threat in the building and the two lycans on the road. They'd survive a car better than another lycan's teeth. And, fuck it, they were mine.

A slow, deep rumble drifted from the growing shadows at the side of the building to my left. Adrenaline poured through me, a familiar well of strength.

"Yeah, you're real fucking scary," I muttered, refusing to let my hand shake as the kill spell coalesced in my mind, humming in my skin.

Just give me a target.

I kept myself low, staying between my lycans and their attackers, but didn't turn to check on them. The girl and the big, blonde lion-like lycan would be fine. If they weren't, I couldn't look away anyway. My boots crunched on the loose rocks atop the bitumen. Moving low and slow, I looked for a target. What I'd give for a team around me.

Fuck Beo for chasing the decoy.

Fury hummed under my skin. A flicker of motion to my right served as the only warning I got. It was the only warning I needed. My heart in my throat, I spun, directing the knife. My target: a black blur. *With this blade, I cut you three by three from top to tail.*

Wet, hard pieces of it pummelled me. Chunks of lycan carried by their own momentum threw me backwards. Blood sprayed from it like a popped water balloon.

Something sharp pressed into my lower thigh, but it was background information, unimportant. Terror was like lava in my veins.

Lycans never worked alone.

I struggled up, kicking off pieces of beast. Not thinking about that creature as a person was easy when they were about to kill me—when another could be about to kill me. They were just obstacles now. Nightmares later, sure, but right now, just weighty, messy obstacles.

I broke free from the hot, stinking mess, heard flesh and bone land on the ground with a squelch. The smell of blood coated the back of my throat. My amphibious boots didn't care about the wet cement. They held me.

There were two more unfriendly lycans, big and brown. I saw the blur of motion, the coiled strength, the fury of them as they leaped onto the road where the blonde lion of a lycan lay prone. The smallest of mine—the girl, shifted now—ran away with her tail between her legs, jumped and cleared a car, vanishing from sight. One of the lycans was in close pursuit.

I leveled my knife and reached for more power. The one left turned towards me, revealing green eyes and a scarred face. The one who wanted to hurt Beo?

Well, I'd already done that.

My heart squeezed as the fallen lycan snapped its jaws towards my opponent, trying to nip at its heels. My lycan couldn't get up, but they tried. From the corner of my eye, I saw them fall and shift.

Callie. Bleeding.

The knowledge settled over me like a mantle as the scarred lycan turned, his teeth bared.

I heard Beo in my head. *Our most vulnerable state.*

Callie shifted back, and I ripped my eyes away before I vomited at the sight, at the overwhelmingly unnatural void that existed in the abyss of a lycanthrope shift.

Over the road, the girl tried to duck and weave, but the big lycan was almost on her. And in front of me, the green-eyed beast stalked me warily, a growl rumbling. Time slowed.

This lycan was a blood relative of Beo.

And Duke.

I watched as it raised a paw, swung it through air like reality was buffering. Even the beating of my own terrified, adrenaline-fuelled heart slowed in my ears. Every whisker on the nose of the green-eyed lycan, every dark green fleck in its eyes, was burned into my mind. My heart beat slow and steady.

I was being sized up, and I knew it.

Casting twice in the time needed was impossible for me, and I knew that too.

I couldn't cast two spells at once.

It was me or the girl.

Brandon's screams echoed in my head. The crunch of bones. The gurgling blood. The spray that too quickly became a trickle. The glint of the bright afternoon light on the red pool as it soaked into the ground.

That was reality now. Not traumatic past. Right here. Right now.

Stalking me.

Stalking the girl.

I couldn't help her if I was dead.

If she was dead, she was beyond anyone's help.

Really, there was no choice to be made…but they didn't know that.

They didn't need to. I moved my lips. Said some rhyming bullshit, something to distract, to misdirect the lycan before me. To buy time.

I tried to get closer to Callie. Tried to circle around to get a clear shot at the lycan going after the kid.

My boot twisted beneath me as I stepped down on the lip of the cement gutter, but I barely noticed, my body correcting, the soles of my shoes finding purchase. From the corner of my eye, another flicker of movement.

More. Fuck. *Keep the girl safe.*

The lycan in front of me lowered its belly towards the ground. The muscles in its shoulders rippled, bunching. I saw a flash of motion from the corner of my eye, big and brown. It was hard on the tail of a smaller, paler blur diving low between two cars.

My arm moved, strong and sure. I swung my knife and felt the rush of power. *With this blade, I cut you three by three from top to tail.*

I was knocked aside before I could see the spell work. The world tilted. I felt my body thrown about, heard the solid thud of my head crack against the bitumen.

There was no pain, but everything was wrong—stood on its end. Flashing lights in my eyes expanded into a grey, heavy mist, and I felt curiously light. It wasn't an unpleasant feeling. I lay there, considering the weird sensations and the car I could see with its doors hanging open, standing on its nose. Both were equally important.

Although the car on its nose was funnier. Or was it? Another car kissed its arse; the doors of that one were open, too, like some sort of giant arse-eating butterfly.

My career had certainly had some twists and turns, but that sight was right up there.

The silver knife had skittered away, useless. Even though it had stilled, now on the far side of the dotted white lines in the middle of the road, I could still hear the way it had scraped across the asphalt. The sounds played in my head like my brain lagged. The scrapes and bumps made me mildly unhappy, but it was done now.

Still, shit was expensive. The knife blurred, doubled, snapped into focus.

It was covered in blood. How had it gotten bloody? If it was scratched, I'd have to get the blood out of the scratches, and that annoyed me, a little. I liked how shiny it was, how sleek.

I remembered when I'd first gotten it. I'd been both utterly terrified and felt super cool all at once. I wondered what the cost would be to repair it. Would Retrievals insurance cover it? Even if they did have insurance, the arseholes probably had a huge excess to pay, and also, fuck paperwork. It was probably worth a couple hundred bucks to me to just get it fixed.

But I was definitely going to complain to Taig and anyone else who'd listen.

The thought of bitching at Taig, at Dad, at Lilith, made me feel better about the situation. I lay there for a moment, looking at it in a puddle of crimson. Everything else was grey, far away, hidden behind the mist. Plenty of folks would point to that and whisper dark magick. And it sure looked like it right then.

I drifted in a sea of mild amusement and even milder irritation, felt a hysterical laugh bubble up in my chest. *Not dark magick, kitchen magick.*

My belly rolled. I was going to vomit. I knew I was. A shoe, right beside me. Black and shiny. Polished. Neat slacks. The butt of a staff. I blinked as alarm bells rang in my head and survival instincts went into overdrive. I looked up. Up. Along the staff, a deep red polished wood.

Arthur.

Fucking *Arthur?*

The grey fled like a tsumani on rewind, leaving everything over-exposed. Pain in my head was blinding. Energy churned through my limbs in a rush that I could feel. The staff was in motion.

I could hear him casting, see light, feel wind and heat. There was the sickening smell of decay.

Shit-lord was using a *decay* curse? That was fucking illegal.

And also left really rank stains.

Not that I knew—it wasn't like I'd ever break any rules.

I tried to get up and saw big black blur of a lycan as it leaped onto a parked car, collapsing the roof of the thing with the sound of shattering glass and twisting steel. It stayed there, frozen in my vision, its massive jaws pointed towards us, its eyes swinging from me to Arthur. I could see the thing figuring out which one of us to ragdoll first.

And then it was in the air. I hadn't seen it jump, but it must've. My heart leaped almost as high as the lycan, into my throat, into my thrice-cursed skull, roaring in my ears.

Before I could shout, before I could do more than focus, Arthur spun his staff. *"Silver rain, silver snow, silver stream, and silver flow,"* I heard him chant. *"Fly fast, fly true, fly until you stop at last."*

And a fucking silver spear pierced it.

The weapon sent it spinning, crashing across the road. How much momentum did the bloke put in his spells? I watched, horrified and awed, as the lycan half-crumpled parked cars over the other side of the road and came to a stop, still.

My head throbbed. Arthur grabbed my arm, and I was hauled brutally to the side. Reeling, I tried to struggle up again and failed. I stopped trying and just stayed on my arse at his feet, trying to see, trying to think.

"You alive, Rory?" he asked, with an ungentle nudge of his foot against my thigh.

"Yeah." Fuck, was I ever.

"Got us a problem," he said, voice hard. "Don't suppose you've got a trick up your sleeve."

I'd used up my fucking trump card. I tried hard to focus, two, three... four lycans.

Fuck. I had no knife. I had no fucking brain.

Where was the girl?

I clutched at my wand. They were circling us, snarling, pacing.

No—communicating.

If they were still here, they didn't have her yet. There was still hope.

I lifted my fist, the bright, hot spark of faith burning bright. So bright, so strong it hurt. *Burn, witch, burn.* And every word coalesced crystal clear. Agonizingly powerful.

A lycan in front of us burst into flame.

The other two lunged. "Go right!" Arthur shouted. And then he was casting, the words so fast he should've been a fucking rapper.

I had nothing, though.

Except the old, the tried, the true.

The lycan on the right was the one that wanted Beo, the one that had scars that matched the picture Taig had shown me a lifetime ago over stolen hash browns and coffee.

Arthur fought. I could hear it, but I couldn't look and tear my eyes away from that pure green gaze as it moved through the air towards me, jaws open.

My ward rose in my head, swam, and settled softly, like dew. *Through this dome, none shall leave or come unless it is with me.* There was no explosion of bitumen, no damage. But the ward was there, invisible, powerful, and impenetrable.

The green-eyed lycan barrelled into the barrier of my spell, folding up like a cartoon animal and landing on its feet with the scrape of claws against tar. It lunged, snarling, attacking the ward, trying to get out.

Pain exploded and darkness rushed forward.

TWENTY-FOUR

"What the hell do you think you're *doing*?" Arthur roared at me.

The words struck me like blows. I bloody nearly vomited. It would've been great. He had me by the front of my shirt and was shaking me like a dog. I couldn't really see him, but I knew who he was. I'd recognize that man-shaped sack of privilege anywhere.

"What?" I managed to say somehow. The darkness skittered along the outside of my awareness.

Grey. So much grey. And I was so heavy.

And then magick punched into me, ripping the pain away. Most of it, anyway. And though my head was still slow, I could see again.

Arthur, his suit dishevelled and his staff beside him, held his wand in the same hand he'd fisted my shirt in, and it jabbed me in the chest. It didn't hurt, but it sure was annoying. Just like him.

"What the hell are you doing, Aurora?" he demanded.

I narrowed my eyes and seriously considered headbutting him. With the pain-block spell he'd thrown on me, I wouldn't even feel it.

"My job."

"This—" His face went from red to purple. "You're a Caretaker, not Retrievals!"

"Actually," I said, the words gravelly, "got a contract."

He gave me another shake, his teeth bared. I lifted an arm and broke his grip. Kicked the arsehole off me. He barely moved. "You can't work two jobs at once!"

Surely not. He'd come after me because of *admin* reasons?

No. I leveled my wand at him. "Talk."

His fingers tightened on his staff. "Don't threaten me, Witch," he said, the words low and hard. "How dare you abandon your duty of care, waste our budget, and drag our coven's good name through the mud—"

"Are you running pixie dust, Arthur?"

"—it'll take me years to live this down, you didn't even declare this on the alternate incomes form! And then I... What?"

I wished I could've kicked him right then, in the fucking jaw. "Are. You. Running. Dust?"

He looked at me like I'd spoken another language. "What are you *talking* about?"

"Did you kill Betty?"

Purple again. "You cannot be serious."

He wasn't lying.

My head spun. "Oh, shit." I dropped my arm and looked around. Callie was there, still on the ground, bleeding. "It's Edward. It's Edward."

"What's Edward?" he demanded furiously. "Did I screw something else when I threw that pain block into you, Rory?"

Tears burned my eyes. I started to stagger towards Callie. Please, please, let the girl be okay.

"Edward killed Betty," I told Arthur, feeling the world spin and sway. I'd played into his hands. "He wanted me to think it was you, wanted to set you up to take the fall." And I'd believed. I'd gone along with it.

Divide and conquer.

TWENTY-FIVE

APPROXIMATELY ZERO-POINT-TWO SECONDS LATER, A LOW WHINE AND THE far-off sound of sirens sent a wave of heat through me. Arthur fell down beside me. Didn't complain when I reefed his jacket gracelessly from him and held it against the big gouge in Callie's abdomen.

The girl. The little lycan.

"If you're here," I said so softly the words were silent to my own ears. "Hide. The back of my car. They will check everywhere else." With much gratitude for my poor, bruised brain, which somehow still managed to work despite the odds, I leaned all my weight against Callie.

"Callie." The cops. The paramedics. "You need to be human so they can patch you up." Also, who fucking knew if they'd shoot first and ask questions later? I didn't want to bet her life on it. Oma's voice sounded in my head: *many a slip twixt cup and lip.*

Not now, Oma, I begged her silently. "Callie, sweetheart." I was upright. Mostly. "There are cops. Ambos. You need to be human." Her form rippled. I looked away, but it was too late. My belly pitched and flexed. I turned my head, half-collapsed, but Arthur grabbed me by the collar before I tasted bitumen again. I heard myself vomiting from far, far away through a high-pitched, irritating ringing. The world blurred.

Slamming car doors. "Police!" Then, again. "Police!"

I lifted an arm. "Here," I croaked, then spat out the disgusting contents of my mouth. Coffee a second time. So fucking bad. Arthur still had me. I didn't have the strength to complain.

I heard them calling to each other, talking into radios. "The threat is contained," I managed as the world swam around me. "He's in my ward. The others are dead."

"Copy," someone said, approaching me warily, gun drawn. Fuck-wad probably had silver bullets.

I draped myself over Callie's golden lycan form. "Not this one."

The cop eyed me, then the lycan beneath me. "Are you Caretaker Aurora Gold?"

"I'm High Wizard Arthur," said good old Arthur, letting me go warily. "This woman is on a Retrievals contract. She is a Caretaker, however, she isn't currently on the clock." And he sent me a hard look. "Since she took a Retrievals contract."

I bet he'd check my fucking time sheets.

I didn't even care.

"This lycan needs medical attention, now." My words weren't a demand. They were barely a mewl.

The cop eyed off the girl beneath me. She wasn't moving, but I could feel the rise and fall of her chest, the heat of her body. I couldn't follow the conversation he had into his radio, crouched there between two parked cars, his gun pointed low in the direction of Callie. I didn't need to. They'd do their jobs. Or else.

I had mine to do, too. I knew a spell to force the shift, but I'd never been very good at it, and there was absolutely no way I could pull it off and also hold the ward.

"This lycan is an Australian citizen," I said to the cop. "You get the paramedics here now, or I will have you, your station, and your whole fucking family hung out to dry. Do you hear me?"

Arthur turned and barked, "Do it." And he held his staff threateningly.

For perhaps the first time ever, I was kind of glad to have Arthur there. I let my eyes drift closed. The pain was held at bay, but my muddled head wasn't. I let it hang off my shoulders against the road. Let my body be a dead weight against Callie. Keeping pressure on her wound, keeping myself going, maybe.

I heard running steps, the crackle of another radio. "Caretaker Gold?" I blinked and tried to sit up. "I'm John. This lycan is a patient, I hear?"

"Her name is Callie," I told him, easing back. "And, yes. She's one of the good ones. Not that it should matter."

"No, Caretaker," he agreed, eyeing her off. "Give me a shot of acepromazine," he said to his buddy, who was pulling on gloves. "Got some pretty serious puncture wounds down here. Going to need to do a transfusion. Radio that through while I get the cuff on her. Callie, you said?"

The world swam. "Don't you dare silver her," I said, or I thought I said.

"No, Caretaker. Blood pressure cuff. We'll sedate her, because it's safest, you understand."

"Yes." That was fine. Wasn't it? I dragged myself out of the way, two cops there helping me to my feet. In the gathering gloom of twilight, I sat on the bonnet of my car and leaned forwards, letting another pair of paramedics treat me.

To the side, Arthur spoke to another officer.

I listened to them as the others loaded Callie in her human form. She'd rippled back and forth a few times. I had full respect for the paramedics' training. They knew not to look. They didn't puke. Another team worked in tandem with them, four people fighting to keep her alive.

I remembered the day she'd spotted for me when I was pissed at Arthur. When she'd pleaded for my help with the girl. I sucked back the tears that wanted to come. I was crashing hard. Coming down from adrenaline was a shit sandwich without bread.

Cops worked around me, securing the scene. I wanted to go with Callie, but I couldn't. When I could stand, when I could walk, I got around to the side of my car and opened the back door.

I saw a small, familiar lump under a bunch of reusable grocery bags and my work clothes.

I almost died from the wave of relief. She was safe.

"Stay here," I murmured. "Beo will come." And then we'd figure out how to keep her hidden. It was a later problem. Right now, she was okay, and that was enough. Zane's place was being searched, but she'd be safe here, in my car, for now.

Twilight had almost given up entirely, and Callie had been taken in an ambulance to the nearest hospital when I glanced up to see Taig, still in that nice charcoal suit, striding towards me.

"You know what?" he said, passing me a paper cup of water. "I'll quibble about your hazard pay on your behalf."

I tried out a smile. "Shit. Might own a house one day after all. Now to stop buying coffee."

His grin was fast and hard. "Give me a rundown." He waved over another suited dude with a notepad in his hand and a pencil poised.

Who still used paper notepads? Weren't they extinct? I shook my head, trying to clear it. "I need a coffee, or I don't know, a bag of chips."

"You got some injuries?" Taig asked, the question clinical. "Excuse me," he grabbed a paramedic who was hustling past. "Is the Caretaker right to eat?"

"Eat, yes. Drive, no. She needs to present herself to the hospital tonight. No loss of consciousness, one vomit, but we suspect it was driven by a close-range Shift, not head trauma."

I remembered almost giggling at the sight of my knife in a puddle of blood and the long stretch of darkness. I kept the thoughts to myself and sipped the water. "All right. I'll send someone to grab you something." Taig's buddy nodded, who then went and grabbed a uniformed cop. Obviously, snack runs were below a detective's pay grade. "Any immediate threats?"

I blinked, looking back at where my ward should have been.

A naked dude sat there—actually, he lolled back on one arm, the other draped over his raised knee. Who did he think he was, Adonis? Now that he wasn't a lycan, or injured, or trying to escape, he'd been mostly ignored. "There's your suspect," I said, nodding towards him. "Blood relative to Duke or I'll eat my wand." It all made sense now. Except... Who sent the fucking faeries?

Arthur was there then. "Detective," he said with a very important nod. "Rory isn't feeling well. Perhaps I can answer your questions."

Taig smiled at him. It wasn't a friendly smile. "Sure you can, Arthur."

Then he turned and eyeballed the lycan in the ward. "Looks like our description. Your ward, Caretaker?"

"No, he just wanted to sit and enjoy the party."

Taig laughed at me. "Yeah, okay. I need to..." He trailed off at the sound of bikes. "Well, looks like word got back to your clients."

"Any idea who the fuck they were chasing, since we have our suspect here?" I jerked my chin towards the warded man who stared at a femme paramedic with far too much interest. "Or who sent fucking faeries after me?"

"Working on it."

The engines cut and bootheels hit the pavement nearby.

"You up to this, Rory?" he asked me quietly as Arthur postured and stepped in front of me.

I groaned, considered getting up. Didn't. "They're fine. They'll have a lot of questions, but they're fine." Beo appeared, skidding across broken bitumen and the rubble from Zane's place. I noticed, for the first time, the nasty lean to the building. "Shit. Looks like something is wrong with it."

"Possibly structurally unsound," Taig said with a brief nod. "Residents were evacuated. Didn't you hear?"

"Oh. Yeah. Sure." I cleared my throat, lifted my cup to Beo and the pack, and ignored the stab of hurt that was utterly inevitable. It would pass. I knew it would. "Callie's in a bad way," I told them. "She's on route to the Alfred. Oh. Um. Maybe she's there. Someone should go, be nearby."

Beo glanced swiftly at Zane, who vanished without a word, running back to his bike. Inspiration struck as a car started up nearby and was reversed out of the mess. "Callie was their target, I suspect," I told Taig, putting a hand to my head to try to keep it level. "When I saw Duke, he ranted about a 'her.' When you told me there was no one small with the lycans, I decided to come back here." The world swayed a little and went grey around the edges. "No. No, it was when you told me there was only one lycan trying to launch an attack." I rounded on Beo. "What the fuck were you thinking? As if one lycan would attack your pack!"

His expression was hard. "Seven. We lost them, then spotted that one."

Oh. So, they'd been led on a merry chase. Some of my indignation ebbed. It left nothing but hurt and sadness in its wake. I wanted the indignation back.

"Someone switched in," Taig said as his buddy took notes. "Your coffee will be here soon, Rory. Maybe you should just sit somewhere quiet."

"Life goals." I drew in a deep breath, then let it out. "You'll need me to lower that ward."

Taig glanced over at it, thoughtful. No longer was the Adonis leaning. He was on his feet, his weight settled, his eyes glued to Beo. If I was any judge, he was ready to shift in the blink of an eye. His posture all but said "I'm shit scared."

"Yeah," Taig said, the word rolling around in his mouth like he enjoyed its taste. "Might see what we can get out of him on the scene, though. If you're up for it, Caretaker, Arthur."

I blinked. Me? "I'm Retrievals. Not—" I flopped a hand in the general direction of the badge on his belt.

"As the witch who cast the ward, I think it's appropriate that you're nearby while we test its integrity," he said, sending me a hard look. The words didn't make sense, but that "play along" in his eyes did.

"Oh. Yeah. Sure." I slid off the bonnet, felt one leg give out, and caught myself on the side mirror. *Fuck. Takes forever to adjust those things.*

Beo was at my side, stabilizing me, before I could do more than get myself upright. "And as her client, I believe it's appropriate for you to be present too, Mr. Velvela," Taig said, lifting a brow at Beo.

He dropped me like a snake. My arm burned from the touch of his hand, but it was nothing next to the ache in my heart. From somewhere far away, I felt a familiar weight in the pocket of my pants, let my fingers skim it. My keys. My wand.

I held myself upright and made myself approach the ward. If it failed, I was fucked, and, right then, with sadness settling in my soul, I didn't care. But it wasn't going to fail.

Inside the ward, the lycan with the scarred face and Duke's brilliant green eyes backed up, his gaze locked on Beo. Detective Taig said, looking at Beo, "I probably can't hold him," he said to us. "Unless he cooperates. You'll be around, won't you? As a lycan leader, I'm sure he'd benefit from your support."

The implied threat there made the trapped lycan's face harden. He glanced from Beo to Taig, clearly decided Taig was the lesser threat, and said, in guttural, heavily accented English, "I help."

"I'll be around," Beo said quietly. "In case he changes his mind."

With a brisk nod, Taig got out a voice recorder. "You have the right to decline to answer our questions. You have the right to Overworld representation and a translator, if you need one," he began.

The lycan was hyper-focusing on the Alpha near me and I wondered how much of his rights he took in. I didn't listen to the formalities, to the give-and-take of bullshit. My head pounded. I felt sick, and sad, and small.

A beat cop passed me a coffee along with a brown paper bag of hot chips that had been doused in salt. I mouthed my thanks as Taig questioned the lycan about his movements that day and the attack this evening.

Adonis didn't give any useful information from my viewpoint, but then, I already knew most of what had gone down, or had guessed it.

"We have information that places you at the scene of another crime," Taig went on, checking the notepad his partner held as if he was reading it. I reached for a chip, saw the gore on my hands and thought better of it.

"A meeting that happened between a witch." He glanced at his partner, who'd already lifted a phone and flashed a picture. "For the record, please note that Detective Smith is showing a photograph of Caretaker Elizabeth 'Betty' Brown. Can you tell us anything about this?"

I watched as the lycan's eyes narrowed. Assault was very different from murder. "No comment," he said.

"I see." Taig nodded slowly, glancing at me, then Beo. "We don't have too many more questions then. Caretaker, perhaps once the pack here is accounted for, we should lower the ward."

Adonis's throat worked. His lips peeled back as he looked from Beo to the pack, who had wandered closer. I saw Frankie cracking his knuckles, flexing his neck.

The lycan in the ward snapped his eyes back to Taig. "A wizard. Paying us to riftrun dust."

Taig held his phone a little higher. "Can you describe this wizard?"

"Tiny dick," the lycan snarled. "Big staff."

Trying to muffle my horrified laughter, I choked on my coffee. Body shaming wasn't okay, but the whole thing felt so surreal that I just couldn't help it. "Hair color?" Taig asked, ignoring me.

He glanced around and pointed at a grey-haired paramedic. "That."

"For the record, the suspect has pointed at a man with grey hair." Taig glanced at me. "If I got you some pictures, sir, would you be able to identify him?"

Edward.

Hadn't Arthur already told him that? Was this, like, more official?

Yeah. Yeah, it probably was. Here was a lycan who could officially identify him. No need for warrants, judges, or innocent until proven guilty. I reached out and put a hand on Taig's shoulder. He glanced at me, puzzled. My head pounded. "We should call in our supervisor before he's moved. This is a major safety breach. I believe it calls for the High District Wizard to be present. Don't you think, Arthur?"

Arthur shot me a level look. He knew exactly what was happening here. "I support Caretaker Aurora's decision."

Understanding flickered across Taig's face. "You're right, of course. I apologize. Policy is still catching up when it comes to how to implement magi in law enforcement. Let the record show the interview will be postponed until the Melbourne District High Wizard, Edward Van Der Holst, arrives." He switched off the recording, eyeballed me, but didn't say anything except to jerk his head towards the paramedics.

I went, leaving Beo standing guard over the trapped lycan. With Taig beside me, I picked my way gingerly through emergency vehicles until he stopped before a car, reached in, pulled out a water bottle, and motioned for my hands. "We can stall until the Retrievals team gets here," he said as I sat the chips and coffee down and offered my filthy hands.

"No." I didn't glance over to my ward, to the lycans. "Let's get this shit done, Taig. We know who it is. Arthur confirmed it earlier. If it wasn't Arthur, it has to be Edward. That lycan punk will give you an ID. We can put him away." I was pretty sure that was how it worked, anyway.

"If he fights…"

But I barely heard the objection. The lycan punk would recognize him with sight but also smell. Would Beo? Was that why Mr. District High-Horse had never managed to meet me in person?

"If he fights," I said, feeling sick to my stomach, "I'll lift my ward on our suspect and drop it on Edward."

Water splashed over my hands, cool and gone all too soon to properly get them clean. *Fuck it. Close enough.*

"Rory," Taig said quietly, "I know this is personal and big. But we have teams for a reason."

I thought of Lilith, of my dad and Oma. Of the old, sweet grey-hairs. My heart swelled. "You're right," I agreed, a weight lifted from my shoulders. "I'll call my coven."

He eyed me warily. "I'm sure they're good at...what they do. This is a high order wizard we're dealing with, though."

My smile was big and cold and utterly mirthless as I reached for a chip and bit it hard. "The hells hath no fury like a coven wronged," I promised him quietly. "Where's my damn phone, O'Malley?"

TWENTY-SIX

Edward fought coming in.

I heard Taig politely talking him into a corner, boarding up all the metaphorical exits. He threw in an extra gambit; we could use this to lure Arthur out. They'd confirmed it was him, we just needed Edward on site to make sure we could take him down.

The good detective was excellent at bluffing.

I let him do his job as Arthur helped my coven get positioned around the area. It had been evacuated, as was appropriate. While that all went down, I tossed back the last of the coffee, even though it writhed in my belly, and went to where my poor little car was still double-parked. I'd left blood smears on it from where I'd sat down. It would take me forever to get my Lupetec armor clean. Stretchy, warm, and tough as all get-out, but not machine washable because…fuck faeries.

Beo intercepted me as I went to my car, all but vibrating with leashed violence.

"It's good to follow protocol," I told him, going around to the passenger side door closest to the buildings where the shadows long.

He said nothing. I glanced in, and some of the foreboding that had niggled at the back of my mind eased. I opened the door, pretending to rummage near where the girl was hidden. "Pack's here," I murmured, then straightened, dusting off my hands.

The world tilted. I grabbed the car door and straightened myself. Beo stood, his hands by his side, watching.

He didn't steady me.

My heart broke properly in that moment. It was over. Really over. But a kernel of anger protected me from the tide of grief.

Yeah, okay, so maybe I'd caused the whole shitstorm.

At least I had the grace to help clean up, right?

I didn't feel much better, though. I pretended to rummage some more in the car, put on some lip balm, used some wipes to clean my hands a bit, and found my phones. Both had more than a dozen missed calls. I grabbed them, slid them into the pockets that ran down the outside of my thighs, and hoped they were blood proof.

A clean-up team had come and was loading pieces of lycan onto a trolley about fifteen meters away. I felt nothing for that life snuffed out. The smell of burned hair, decaying flesh, and blood still lingered.

"Get her out," I murmured to the pack. "I'll cover."

But there were no shouts of discovery, not even a murmur of interest. My support wasn't even needed.

A few of the pack, deep in conversation, loitered near my car where I'd left the back door open. I went over to Taig, watched him getting out the silver cuffs and harness, and when I glanced back, there were three less pack members and my car door was closed.

The girl was gone. She was safe with them.

My witches knew their shit. Lilith did their disguises as trees and lampposts. Cici was a fucking car. Janet did her own, blending in with the land. Wards were cast, protective spells. Salt was trailed, herbs cut, eaten, or burned. Bernie offered me a sip of whiskey from her hip flask, her eyes glittering fiercely, before she went and became one with the graffiti-enriched fence. Arthur took up a protective position near emergency personnel.

And when Edward finally arrived, staff in one hand, expression trained in lines of concern, he walked straight to me and clasped my shoulder.

He was shorter than I'd expected. That was all my tired brain could think.

"Sorry they had to call you in," I said. From my angle, I could see where Beo prowled near the ward. And I knew the moment he scented Edward. From the corner of my eye, I saw his body stiffen, his head swung towards us.

I didn't have the courage or the heart to meet Beo's eyes, but I knew.

"I can't cast more than one spell at a time," I told Edward, not even lying and sounding as wrecked as I was. "And I've taken some hits. We need to transfer the lycan, and Elders-know when Retrievals will arrive."

His expression was still fixed in a concerned mask that didn't look like it quite fit his skeleton. "Of course. It's my job, isn't it? I hear Arthur..."

I tried to look sad. Tried to look sorry. "I know he's your nephew," I said as gently as I could. "And I'm wiped out. I'm sorry I can't help."

"No, Aurora." His smile was gentle. "You've done enough, my dear. More than enough." He rubbed his hands together. "I'll speak to the detective then. Bring that boy in."

I didn't say anything, just stayed where I was, nursing my fresh coffee as Taig crossed to us. He looked worn and worried as he shook Edward's hand and began to lead him towards the warded lycan while he talked.

I'd seen Taig saying something to the lycan earlier, something off the records, something, no doubt, designed to help him sing. So, I just watched and waited and relaxed. It was over. Almost.

"Him!" The lycan shouted, pointing. "The wizard! The dust!"

From my angle, I saw the expressions of shock and confusion on the faces of a dozen or so emergency service workers who'd been quietly instructed to listen in.

Edward's staff struck the ground once and it rippled, rocked, shattered. Cars spun backwards. An ambulance flipped and its siren started up. The noise from every window in the street shattering made nausea grab me by the throat, and I doubled over, clutched at my belly. I was safe from the last of his magick, thanks to Janet's protective spells, but not the noise or the chaos of it.

When I straightened, I saw some emergency workers and pack

members had all been thrown back. But not my coven. And not those around Arthur as he strode out between ambulances, staff in hand.

Edward's mouth opened, and I reached for my magick, trying to think of a spell, even as his tie suddenly loosened around his throat and filled his mouth to overflowing.

The sheer hilarity of the sight was surreal. Around us, my coven, my grey-haired, friendly-faced veterans, worked untouched by his spell.

Edward tried to run, but the ground sucked at him like uncooked cake batter. His jacket shrank, popped at the seams, and reformed like a straitjacket. A snake appeared, fat and long, and coiled around him.

And, as he struggled helplessly, making furious, muffled noises as he sank ever deeper in the now-sticky road, his staff lifted and rapped him smartly on the back of his head, then again on his backside, before it burst into flame.

"All right, all right," Taig said, and I wanted to laugh as he gingerly picked his way over to where Edward lay, stunned, in the batter that had been road, the snake peacefully resting with him in its coils. "You have the right to remain silent."

"As if he can manage that," Cici said, her hands on her hips, still looking like car doors propped open.

"Wizards," I agreed, taking a sip of the coffee.

They could do a lot of damage from the shadows, from their high thrones in positions of power. They were terrifying one-on-one or when they could keep us isolated. But, united? No chance.

Halfway through a sip of overly bitter swill, I saw Beo coming out from where he and his pack had sought shelter, and he headed my way. My heart skittered and rolled. He looked me over for injuries.

Why was he looking me over for injuries?

Lilith appeared beside me, her expression more than satisfied. "He didn't see us coming."

"They never do," I agreed, my mouth dry. "Hi, Beo."

Lilith's eyes widened a fraction. She cleared her throat and glanced between us. "I'd better go check on Bernie."

Beo didn't acknowledge her. Those green eyes were burning, branding my skin. I tried to swallow around the lump in my throat. I didn't know what he wanted. I didn't know if I'd be able to give it to him. And I couldn't even muster up enough thought right then to form the words to check in about Callie.

Or the girl.

"I heard you need to go to the hospital," he said eventually.

My heart hurt. The hospital was the least of my problems. "I can wait."

He shrugged, pulled keys out of his pocket, and considered them. "Tram might be safer. Secondary bump to your head wouldn't be good. I can get one of the pack to come pick us up later."

Us.

"What?" I asked, disoriented. Hope and terror warred inside me, brutally.

"From the hospital," he explained, his eyes narrowing a little. "I'll take you. Get you there safe."

Repayment was all this was. I felt sick and was, for once, pitifully grateful to see Arthur striding over. "Mr. Velvela," he said, briskly. "You're free to go. But if you'd linger until we transfer"—his eyes cut to the lycan still in my ward, and he paused for a fraction of a second while I just sat there, feeling like six kinds of crap—"the suspect, it might make things smoother."

Beo's mouth tightened, just fractionally, as he looked at Arthur. "Fine. But I'm taking Rory to the hospital as soon as it's done," he said flatly. "I'm not escorting him."

"I...Caretaker Aurora can go with paramedics or..."

Beo's brows raised. "They're pretty busy, Arthur." And they were. Arthur hadn't protected all of them, just those clustered nearby. Minor injuries were still injuries.

I watched the color rise in Arthur's throat. He looked, somewhat accusingly at me. I could almost *hear* him quoting some policy or procedure we were breaching. Almost. The drumming of my own heart drowned it out. "As kind as your offer is—"

"She's my witch, Arthur." Beo's expression was painfully neutral, and my heart—my poor heart. It didn't need this.

I straightened and shook my head a little, regretting it instantly. "I'm fine. I'll get there later." Arthur kind of had bailed me out. Even if it was just to cover his own arse.

When I wobbled, Beo's hand was on my elbow, until I had my feet again. *Oh, fuck.* I was tempted to wobble just so he'd do it again. Shit, I could faceplant. It was what my body was trying to do, anyway. Maybe he'd pick me up. Maybe he'd hold me.

I steeled myself and didn't let myself fall in a pathetic heap. *I can do this.* It was all but done anyway.

"It's fine, Beo," I said and willed it to be so. Fuck it. I'd make it fine for now and fall apart later. "I'm just doing my job."

"Which one?" Arthur asked under his breath.

I ignored the jibe and wandered to my captive Adonis. We stopped at the edge of the ward. The police were still restraining Edward. I didn't bother watching the spectacle. Keeping wizards in one spot when they didn't want to be was a whole dance—gags, restraints, removal of all foci. I'd been trained to do it and knew the drill. And I took no pleasure in knowing that was happening to Edward.

"It's my job to look after my pack," Beo said quietly from beside me. I couldn't read his tone or his body language. He didn't say anything else, just stood there beside me, silently while the aftermath of the operation unfolded until, finally, we could leave.

It was over.

Everything was over.

EPILOGUE

BEO GOT ME TO THE HOSPITAL. I STUCK TO MOSTLY WESTERN MEDICINE TO reduce my downtime, but I accepted some healing magick for my concussion. Seemed like a solid option, since I'd be wiped out from that either way.

Exactly how I got to the tram to go home, I wasn't sure. I know I fell asleep while it rocked along.

And I know he kept his arm around me while I was down and out.

The steps to my apartment seemed endless. Beneath my Lupetec gear, I'd be black and blue. Still, it was pretty light punishment for my crimes.

"You don't have to wait with me," I said as he stuck beside me with outward patience while I climbed the stairs at a snail's pace.

"I know."

I couldn't read anything into those two words. I didn't have the energy or enough brainpower to try to figure out what was going on. And, right then, I wasn't sure I wanted to know.

Eventually, I got to my apartment. I realized I didn't have my keys. Or my bag. Or anything, barring my phones. Because fuck my life.

Arthur was going to be pissed if I was off work tomorrow. And, for once, that thought didn't give me a jolt of pleasure.

Beo reached past me, fitting the key neatly into the lock. I blinked at it, trying to remember when that had happened. I followed his arm up to his shoulders where my head had rested. I wasn't done yet. But if he was, I'd manage.

My bag was on his shoulder. He opened the door, then turned on the lights. "No one's inside," he told me, dropping my bag. He took the keys and put them in my hand.

He wasn't coming in.

Of course, he wasn't coming in. Callie. The child. Duke. Shit, bystanders who'd seen him, probably knew he was a lycan. And would he face pushback from other lycans for working with the police?

I cleared my throat. I wished I could clear my head as easily. The fog was thick. "Look. I'm sorry about—"

"Not now." He reached up. Stopped. Dropped his hand. And, shit, the torment on his face nearly brought me to my knees. "We need to talk. You can't, now. I can't. So…"

The lump in my throat resisted being swallowed and made my voice thick when I said, "Yeah. Thanks, anyway, for getting me home. I'll see you."

Shit, that sounded weak.

He didn't move, though. Just stood there in my doorway next to the new door I hadn't even known I had. I didn't care I had.

"Send my best to the pack." I stepped back. Couldn't meet his eyes. *Keep it simple. Keep it easy.* I was terrible at good-byes. "Don't feel like you need to come by again, Beo. It's fine. I get it."

He put his hand on the door I hadn't yet tried to close. I stared at it. Those strong digits spread with easy strength. "Rory…"

I braced myself. "Honestly. There's no point drawing it out." But, fuck, if I could just have one more night. Or decade.

"I don't want this to be over," he said, and the words were rough, guttural, thick with the accent I couldn't place. "Do you?"

The idea swam in my head. Forgiveness. I met his eyes and saw them full, glistening. *Oh, fuck.* My heart broke. "No."

"Then we talk," he said, and his breath shook as he let it out. "Like we should've talked before."

I watched, hypnotized, as the tears spilled over.

"We can do that. We can try to fix this." He looked at me like he was willing it to be true. "You're in my bones, Rory," he said, and the words were agonized.

My head ached. He couldn't mean… "I don't understand."

He swallowed, glancing down at my battered boots. "Bones, Rory. They…hold you up, even when nothing else is working. Keep you from being…nothing." He looked up and my heart twisted, shuddered. "You're in my bones," he repeated, softly.

My body weighed a million tons, and still I managed to lift my arms. He crushed me to his chest.

He loved me.

We would figure this out.

His breathing was ragged, and I clung, the pain far away and unimportant. We fitted together like we'd grown entwined over centuries. Dips and curves, softness and steel, strengths and weaknesses. His lips were crushing mine, and I took everything he could give and gave him everything I had. My heart swelled, shattered, and bled.

There was a future.

There was hope.

This wasn't the end.

***

Thank you for reading! Did you enjoy? Please add your review because nothing helps an author more and encourages readers to take a chance on a book than a review.

And don't miss VILLAINS BY NECESSITY, book two of the *Something Wicked* series, available now. Turn the page for a sneak peek!

Also be sure to sign up for the City Owl Press newsletter to receive notice of all book releases!

SNEAK PEEK OF VILLAINS BY NECESSITY

Arthur walked about half a stride ahead of me, his handsome face totally blank as we headed back to the East Melbourne Coven. We'd survived what should, hopefully, be the last official interview with the police after all the shitfuckery with his uncle Edward Van der Holst. Drugs. Murder. Riftrunning. Faeries. Lycanthropes. Egos. All that good stuff.

I kind of felt for Arthur. Edward had done a pretty solid job of setting him up to take the fall if the cops ever got close. So much for familial loyalty.

If I hadn't stuck my neck out to back him up, he'd have copped an accessory to murder charge and a bunch of others, too.

Of course I *had* stuck out my neck, because that's the kind of witch I was. And my thanks? Not even him acting as my thrice-cursed windbreak on the way back. I huddled lower in my jacket and scowled at his back.

Maybe I could call up Detective Taig O'Malley, bat my eyelashes, fan myself. "I'm so sorry, Detective," I could sigh. "I don't know what came over me. I think Arthur must've scared me right out of my senses. Why, he must've been in on it all along."

Except I wouldn't. Because I wasn't *that* shit. Even if he was.

But thinking about it didn't cost me my high moral ground.

The amusing part was, despite all his petty posturing and puffing, my legs were still longer than his. He was working *hard* to stay ahead.

As if hearing my thoughts he paused at the slightly wonky post box beside the walkway to our coven, his hand on the recently graffitied gate. His gaze swept me, lip curled in derision. I stopped and planted my hands on my hips.

I could think of comfier places to confront the jerk. But I could think of worse ones, too. At least out here there weren't any nosy witches listening. Aside from me.

"If you'd just done your job—the job you were actually *hired* to do!—this wouldn't be happening."

"Thanks," I said, brightly, and smiled with lots of teeth. "Did it occur to you I *did* do my job, and now *I'm* being punished for it?"

"The way you fawn over Taig," he said, disgusted. "No, it hadn't. You obviously like the attention. Is that why you did it?"

Rage pulsed in my veins. There had been zero fawning. Taig and I were friends. I was very happy snuggling up to Beo Velvela, even if he *was* technically my client and theoretically off-limits due to my alleged power over him.

I mean, I *hoped* I had some power over him, since I was halfway in love with the big lump.

"Oh yeah, King," I shot back, mockingly. "Spending hours with cops just makes me *so* happy. It's not like I'm now about four days behind in my observations. It's not like now I need to put in extra hours to make sure the leprechaun family who's just transferred can get uniforms and devices for their kids so they can start school on—"

"As if you even care!" he half-shouted, throwing his hands up. "You're in it for the fame! And now *me* and *my coven* have had our names dragged through the mud!"

The fury at my temples drummed. I could so clearly see the way my fist would cut through the air. The force would reverberate down my arm, nestle in my shoulder, burn in my knuckles. "*Your* coven," I repeated, mockingly.

"Yes!" And he raised his hand, one finger drawn in threat. "*My* coven!" And the finger jabbed forward in accusation and attack.

My wrath was red-hot. In that moment I gave exactly zero shits that he was a bad-arse wizard.

My body knew the moves. I shifted, felt my shoes on the wet cement with the slick leaves and grit as the soles gripped faithfully. And as I rotated, I felt the damp, icy wind pick up my hair and toss curls into my face.

Fuck you, wind.

Fuck you, wizard.

I knocked his finger aside but crushed the urge to grab that wrist. I knew exactly how it'd feel when it broke and oh hells it was *right there.* "Don't you *dare—*"

An arrow bloomed in his chest.

My heart stopped for an instant. His face was frozen and if it wasn't for the way his pupils dilated as he stared, I would've sworn time stood still.

My cold fingers coiled around my wand. Traffic rumbling along the street, ignorant. Proof that the world still turned as I reached for my magick. His hand swept up like it was pulled by a string, past the lapel of his charcoal woolen designer jacket to the shaft protruding from low in his shoulder.

Through this dome none shall leave or come unless it is with me. The spell rippled and flowed from me. Blood bloomed in the fabric of Arthur's shirt and the song of a bell ringing met my ears.

With the breath still frozen in my throat I cut through our surroundings with my gaze. There weren't any obvious culprits but every detail jumped out at me. The light was almost gone, partially due to the hour but also because of the thick clouds gathered overhead. Parked cars sat in the gloom, unmoving. An older woman toddled down the road towing a cart of groceries, her big coat wrapped tightly around her bent frame. A young guy with headphones over top of his blue and white striped beanie walked a dog and scrolled on his phone.

Fuck.

"All right, Arthur," I said, grimly, turning back to my jerkoff line manager and digging out my phone. "Don't pull out that arrow. I'm calling the ambulance." And whoever had shot him—with a medieval fucking *arrow,* no less—was probably long gone since their second attempt had just hit my ward.

It'd be less paperwork in the long run if they'd had better aim. I could hear my Oma's voice in my head. *Measure twice, cut once.*

He collapsed, right there. Plonked down on his arse on the wet cement like some sort of cartoon character. With his mouth hanging open he stared up at me like he'd never seen me before.

Something about that made unease crawl up my spine.

The wound was too high on his chest to have hit anything *incredibly* critical and there sure wasn't a geyser of blood, but maybe my judgement was clouded by the liberal amount of adrenaline I was currently enjoying. Still, while his color was a bit high, it sure wasn't the white of shock. "You okay there, King?" I asked, resisting the urge to shove him at some paramedics and get home to a bucket of ice cream and forget this whole shitstorm.

He blinked owlishly. "You're beautiful when you're in action."

I froze. I was *what?*

And then the arrow just fucking *vanished*. Right there. From his chest. A hole remained in his shirt, welled and overflowed with blood. And he just sat there staring at me with wonder.

Okay, I'm going to need more than ice cream.

Gracelessly I yanked the scarf from around my throat and felt it catch on my keys, then the edge of my wand. The concrete was wet under my knees and I focused on that, not the pounding frustration. *I just can't get a fucking break.*

"Who's on this afternoon?" I asked, trying to distract him, keep him calm, and also avoid saying anything that'd cost my high moral ground. I liked the view.

Someone had just attacked him *on the street.* Would the second shot have killed him if I hadn't been there to throw up my ward? Maybe he'd back off, now, if I'd just saved his measly life.

And maybe he wouldn't.

Well, my own reflexes just made shit harder. I tossed the nub of my wand to my other hand so I could grab him in a vice. The silk scarf I pressed hard against the wound. I'd *absolutely* get done for murder if I didn't get this oxygen waster some help. Because that's how my luck went.

"On?" he repeated, the word strangely light. "Your hands. So warm. So strong. Oh, hells, Rory. Oh, please." He let out a long, shaky breath, tears welling in his eyes as he stared at me like a lost puppy. "Please," he said, the word shaking as his hand locked over mine but did nothing to increase the pressure on his wound. "Oh, please. Never let me go."

Well, shit. This arsehole wasn't bleeding out and he didn't seem to have a punctured lung. "Not letting you go, Arthur," I told him, though I really, *really* wanted to. "But I need you to keep the pressure on while I call for help." And then scrubbed away his touch.

"Yes," he breathed, his expression tender.

I had no idea what he was agreeing to. Or maybe he had no idea what he was agreeing to. My head was spinning. There had been no more bell-like noises, so whoever had hit us wasn't trying again. And Arthur was just sitting there, staring at me like I was the answer to his every hope and dream.

Not me. I was a fucking nightmare.

"Left hand, King," I demanded of him.

He lifted it and I took it with my wand hand, juggled until I had him holding on the pressure. Where were my thrice-cursed helpful bystanders? How was a Melbourne street so *quiet*? The one fucking time I needed a nosy neighbor and instead I got...*this*. Arthur. Gazing at me with utter adoration.

I pulled out my phone but hesitated once I got there. He wasn't in any immediate danger of dropping dead. Unless he told me I was beautiful again. Then all bets were off.

Opening my call log, I brought up the number for my most useful connection and hit call. "Detective Taig O'Malley," the sexy, up-all-night voice declared from the other end.

"Hey, Taig. Rory. I got a problem."

A chair squeaked in the background. "Where and what?"

"The coven. Arthur's been shot. By an arrow, not a gun."

"An—okay. Hey, Clint, got us a situation at the coven. Grab a car, meet me out front." Arthur leaned closer, his expression one of bliss. I leaned back and his face fell. Tears welled.

The *fuck?*

"What're we looking at?" Taig asked me. Background noise rose and fell on the end of the phone. "Doesn't sound like magick."

"It was absolutely magick," I said, irritated. "The arrow vanished after, I don't know, some seconds. Or minutes. And Arthur is really weird."

"Weird?"

"Yeah. Weird. You'll see."

"I'm not weird," Arthur breathed. "I love you, Rory."

Oh.

Oh, *no*.

Don't stop now. Keep reading with your copy of VILLAINS BY
NECESSITY.

Don't miss VILLAINS BY NECESSITY, book two of the *Something Wicked* series, available now, and find more from Elisse Hay at www.elissehay.com

I follow the rules when they're fair, but since when has love ever been fair?

There's a power vacuum triggering issues between the magi and vampires that's threatening to unleash a nightmare. Vampires, witches, and fae I can fight. That's all in a day's work. But my enemies' choice of weapon is the most terrifying of all—love.

I'm paid to guide the magickal members of our community. I won't have an obsession-fuelled team of witches running an abusive, Cupid-esque racket. And I definitely won't let my client be drawn back into their horrific web.

One thing's for sure, love has a dark underside, and it's coming for my client—but first, it'll have to go through me.

ACKNOWLEDGMENTS

The team at City Owl Press have been patient, kind and unflaggingly supportive. I haven't interacted with a single person who hasn't been wonderful and I'm so grateful to be part of such a wholesome organisation. Particular thanks to Lisa Green, whose ongoing support has helped me enhance the story I want to tell.

Thank you for Oleander Blume and Kim Smith, whose suggestions helped me create something I was proud of, and whose belief helped me stay grounded when things got hard. I contacted you both to help me with my writing, but your influence has reached far further than that.

My family have always been an amazing cheer squad and I'm so grateful to have you in my life. Dad, you even read the draft – first book in how long? A special thanks to Sharon for sharing my excitement, and for James, who has made it clear that you're always on my team.

I have some pretty top-tier supportive friends, too. Corinne, your mix of creativity, calm and consideration never ceases to amaze me. Mez, you put up with me figuring out the early details of Rory *and* you made sure I got French champagne, even though Aspen didn't end up having pet rabbits. Naomi, I've valued the wine nights, afternoon 'smoko' chats and gaming sessions more than I could ever say. In fact, I think we need another! Howard, life isn't the same without you; I guess that shows the sort of person you were, and the impact you've had on me and mine.

Acknowledgements wouldn't be complete without Wayne, my anchor and partner in crime. In addition to being the best husband I've ever had and a joy to be around, he is always happy to not just listen but discuss my latest hair-brained plot and has read almost all of the hundreds of thousands of words that I've typed. I have also been cheered on by three fantastic miniature humans who have taught me what it means to be brave. I'm so grateful you're all in my life.

ABOUT THE AUTHOR

ELISSE HAY lives on the unceded land of the Kulin Nation in so-called Australia. She loves hanging out with her three awesome kids, plays a variety of the nerdiest games she can find with her partner in crime, and considers a week incomplete if she hasn't eaten pesto. You'll most likely find her somewhere comfy with a coffee, a cat or dog and space to share with good humans.

www.elissehay.com

instagram.com/elissehayauthor
tiktok.com/@elissehay

ABOUT THE PUBLISHER

City Owl Press is a cutting edge indie publishing company, bringing the world of romance and speculative fiction to discerning readers.

Escape Your World. Get Lost in Ours!

www.cityowlpress.com

facebook.com/CityOwlPress

twitter.com/cityowlpress

instagram.com/cityowlbooks

pinterest.com/cityowlpress

tiktok.com/@cityowlpress

Made in the USA
Middletown, DE
01 October 2023

39732303R00161